Désirée Broussard

by

Lee René

Désirée Broussard

Cover Art by *Debbie Taylor*

The Wild Rose Press, Inc.
PO Box 708
Adams Basin, NY 14410-0708
Visit us at www.thewildrosepress.com

Publishing History
First Vintage Rose Edition, 2019
Print ISBN 978-1-5092-2638-2
Digital ISBN 978-1-5092-2639-9

Published in the United States of America

"What's wrong, Patrick?"

"Nothing, really. That girl in purple is my father's, uh, special friend. She used to dance here, but Daddy made her his hostess. She, uh, has an affinity for a certain type of woman."

His words confused her. "But why?"

"Daddy doesn't care. He's attracted to the…uh…unusual."

"Oh." Mistress Adele's words about Patrick Sr. danced in Désirée's head.

The dark beauty in the amethyst gown signaled Frankie with a wave of the hand, then slithered away from the table. The two women disappeared behind a red velvet curtain.

Lilly gyrated across the stage, undulating to the primitive rhythm, her tiny feet moving at lightning speed. She swung her head around, tossing her platinum hair in a frenzy of passion. After a series of bumps and grinds, the dance ended. Lilly turned her back to the audience, unhooked her bra, and flung it across her shoulder. She swiveled her head toward the crowd and gave the gents an over-the-shoulder wink. Then the stage went black. Thunderous applause, shrill whistles, and catcalls from the cruder members of the audience filled the room.

Praise for Lee René

"*DÉSIRÉE BROUSSARD* captures the dark, inner pulse of the smoky labyrinth called New Orleans. Each page celebrates the sordid beauty and haunted soul of America's most exciting yet decadent city."

> ~*Asif Ahmed, Executive Director of the New Orleans Vampire Film Festival*

~*~

"After just a few pages, I was invested in the tale. Her imagery conjures a sensory experience of America's most exotic city in the 1950s."

> ~*Kenny Ard, King of New Orleans pianists*

~*~

"What a meticulous portrait of vintage New Orleans. I could smell, see, and taste every scene. Beautifully drawn characters. Plot has as many turns as a Vieux Carré alley."

> ~*Fleeta Cunningham, author of the Santa Rita series*

Dedication

This novel is dedicated to my mother,
Thora Pradia Miller,
a true flower of Louisiana and Texas,
and my father,
William Miller,
who instilled the love of reading and storytelling in me.

Acknowledgements

Thanks to my mother, Thora Pradia Miller, for sharing her memories of New Orleans, and to my friend Patrick Sullivan, who introduced me to both the marvels of the city and witnesses to New Orleans' history. Thanks go to Kristine Peterson for pushing me on my journey, and to beta-reader extraordinaire Kristin Aragon, who was invaluable in helping me rewrite my manuscript, and to editor Windy Goodloe.

A special thanks to Sergeant Barry Fletcher, formerly of the New Orleans Police Department, for his assistance in the historical research, along with my New Orleans friends: the late Skipper Jordan, Kenny Ard, Jeff Laque, Sal Perricone, the legendary Chris Owens, and many more who guided me through a city of darkness and enchantment.

Special thanks to activist Joan Nestle, who introduced me to the words of the late Blue Lunden, a teen sex worker in 1950s New Orleans.

I would have been lost without the encouragement I received from writer Cat Winters and from my friend Dr. Caroline de Costa. Hugs and kisses to my dear friends and relatives Lee Pradia Miller, Denise Sullivan, Flora Racely, Tim Cogshell, William James, Caroline Jefferson, Selma Betton, Jack and Donna Salem, Peter Taubkin, Lorrie Marlowe-Hooks, and Robert Hooks, all of whom motivated me through the years.

Tears and fondest remembrances to the late writer Bridget Morrow, who never saw *Désirée Broussard* in print.

Chapter One

Bourbon Street, July 4, 1955

"America has only three cities: New York, San Francisco, and New Orleans. Everywhere else is Cleveland."

~Tennessee Williams

The evening humidity trapped the street in a pungent mélange of vomited-up Hurricanes and fried oysters. Young men strolled down Bourbon, leaving whiffs of Brylcreem and Aqua Velva in their wake. The stink of hot piss floated from an alleyway on the evening breeze. It mingled with the smell of burning sulfur, mixed with charcoal powder from spent firecrackers. The stench cut through the moist air like a switchblade.

Désirée Broussard scanned the banquette from a darkened portico and wrinkled her dainty nose at the foul air. She gave her ponytail a toss, and then trounced through the masses of bodies cramming sidewalks canopied in wrought iron. Dixieland and race music spilled from every doorway. Crowds packed the street, but Désirée sashayed past them, ignoring the musical cacophony and the hoots and catcalls from horny sailors.

The pandemonium increased with the din of

exploding fireworks. Whistling pierced the air, warning her to take a step back. A firecracker popped close enough to her sandaled feet for the burning sparks to scorch her bare skin. The culprit, a teen boy, dashed away before she could utter anything stronger than a furious, "Damn it, you son-of-a-bitch!"

A matron in a red, white, and blue sundress gasped at her language. Désirée ignored the woman and tromped off. She'd never been fond of evening jaunts in the Quarter, especially when holiday revelers packed the Vieux Carré. Désirée had once fantasized about abandoning New Orleans for life as a bohemian writer in Greenwich Village. Tragedy had dashed those dreams, and the Quarter held her captive.

Her uncle owed her sixty dollars. He'd borrowed it as soon as he blew into town. He insisted she meet him on Bourbon Street to pay her back. If she hadn't needed the money, she wouldn't be here, trapped in a maze of neon signs, dodging exploding firecrackers. Instead of sweating in the Quarter, she'd be relaxing in her little flat, reading *Auntie Mame* beneath the coolness of a ceiling fan.

Désirée cursed under her breath, "Damn it, Uncle Louie. Where the hell are you?" She adjusted her peasant blouse, and her wooden bangle bracelets clattered as she pulled at the red shoulder ruffles. She glanced at her timepiece, a tank-watch her grandfather had brought back from the War. The hands read nine on the dot.

When two burly cops plowed through the crowd, brass knuckles and blackjacks dangling from their belts, her pulse quickened. Although the police had never messed with her, they'd done horrible things to those she loved.

Désirée backed into the darkness once again. The racket from the clomping police horses and strident sirens caused her jaw to tighten. Perhaps the cops had already nabbed her uncle. But then the scent of Canoe aftershave engulfed her.

A Zippo flared in the darkness as a voice whispered, "Hey, Désirée. Over here."

The cologne's sweetness alerted Désirée that her uncle had finally arrived. She locked her gaze onto the handsome face of Mr. Louie Favre, pimp and stick-up man extraordinaire. "Where y'at, girl?"

Désirée whipped around, her eyes flashing like two flares. "Why are you so late, Uncle Louie? I been waiting a whole hour."

Perhaps his stint in Angola had influenced his choice of attire, but she'd never seen him dress so conservatively. Instead of his usual iridescent suits, the flamboyant garb of the musicians he loved, Louie had donned a black satin shirt and pleated trousers. "Are you duded up for a funeral or something?"

He took a drag on an Old Gold cigarette and grinned as if he hadn't a care in the world. His Brylcreemed pompadour stayed in place when he gave his head a toss. "I'm trying to look professional. I have to meet an important fellow tonight."

Bullshit rolled easily from her uncle's lips, and she couldn't stop herself from uttering a snide remark. "What meeting, the pimps' cotillion? Maybe you got time to lollygag, but I don't. I've been twiddling my thumbs here for over an hour. Why did you want to meet on Bourbon anyway? Cops are swarming all over the Quarter like roaches, and you just got out of

Angola."

Louie took another drag of his cigarette before planting a cursory peck on her cheek. "Cops ain't nothing."

She didn't bother to conceal her annoyance at his flippant attitude. "Cops ain't nothing? Remember when Jim Dandy got drunk last Mardi Gras? The flatfoots nearly beat him to death. Let one of those thugs kick your ass like they did his, and then tell me they ain't nothing."

Louie grinned at his niece as if things were hunky dory. "They've knocked the shit out of me before, but they wouldn't hurt a pretty gal like you." His charm wasn't working on her. When she rolled her eyes, he trotted out his most contrite expression. "I'm really sorry about being late, boo, but a big shot needed somebody to show a few fellows around the city, you know, take them to places of interest."

She snorted an angry retort. "Stop the crap, Uncle Louie. Nobody's using you as a tour guide. I'm here for my money. I've got rent to pay. Where is it?"

He took another drag, tossed the half-smoked butt to the ground, stubbing it with the toe of his Stacy Adams two-toned wingtips. "Baby, please don't tell your mama you loaned me the coin. She's pissed enough, and I don't want her raising Cain with you for helping me. I got half your money."

Louie pulled three ten-dollar bills from his pocket and jammed them into her hand. "We've got to go to the Lucky 13 to get the rest."

At the mention of the Lucky 13, Désirée's face lost its color. "Huh? You said the Lucky 13?"

Everyone in New Orleans knew the place.

Strippers with drooping breasts and paunchy stomachs performed there when they couldn't find work elsewhere. Still, it didn't matter what the exotic dancers looked like. No one cared about the floorshow since the back rooms brought in the business and, on occasion, the coroner.

"Uncle Louie, you just got out of Angola. If the cops catch you in a place like the Lucky 13, they'll send you back. Swear to me you aren't doing anything wrong, or I'll be through with you, just like Mama is."

The moment he averted his face, Désirée knew he'd involved himself in something nasty. Her anger swelled up once more. "You should be ashamed of yourself, but I know you aren't."

She glared at him and shrugged her shoulders before stomping away. Louie followed, entreating passionately all the while, "Désirée, don't do me like that. You know you're my heart, girl. Please, darling!"

Her pace slowed. Despite his trifling ways, Désirée held his heart in her hands. No matter how much he lied to those who loved him, he certainly held hers.

The moment Désirée's face softened, Louie saw an opening and pressed his case. "I got something to tell you, something nobody knows. The new owner of the Lucky 13 is Mr. Patrick Renaud."

At the mention of the name of the most powerful man in the city, Désirée came to an abrupt halt. "Renaud?" She nearly jumped out of her skin at the mention of the name. Like everyone in New Orleans, she'd heard wild tales about the Renaud fortune, their fabled parties, and opulent masked balls. Maison Renaud had stood in the Quarter since the early 1800s, and folks swore the insane patriarch had buried trunks crammed with golden doubloons throughout the property. She'd heard about the rich slumming, a reality of life in New Orleans, but couldn't image anything as ridiculous as a Renaud-Favre connection.

"Uncle Louie, I read in the paper that Patrick Renaud almost died of a heart attack and is getting treated in Europe." She shook off his restraining hand on her wrist. "Besides, what kind of a sucker do you think I am? Patrick Renaud wouldn't have anything to do with a dive like the Lucky 13, and he wouldn't wipe his shoes on the likes of you."

She stormed off once again with Louie at her tail. He overtook her before she moved to Dumaine Street. "Cher, I ain't talking about the old man. It's his son, Patrick Renaud, the one they call Junior. I tell you, he owns the Lucky 13, just took it over. Come with me. Won't take a minute of your time. I'm out of Angola for good. I've turned over a new leaf, I swear."

At first, she couldn't read his face in the darkness. "For true?"

When Louie moved into the light, she noted the self-satisfied grin plastered on his mug. "For true. I ain't pimping no more, just selling a little reefer to friends and playing craps with some of the guys. Come on, baby."

Désirée had already wasted an hour. What else did she have to lose? "All right. I'll go with you."

Her gut told her to run in the opposite direction, but she followed anyway.

Chapter Two
The Lucky 13

Désirée and Louie made their way down Rue St. Marc, a street that welcomed the most avant-garde, offbeat, and twisted the city had to offer. Bar owners never regretted paying the police to look the other way at the antics of the free spirits and the depraved who congregated there.

Uncle and niece strolled past bookstores, coffee shops, and dark alcoves where bohemian poets spouted their verses. Folk musicians competed for nickels and dimes with the blues singers and tap dancers who performed on street corners.

Red, white, and blue streamers festooned the Creole townhouses. American flags fluttered next to the blue bars and scarlet of Confederate banners. A plaster figure of Uncle Sam sat perched on a wrought-iron balcony where drunken revelers tossed confetti onto the street below.

Désirée took a sniff of the night air. "Somebody's frying oysters and smoking reefer."

He gave a shake of his head. "I don't get a whiff of nothing, boo."

Except for the perfume of female essence, Louie didn't possess a sense of smell. Désirée, however, had waxed poetic about the scents of the city from the time she could talk. "I do. Maw Maw said I could tell when milk was spoilt before they opened the bottle."

They moved toward a dark, soulless building that loomed out of the evening like something from a voodoo nightmare. She sniffed the air and winced. Even the fragrance of narcissus couldn't overwhelm the potent musk of the Lucky 13.

No one remembered how the place got its name. Désirée gave the dark, windowless building a fleeting glance. One look gave credibility to the tales of degenerate acts that occurred in the back rooms. The most jaded and dissolute in New Orleans crossed its threshold, like Moslem pilgrims traveling to Mecca.

Three bar girls in brightly colored satin dresses with matching stilettos stood at the entrance. They'd plastered themselves with Pan-Cake makeup, their mouths slathered with Max Factor lipstick. Cigarette smoke plumed around their heads. The siren's song of swishing crinoline and throaty laughter accompanied their every movement. All were clearly past their prime, yet they moved like nubile seductresses, unaware their best years were behind them.

When Louie flashed his procurer's smile, the B-girls sniffed the air, finished their cigarettes, and reentered the club. Désirée could barely contain a giggle. The pungent aroma of her uncle's aftershave couldn't disguise the pimp stench dripping from his every orifice.

Louie sneered at the women as they entered the club. "Sorry bunch of broken-down whores. Come on."

Louie's displeasure stemmed from the fact none of the women had fallen for his greasy charms, but Désirée didn't say a word. He steered her into the club, the place reeking of smoke mingled with bleach and

Lysol. They walked past a few rum pots huddled at the bar, moved through the smelly gloom, stopping at a beaded portal. A stocky tough in a sharkskin suit barred their way. "What are you doing here, Louie, and who's your friend?"

Although the goon directed his words at Louie, he'd fixed his leer on Désirée.

Louie locked Désirée in a protective clinch, so firm it felt like a death grip. "Leave her alone, man. She's my niece."

The fellow grinned, his smile hollow and mirthless, his gold tooth flashing in the dim light. "Your niece? Why the hell did you bring her to this dump?"

"I got an appointment with Mr. Renaud."

The thug extended his arm toward a dark void. "He's in the office talking to the police, so I'd tread lightly, if I was you."

Louie hesitated before stepping into a smoky labyrinth of dark corners, alien sounds, and smells. Désirée trailed him through the darkness. A purple light illuminated a floor sticky with the product of a thousand ejaculations. A door creaked open, spewing out carnal moans. Désirée couldn't stop herself from looking inside.

A single lightbulb illuminated a petite woman standing over a man and swinging a leather paddle with one hand. She was dressed in fetish garb—black leather bustier, black panties, fishnet hose, and stiletto pumps. Her supplicant, a muscular fellow with a graying crew cut, had stripped to his skivvies. A leather collar encircled his neck. He groveled at her feet.

The woman in black tossed her mop of flame red hair. She raised a small leather whip over her head and placed a dainty foot in front of the man's face before addressing him in an earthy growl. "My poor little sugar, so big, but such a baby, a big baby who needs a good spanking. If you're a good boy, I might let you kiss my shoe."

He embraced the woman's foot, sliding his lips over her ankle.

Louie grabbed Désirée's hand and pulled her forward. "Come on. Ain't nothing here you need to see."

Désirée shook from the power of the woman's words, her heart pumping like a conga drum. "I'm a writer, Uncle Louie. I have to see life at its rawest." She remained in place, her feet rooted to the floor.

"Not this raw, boo."

Louie pushed her farther into the darkness.

A stream of light bled from an open door. Désirée heard masculine laughter float into the dimly lit corridor, then a fellow spoke in a youthful baritone. "Mr. Renaud, sir, if it was anybody but you, I'd swear they were blowing smoke up my ass."

Even in the barely-there illumination, Désirée could see her uncle's face had turned stark white. "What's wrong, Uncle Louie?"

Louie made an abrupt stop and pulled her into a shadowy alcove across from an open door, a pebbled door glass etched with the word OFFICE.

Her uncle's customary air of bravado abandoned him, and the acrid perfume of dread cut through the sweetness of his aftershave. He placed his forefinger to his lips, signaling her to be silent.

She nodded, then peered into the office, a jumble of cheesy furnishings and tacky décor. A cheap steel desk covered with neatly stacked piles of paper sat atop the spotted linoleum flooring. The plaster walls were bare, except for yellowed eight-by-tens of exotic dancers. Fluorescent lights painted the room an anemic shade of tan, bathing the room in a jaundiced glow. An electric fan sat on the desk, moving back and forth at a languid pace.

Two men, their backs to the door, obscured her view of whoever sat plopped behind the desk. She stared into the squalid office and questioned why such an important man would waste his time with a rat-hole like the Lucky 13 and a pimp named Louie Favre. Her skin turned to gooseflesh at the thought. The room buzzed with enough potent masculine energy to push Désirée farther back into the darkness.

One of the men, a beefy young fellow in two-toned shoes and a wrinkled seersucker, took a step toward the desk, but his bulk still blocked Désirée's view. When he stepped into the harsh light, she noted the guy wore his brown hair parted on the side and slicked in place. He fiddled with his hat as he spoke, his nerves obviously on edge.

"Mr. Renaud, if you don't mind me asking, what are you fixing to do with this place? If word got out that you owned it, it wouldn't be good for you, sir."

Mr. Renaud sat behind the desk, holding court like some benevolent potentate. Although she couldn't make out his face, she watched him twirl a pencil between his beautifully manicured fingers. "Glad you asked, Lieutenant DeLuca."

Renaud dropped the pencil before extending his hand to the heavyset fellow, who shook it with great enthusiasm.

11

"Your name is Gino, right? Please call me Patrick, never Junior. Lord, I'm tired of that name. I bought the Lucky 13 because I thought it would be a good idea to keep the freaks of New Orleans in one place."

Patrick Renaud's voice, a chocolatey baritone, piqued Désirée's interest, and she craned her neck for a better view.

Unfortunately, DeLuca took another step toward Patrick Renaud, blocking her view with his bulk. The guy who'd accompanied Gino moved closer to the desk, too, further obscuring her view of Mr. Renaud. With his back to Désirée, she couldn't see his features, but he appeared to be over six feet tall, with a muscular body. She watched as he reached over and pulled a cigarette from a velvet box.

Without warning, Louie gripped her hand.

"Problem is the mayor's lovely wife and the ladies of the historical society want to keep the Quarter quaint and charming. They want to start their efforts here on St. Marc. Me and Gino have what you'd call a quandary. Understand what I'm saying?"

The fellow swiveled around as he lit a cigarette. "One day I've got to give up these coffin nails, but not tonight."

Désirée could barely stifle her gasp when she caught sight of the handsome, blue-eyed fellow with teeth that glinted white and feral under the urine-colored light. Self-assured and cooler than an iced-lime daiquiri, he wore a gray summer suit with an orange pocket handkerchief. In spite of the heat, his presence chilled Désirée to her core.

Her uncle suddenly squeezed her fingers with such force she feared he'd pulverized them. She managed a whisper through gritted teeth. "You're breaking my hand."

He relaxed his grip. Désirée ignored her aching fingers and looked deeper into the room. Although she still couldn't see Patrick's face, the velvety resonance of his voice continued to intrigue her.

"Captain Vitale, your name is Eddie, isn't it?"

Vitale nodded in the affirmative.

Although she couldn't see Patrick Renaud, the honeyed tones of his voice mesmerized her. "Eddie, you're Lula Vitale's boy, aren't you?"

Eddie nodded, a huge smirk on his handsome face.

Patrick's unforced laughter warmed the room. "Uh-huh, I knew it the moment I saw you. Your mother has been a friend of my family's since I was in diapers. Yes, the ladies want a pristine Vieux Carré, but man to man, as long as nobody knows about the specialty acts, what's the problem?"

The detective took a drag on his cigarette before snuffing it out. "They are the problem, sir. Everybody knows about the specialty acts. You might could get away with the peep show, and that lady with the leather whip, but, sir, the other stuff that happens in the back rooms, the beatings, the brandings, and all that other mess, is what they call 'beyond the pale.' And how about cleaning up that nasty kitchen while you're at it?"

The host's laugh suddenly became cold and mirthless. "Eddie, the fellows who frequent the Lucky 13 don't come for the food. They're men of peculiar tastes, peculiar indeed. I figure, if I keep them satisfied here, they won't roam around the city, getting into mischief."

The room went silent as the two detectives digested

Patrick's words.

Eddie nodded at Gino, then focused his attention on young Mr. Renaud. "You might be right, sir, collect all of New Orleans's shit in one place. I'm taking you at your word that nothing will happen upfront, and you'll keep an eye on the mess in the back rooms. I don't want to have to drag a corpse out of here. I'll let the superintendent know. We got us an arrangement?"

The detective pumped Patrick's disembodied hand, the two men bonding in a palm-to-palm agreement.

"Yes, Eddie, as long as Gino agrees, we've got us a deal. Since the police are staying away, let us show our appreciation." Désirée watched as he handed Vitale a small wad of bills.

Patrick chortled, his laugh deep and resonate. "Have to say, your smile is just like your mama's, a dead giveaway. My parents and Lula go way back." He paused for a moment. "I think Daddy knew your brother Sal, too. Sorry about how things went down with him."

Once again, Louie gripped her hand like a vise. When she opened her mouth in protest, he slapped his palm over it. He'd muted but not blinded her, and she looked into the office from the dark recesses of the corridor.

Eddie Vitale went silent, his face impassive.

A nervous Gino DeLuca glanced at his partner. "Eddie don't like talking about Sal."

Eddie laid a restraining hand on his partner's arm. "It's all right, Gino. Patrick knows the story, just like everybody else in New Orleans." He focused his blue gaze on Mr. Renaud. "Yes, sir, I'm afraid Sal got in with the wrong crowd, hung around with vermin, but there's nothing we can do about it now."

Patrick Renaud spoke in silken tones. "I know your mama took it hard, but she's a strong woman. Daddy always swore that if Lula Vitale had been born a man, she would have been mayor by now, but of course, she has you."

Gino jammed a stick of Juicy Fruit gum in his mouth and remained silent. His bulk continued to block Désirée's view. "Eddie, didn't I see you decked out in your uniform on the front page of the *Picayune*?"

Even though she still couldn't make out his features, Patrick's voice sent a shiver down her spine.

The young detective glanced at DeLuca, a smirk on his handsome face. "Yes, Patrick, that was me."

At that moment, Eddie moved closer to Gino and allowed Désirée to get her first glimpse of a smiling Patrick Renaud. She stood stock still, gazing at a man who looked as if a master sculpture had molded his face. Her heart palpitated wildly. So this was Junior Renaud.

Patrick stood, his muscular body clad in a carefully tailored tuxedo, his height more than a match for Eddie Vitale's. His face managed to be strong yet boyish. Despite the symmetry, Désirée noted a flaw in his perfection. The sensuality of his full lips belied his aristocratic features. His dark beauty rivaled Vitale's, but the young detective's face lacked the air of entitlement of Renaud's.

The room's horrid lighting couldn't diminish his most arresting feature, eyes like pools of still water, framed by heavy brows and lashes. They were the kind of orbs women swore Mother Nature wasted on a man.

Her heart stopped or, at least, she thought it had.

After a few seconds, it began pumping again, her pulse surging so violently she feared she'd pass out. Désirée had never seen a fellow like him before, except for a matinee idol plastered across the screen of the Saenger Movie Theater.

The room went silent once again. Patrick appraised Eddie for a moment, and his lips spread into a lazy smile. "Eddie, I can tell you're an ambitious guy. I admire ambition because I'm a driven man myself. You're climbing the ladder fast."

The young detective laughed off the compliment, but his "aw shucks" demeanor was patently false. "Sir, I mean Patrick, I'm a lucky man."

His host greeted Eddie's words with a snort. "Come on, Eddie. Modesty doesn't become a cool cat like you. You're smart, made your way up the ladder through hard work and gumption." Patrick sat down once again, reclining in his chair, a grin spread across his face. "By the way, we have a mutual friend, Willie Corolla."

The young detective's smirk broadened. "Yes, I know Willie very well."

Their host suddenly stiffened, and his demeanor chilled. "I believe you're courting his daughter Bianca. She's a lovely girl, Daddy's goddaughter, a sister to me. I'd hate to think someone might hurt her."

Eddie's grin magically disappeared. "No, Patrick, I'd never hurt her."

Patrick leaned back in his chair, his attention still on Eddie. "I see politics in your future, my friend."

The young detective's grin returned. "Yes, sir, Patrick, Mama is determined that I get into politics."

Young Renaud slapped the top of his desk. "I knew

it. I'm never wrong. Eddie, I saw drive written all over your face the moment you stepped in my office. Since our current mayor keeps running for governor, who knows, maybe you will be mayor one day. I'd like to converse with you about your future when you have a minute."

Eddie strode over to Patrick and pumped his hand. "Mr. Renaud, uh, Patrick, anytime, sir, anytime."

Désirée noted that Renaud scribbled on the back of two business cards lying atop his desk and handed one to each officer. "I didn't mean to leave you out, Gino. If y'all want to stop by the Mason-Dixon tonight and celebrate the birth of our great nation, everything's on the house."

Eddie glanced at the card; his lips spread in a wide grin. Désirée wasn't close enough to smell him, but she was certain he reeked of ambition.

"Thank you, Patrick." Eddie pocketed the cash, straightened his tie, and ran his fingers through his dark hair. "It sure was a pleasure doing business with you. Come on, Gino."

When the two detectives exited the office, Louie pulled her farther into the darkened alcove.

Eddie walked past them. The whiff of his lavender cologne slashed through the club's funk. "You heard that, Gino? Junior Renaud, the son of the richest fellow in the city, wants us to call him by his first name."

The young detective's elation seemed to be limitless, and he continued crowing. "Not only did we meet Junior, but he even talked about me being mayor, mayor of New Orleans."

Gino chomped on his gum. "Yeah, I heard the man."

The detective ignored his friend's lack of enthusiasm. "Gino, if we play this right, we won't have to deal with the scum of the earth no more."

"Ain't having a good job enough for you?"

Eddie stopped dead in his tracks and shot his partner a poisonous look. "Hell, no, it's not enough. You might be happy with a houseful of screaming brats and think you hit it big with some cracker box in Jefferson Parrish, but that's not enough for me, man."

Eddie's face suddenly took on a beatific glow. "I got me a girl with a rich daddy and another on the side. Having fellows like Junior and his daddy in my corner makes everything aces. Mama says strike while the iron is hot, so I'm striking. Think big, Gino, think big."

As the two detectives trudged down the hall, Désirée heard her uncle's heart beating out of his chest.

Chapter Three
The Crown Prince of New Orleans

Désirée wrenched away from her uncle the moment Eddie and Gino disappeared down the corridor. "What's wrong with you? Trying to break my hand or something?"

Even in the dim light, Désirée noted that all color had left his face. "Sorry, boo, but that son-of-a-bitch, Vitale, put me in Angola. Why the hell did I have to run into the bastard?" Then, without warning, his mood lightened, and his smile returned. Louie took her hand in his, but gently. "Let me get your money, and we'll be on our way."

He gave her a sideways glance, and his face darkened. "Boo, I, uh, never mind." She knew something important sat on the tip of his tongue. Instead of spitting it out, Louie sprinted from their hiding place and tapped on the half-open office door.

A warm, "Come on in," greeted him. Louie strolled into the office while Désirée watched from the corridor.

Patrick continued perusing his paperwork when Louie entered. He'd planted the fan directly in front of him and appeared to relish the coolness. His charming demeanor vanished the moment he looked up. "Oh, it's you, Louie. I know what you're here for."

Her view unimpeded, she examined his face. He looked to be in his mid-twenties, surprisingly youthful for someone so comfortable with power. The young man rose from his chair, sauntered over to the office safe resting in a corner, pulled out a small wad of bills, and handed the roll to Louie. "Here you go. Thanks for helping my father's guests get their taste of brown sugar. Goodbye."

Louie grabbed the cash and shoved it into his pocket. "Excuse me, sir. I noticed you had two cops in your office. Vitale is a bad actor, sir. If you don't mind me asking, Mr. Renaud, what was he doing here?"

Patrick, his eyes throwing darts at Louie, plopped in his chair. "I do mind you asking." He tossed her uncle a cigarette, then spoke in tones as dulcet as Karo syrup. "Louie, since I acquired this place, I've probably had as many encounters with the police as you've had, a necessary evil if you do business in New Orleans. The one called Gino seems malleable enough. I can use him."

"Sir, Vitale is as big a thug as his brother Sal."

Patrick chuckled at the comment, his voice dark and sensual. "I know he is, but there's ambition there, brains, too, and he has connections. The bastard will be useful. Remember what Shakespeare wrote about vaulting ambition?"

The room went silent, as Louie turned scarlet with anger. His words tumbled from his mouth in a rage-filled rant. "Shakespeare? I don't know Shakespeare, sir. Hell, I barely made it through the third grade. Vitale is a son-of-a-bitch who can't be trusted."

Patrick hesitated before speaking. "Louie, isn't that a case of the pot calling the kettle black? I don't like Vitale, but I know men, and I can work with the prick, at least, for now."

Louie's hands shook so violently he couldn't light the cigarette. "Mr. Renaud, it's like I said, he's a conniving, evil bastard. If you ever need help getting rid of him, I'm the man to do it."

Her heart pumped at full speed. Her uncle may have been a liar, a thief, and a pimp, but Désirée had never heard him declare he'd rub someone out. The thought of him murdering someone, even a skunk like Vitale, made her want to dash out of the Lucky 13.

The young man waved Louie closer and spoke softly into his ear, over-enunciating each word. "Louie, let me speak in a language you understand, you frigging jailbird pimp. I need that bastard. He's with the police, he's a smart son-of-a-bitch, and maybe one day, God willing, Daddy and I can make him mayor, so we can run this town. Now, don't ever say anything like that again."

Louie's eyes widened after his massive *faux pas*. "I didn't mean it, I swear."

Patrick shifted the chair and stared down at the paperwork littering his desk.

Her uncle shifted nervously in place. "Before I leave, sir, I'd like to introduce you to my niece." He called out to Désirée. "C'mon in, *cher*, and meet Mr. Renaud. C'mon, baby."

Despite the tongue-lashing Patrick Renaud had given her uncle, Désirée ambled into the office as ordered. Patrick looked up at her, his beautiful eyes moving north until they fixed on her face.

"Well, well, who would've thunk it? How could someone like Louie Favre be related to this beauty?"

He rose and sauntered toward her, a lazy smile on his lips. Her resolve to be strong disappeared the minute his dimples emerged. Her mother swore dimples were the result of an angel's kiss. If that were true, some cherub had planted humdingers on each cheek.

His eyes narrowed as he perused her face, and he extended his hand.

"Well, hello, I'm Patrick Renaud. Just who might you be, pretty lady?"

Her face warmed from the potent heat of his gaze. She extended her arm, gave his hand a shake, all the time praying he wouldn't notice she was blushing. From his smirk, she knew he had. "Désirée. My name is Désirée Broussard."

He took her hand in his. "A beautiful name for a beautiful damsel. It's lovely to meet you, Miss Broussard."

She prayed she wouldn't collapse from the power of his proximity. *Be still my heart.*

He released her hand, his tongue slid over his lips, and his indolent grin returned. "May I ask what brought you to the Lucky13?"

Louie pushed Désirée behind him before she could answer. "Chief, she don't know nothing about nothing. I got into a jam, and she loaned me some coin when nobody else would. I need to pay her back because she just lost her job."

The young man's grin transformed into a scowl when his eyes rested on Louie. "You didn't need to worry. I wasn't going to bite her."

Patrick turned his attention back to Désirée, looking her up and down, examining the girl like a prize heifer, but stopping short of checking her teeth. He broke out into another dimpled smile. "What kind of work do you do, Miss Broussard?"

The intensity of his gaze made her head throb. She felt as if someone was pummeling her skull. "Secretarial, sir, and a little bookkeeping, too."

His head moved from side to side as he scrutinized her. Then he smirked. "For true? I need a secretary. Do you know how to type?"

Dimples or no dimples, his words felt like a slap in her face. She felt her spine go rigid and bristled at his dismissive manner. Although it took strength, she remained calm.

"Mr. Renaud, I led my class in secretarial school and can type over a hundred words a minute with no mistakes. I mastered Gregg shorthand and own a Smith Corona electric typewriter…sir."

"Very impressive, Miss Broussard. Tell me, how did you lose your job?"

At that point, her nerves got the best of her. She tittered, shifted her feet, and finally averted her face. "Well, you see, my previous employer, a very distinguished lawyer, had this lady friend who, uh, misinterpreted our relationship. He had to let me go, but he gave me a really good letter of recommendation."

Patrick's eyes twinkled like two dark stars. "You seem quite capable." He bowed in her direction. "Miss Broussard, shall we discuss the job on Wednesday, day after tomorrow? I'm afraid I might need time to recover from tonight's festivities. I'm sure you know where Maison Renaud is located, don't you?"

She gave him a curt nod. Everyone in New Orleans knew Maison Renaud, a walled mansion on Governor Nicholls Street. "Yes, Mr. Renaud, I'm familiar with it."

His teeth glinted in the urine-colored light. "Good.

I'll see you at ten on Wednesday morning. Please be prompt."

With that, he scooped up the papers from the desk and turned his back on Louie and Désirée. She felt her pulse rise at the abruptness of his dismissal and struggled to remain calm. *You heartless son-of-a-bitch.*

Désirée answered with a curt, "Thank you, Mr. Renaud," and moved toward the door. She'd prayed he hadn't heard the anger concealed behind her faux smile. On any other day, she would have told Patrick Renaud to bend over and stick his job where the sun don't shine. Unfortunately, she needed the work, so she said nothing.

Louie and Désirée turned to leave, and Patrick called out to her, his voice as warm as a glass of bourbon. "Miss Broussard, I have a special gift for reading people. Louie may be your uncle, but I doubt you have anything in common with him. Take this in the event you have to contact me."

Patrick held out one of his business cards.

Louie mouthed, "Take it." She had nothing to lose, so she dropped the signed card into her pocketbook. "Thank you, sir…I, uh—"

Before she could utter another word, Louie grabbed her arm and wrenched her out of the office. "Goodnight, Mr. Renaud."

****

Neither Louie nor Désirée made a peep until they knew the coast was clear. He handed her the cash, his lips spread into a knowing leer. "That Renaud fellow really liked you, boo. I could tell. Play your cards right, and maybe you'll get something good with him."

She snorted at his comment. "Once a pimp, always

a pimp. Forget trying to fix me up with Patrick Renaud. By the way, what was that bullshit about you rubbing out a policeman? Are you crazy?"

Uncle Louie stopped to light the cigarette he'd been too nervous to smoke in Patrick's office. His hands still shook, but he managed to take a long drag. "Girl, I was just jiving. He ain't nothing to me."

Désirée folded her arms, her anger obvious. "Well, you better be jiving. I don't need you getting your ass fried in Angola for killing a cop." She stepped in front of Louie, barring his way. "Swear to me. Swear you were only joking."

"I swear."

Louie Favre may have been a world-class liar, but for once, she believed him. Her uncle took a shaky drag off his cigarette. "Of all the bad luck in the world, I'm back in town for two weeks, and who do I run into? That wop. I was tight with his brother. We got into a little trouble one night, and Sal got himself killed. It wasn't my fault, but Vitale swore he'd see me dead."

In a bid to comfort him, she placed a hand on his arm. "What are you fixing to do?"

He threw down his cigarette, stomping it into the filthy linoleum. "Don't know. I'll think of something."

Désirée pulled the sixty dollars from her pocketbook and held it out to him. "Take it. Take the money back. You need it more than I do. Use it to get out of town. I have more in my savings, if you need it."

He shook his head, his tone defiant. "Damn it. I ain't going nowhere."

Désirée knew nothing she said would convince Louie to leave. "Where you staying?"

Louie mumbled a reply. "I don't know yet, but that

big-ass bulldagger, Tinkerbelle, will know how to find me. She hangs out at your mama's place sometimes."

Désirée shuddered at the name because she knew Tinkerbelle, but only by reputation. It wasn't a good one. "If I see her, I'll ask her where you are."

They strolled through the smelly darkness of the corridor before ambling into the musty bar illuminated by votive candles and lit cigarettes. Johnny Ace crooned "Forever, My Darling" from the jukebox. Drunken laughter emanated from a corner table covered in half-empty glasses. A trio of B-girls were entertaining a group of business men. A couple danced an erotic grind on the tiny dance floor. The smoke from thousands of Old Golds and Lucky Strikes had drenched the ratty brocade cushions and threadbare carpet in tobacco funk.

Désirée heard a coquettish giggle and turned her head toward a dimly lit booth. A delicate girl sat between a muscular youth bristling with male swagger and a hulking, red-faced fellow in a tuxedo. The remains of a plate of fried shrimp and a tumbler of bourbon sat on the countertop.

Candlelight illuminated the trio. The boy sitting with the drunk was minus an Adam's apple, sideburns, and five o'clock shadow, a handsome young woman rather than a male. She wore dungarees and, despite the intense heat, a jacket over her T-shirt, her breasts tightly bound.

The young butch placed a proprietary arm around the waifish beauty with soft blue eyes and long blonde hair curling about her face. Rhinestones glittered from her ears and Max Factor makeup enhanced her delicate features. A strapless bodice of sea-foam green chiffon accented her neck and shoulders. Désirée had seen the girl in passing, the lovely Baby Ruth, once the Lucky 13's biggest draw. Baby Ruth supposedly possessed an enormous member, rumored to be one of the largest in New Orleans.

The young butch refilled her companion's glass with bourbon. "Here you go, captain."

Baby Ruth tilted her face toward the drunken man but kept her attention riveted on an oversized ruby that flashed from his left pinky. The john slammed his glass down on the tabletop, his focus on Baby Ruth.

"Darlin', the name's Boyd Yates. They call me the Cadillac King. We don't have nothin' like you and that big candy bar between your legs in Memphis."

The butch winked at the bartender and yelled, "Another round, barkeep!"

The gorge crawled up Désirée's throat, and she wanted to scream a warning to Mr. Yates. He may have been the Cadillac King in Memphis, but he'd been taken in by the oldest con in the Quarter, paying for overpriced bourbon while Baby Ruth and her companion sipped cold tea. The B-drinkers would split the difference with the bartender, and the drunk would be none the wiser.

Désirée hissed at Louie under her breath, "They're going to roll that fellow."

When she took a step toward the booth, Louie grabbed her arm and pulled her back. "You ain't doing shit, Désirée."

She pointed to the drunken man. "But what about him?"

He pushed her forward toward the exit. "Who cares if Baby Ruth and that dagger roll the chump? It just might teach the bastard a lesson."

Désirée realized the fruitlessness of trying to stop the inevitable. She shrugged, took a step toward the threshold, but a familiar scent stopped her from crossing. A sudden shower brought on by the intense humidity had washed some of the noxious stench from the alley and slickened the asphalt. The sweetness of lavender cologne cut through the cigarette smoke. Eddie Vitale and Gino DeLuca huddled together, having a smoke near the club's entrance.

She murmured to her uncle. "Vitale's out there."

Louie's eyes widened with panic. Instead of returning to the bar, he ran outside. *"Au revoir*, Désirée!"

It took a quarter of a second before Gino recognized the wiry man who rushed past them. "Hey, Eddie, ain't that Louie Favre?"

Eddie dropped his cigarette and looked at Louie's retreating form. "I'll be a monkey's uncle. It's Louie, all right!"

The pair took off, chasing Louie as he ran for dear life.

Désirée watched as the trio raced away into the night, then mouthed a prayer, "Virgin Mary, please intercede with your Son on behalf of my uncle. I know he's a sorry sack of shit, but I love him and don't want to see him killed."

She turned and made her way down the street.

Chapter Four
The Starlight Bar and Grill

A tune sung in a lusty contralto wafted down Rue St. Marc. Even exploding firecrackers couldn't drown out the street singer as she belted out a ballad of lost loves and broken hearts in the Creole-French dialect. Some called it *Le musique Creole*; Désirée knew it as la-la music, and everyone in New Orleans recognized the singer.

Madame Ruby had performed on Quarter street corners for decades. Despite her blindness, she outplayed half the musicians in the city. The stubborn old woman insisted on singing her heart out in dark alcoves and corners instead of in the comfort of a club. She'd enthrone herself in a folding chair and finger her accordion for hours on end as she stomped out the rhythm with one foot on a pedal attached to an old snare drum.

"Madame Ruby, what you doing out so late?"

When she heard a familiar voice, Madame Ruby flashed her teeth, their pearly whiteness in deep contrast to skin the color of chocolate velvet. People around the Quarter who'd grown up listening to her music figured she had to be at least eighty, but with her unlined face, she didn't look a day over fifty.

"Is that you, Désirée? I'm waiting for Willie to pick me up. The lazy bastard ain't made it here yet."

The old woman gave a toss of her head, an invitation to move closer. When Désirée inched nearer, Madame Ruby whispered in her ear. "Darling, I heard your uncle is in town, and, little girl, I'm about to catch me a heart attack. You tell him to get his scrawny ass out of New Orleans before the cops get him."

Désirée felt her gut knot up. "No one was supposed to know he'd come back. Do you carry a crystal ball in your accordion case? How did you find out about Uncle Louie?"

The blind woman's cackle rolled down the street. "The glaucoma took my eyes, but my ears is twenty-twenty. The police told me they lookin' for him, but if you run into him, don't tell him you heard it from Madame Ruby. No, sir. Uncle or not, that rascal would be madder than a wet hen if he knew I talked to the police. He'd sooner cut me as look at me."

Désirée knelt next to the singer's chair. "Ah, come on, Madame Ruby. Uncle Louie may be a skunk, but he wouldn't do anything to you."

When the old woman turned her gaze toward her, Désirée felt energy emitting from her sightless eyes. "Don't know about that. He's one mean bastard. Tell your mama to watch out for the cops, too. They going to start raiding the queer bars soon. Now, you go on, I got to sing."

Désirée dug into her pocketbook, found a fifty-cent piece, and dropped it into the accordion case before walking off.

Madame Ruby pounded out a two-step rhythm on the drum pedal, tossing her head back as she belted out a tune.

****

A casual observer strolling into the Starlight Lounge couldn't immediately distinguish it from any other bar in the Quarter. Dank and threadbare, it reeked of tobacco smoke, stale beer, and sweating bodies. The décor appeared to be an afterthought, embossed stars patterning the linoleum flooring, mustard-colored Naugahyde enveloping the booths. Star-shaped Christmas lights festooned the mirrored wall behind the solid-oak bar.

The flag-draped portrait of a young man dressed in a Marine uniform sat alongside a Purple Heart and Gold Star. It appeared out of place, nestled among the bottles of rum, bourbon, and scotch behind the bar.

Désirée elbowed her way through a mob of rowdy, muscular youths and a few fawning femmes. These sexual outlaws pursued their own version of the game of love, one that aped male/female relationships. Masculine young men flirted with effete boys who dared to wear makeup and nail polish. Drunken sailors on leave frolicked with lads doused in perfume, lipstick, and rouge. A few young ladies clustered together, their maleness concealed beneath swishy chiffon.

Désirée had grown up with such relationships, which were *de rigueur* in queer clubs throughout the country. Some of the rougher boys were actually girls garbed in dungarees and penny loafers, their cropped hair styled into ducktails. "Saturday night" butches would exchange their shirtwaist dresses for dungarees and T-shirts and search for feminine women who shared their proclivities. The law prohibited cross-dressing, so police raids were a constant threat. Sometimes, a respectable married man would take the chance of spending a few stolen moments in a queer bar. In the event of a blitz by the cops, the results could be disastrous—night court, the fellow's name in the paper, job loss, and total social ruin. Désirée couldn't help respecting the men and women who literally took their lives in their hands in their search for romance.

After fighting her way through the crowd, Désirée finally reached the loveliest bartender, a blonde beauty of about thirty-five.

Women weren't supposed to serve liquor in New Orleans, but no one dared to deliver that information to the loveliest barkeep in Louisiana. She'd once been first runner-up for Miss New Orleans and had picked up the nickname "Young Miss" from her time on the beauty contest circuit. People swore she favored the film star Lana Turner, but Désirée thought her much more beautiful.

"Hey, Ma…uh, I mean, Young Miss."

They shared the same full lips and brown eyes, but her mother had bleached her locks to the color of lemonade. Her tapered hands glittered with jewelry from admirers, and she'd lacquered her nails Fire & Ice red. She smoked her Lucky Strikes with an ivory cigarette holder.

Young Miss plopped a Coke in front of her daughter. "Désirée, what are you doing here?"

Before Désirée could answer, a fellow aimed a Brownie camera at a group of young men clustered around the entryway. "Stand still, y'all, and say 'cheese.'"

An agitated Young Miss rushed to the edge of the counter and called out to them, "Hey! Get that thing out of here. Surest way to empty a queer bar is to point a camera at somebody."

Désirée took her place next to an old butch named Claude who sat alone at the bar. Claude ignored everyone, concentrating instead on her bourbon and branch. Pruned out from years of smoking and drinking, she was a strange old bird, even by New Orleans standards. Claude kept her story close to the vest, but rumors of a husband and child circulated, incredible to anyone who looked at her now. When people discovered she worked as a morgue attendant, some questioned how anyone could distinguish her from the stiffs. Folks only realized she had a pulse and a working heart when she pounded her shot glass on the bar and yelled, "Barkeep, I need another drink."

Except for the few who sported crewcuts and dress shirts, most of the fellows garbed themselves in dungarees and taut T-shirts that displayed their pectorals. Bill Hayley's "Shake, Rattle and Roll" blared from the jukebox. New Orleans law made it illegal for queers to dance together in public, but two boys thumbed their noses at the law and bounced to the spirited jive. They rocked and rolled to the cheers of patrons until a skirmish broke out between two drunken sailors.

The battling seamen provoked Young Miss's ire once again. "Take that mess outside."

Désirée looked up from her Coke and saw a reflection in the mirror behind the bar. At any other time, she would have backed away, but not that night. She jumped up from the stool and, once again, pushed her way through the crowd.

The crowd parted for a beefy gal in dungarees, a pack of Camel cigarettes rolled into her shirt sleeve, her fingers and teeth stained yellow by nicotine. Even from a distance, the woman smelled as if she'd marinated herself in booze and cigarettes. Her eyes glared pale blue and bloodshot in her red face, her nostrils flared like an enraged steer. The whispers that every barkeep in the Vieux Carré had eighty-sixed her seemed to ring true.

No one knew her real name, but locals referred to her by various appellations, including "the bull bitch," "that crazy dyke," and "Tinkerbelle." For some unknown reason, the nickname Tinkerbelle had stuck, though there was nothing elfin or the least bit Peter Pan-ish about her.

A hip cat, his hair sculpted into a pompadour, took the large woman by the arm before Désirée could reach her. The crowd hemmed her in and she couldn't make her way to the butch. She watched as Tinkerbelle pulled a roll of pills wrapped in tinfoil from her pocket and exchanged it for cash.

Young Miss caught Tinkerbelle's eye and flagged her down.

Tinkerbelle lumbered over to the bar, her lips spread in a mad smile. "What you know good?"

Young Miss spat out a reply. "The police have been around inquiring if we're selling reefer and Benzedrine in my establishment. That's what I know good. I'd be obliged if you'd take your musty ass out of here and don't come back."

Tinkerbelle locked the barkeep in a death glare before lunging, but Young Miss had speed and sobriety on her side. She pulled a small caliber pistol from beneath the bar and aimed it directly at Tinkerbelle's head. All the patrons, with the exception of Claude, moved away.

"Tinkerbelle, take one step, just one little step, and your troubles will be over forever."

The butch broke into a hellish grin. "I'll get you, bitch. Maybe not today, but I'll get you!" She shoved her way through the crowd and disappeared into the night before Désirée could stop her.

Désirée returned to the bar and collapsed onto a stool. "Mama, I needed to talk to her."

For Désirée's entire twenty years on earth, her mother had ordered her to address her as "Young Miss." She reminded her daughter with an angry hiss. "Haven't I told you a million times not to call me 'Mama' when I'm working?"

Young Miss arched a drawn-on eyebrow and replaced the pistol under the counter. "What the hell do you want with trash like Tinkerbelle?"

Désirée's shoulders slumped as if they carried all of New Orleans on them, and the words flooded from her mouth. "Uncle Louie is in town, and the police are after him. I saw him tonight. Before he ran away, he said Tinkerbelle was the only way I can reach him."

Young Miss crossed herself, and her eyes rolled up to the heavens. "Lord, have mercy. Louie is in New Orleans? For true? Listen, if you see the bastard again, and I hope to hell you don't, tell that son-of-a-bitch to keep his scrawny behind away from here. He's only my half-brother anyway. I swear, he's worse than his no-good daddy, and they sent that piece of scum to the chair."

One of the bickering sailors screamed at the top of his lungs, "You motherfucker!"

He pounded on a countertop, interrupting Young Miss's diatribe. She pointed the pugilists out to a burly, tattooed fellow, her third husband, Jim Dandy. "Baby, take care of them."

Jim Dandy raced from the bar, grabbed the offenders by the scuffs of their necks, and pushed them toward the exit. "Get out of here and don't come back!"

Young Miss snorted her rage, obvious when she snapped at her daughter. "Désirée, I've told you a million times, I don't want you associating with Louie. I swear, if you wasn't related to him, that pimp bastard would've tried to turn you out years ago."

"Yes, Ma, uh, I mean, yes, Young Miss."

The Fourth of July hadn't turned out as she'd planned. No adventures with *Auntie Mame*, but Désirée did have one bit of brightness to share with her mother. "Ma, I mean, Young Miss, I have a job interview on Wednesday."

Young Miss's beautiful lips finally widened into a smile. "That's wonderful, darlin'."

"I have to share the best part. Can you believe it? Mr. Patrick Renaud Jr. is interviewing me."

Her mother's smile grew even bigger. "For true? How did you manage that?"

Désirée chose her words with care. If Young Miss knew that her daughter had crossed the threshold of the Lucky 13, especially with Louie, she would have beaten her within an inch of her life. "Well, uh, the secretarial school called. They said Mr. Renaud was looking for someone to take dictation and type his correspondence, and they recommended me."

Young Miss smiled at her daughter's answer. "Good for you, baby. When are you going to meet Mr. Renaud?"

Before Désirée could sputter another lie, a girlish

giggle caught her attention. She turned just as the trio from the Lucky 13 entered the Starlight.

The young butch and Baby Ruth plodded through the crowd dragging the drunken Mr. Yates with them. The masculine girl led Yates to the booth vacated by the sailors and eased the drunken man onto the Naugahyde-covered bench. The butch patted the old souse on the back. "Come on, chief. It's time for another drink."

Baby Ruth slid next to Yates. The drunk grinned at the demure girl, bellowing over the din. "Hey, bartender! Get me a beer, and a bourbon and branch for the gentleman, and a Brandy Alexander for the young lady."

Yates turned to Baby Ruth, a sordid endearment rolling off his tongue. "I sure would like to play with that big sucker between your legs, sweet pea."

Baby Ruth broke out in titters. "Mr. Yates, you're very naughty. What would my mama say?"

The drunk pulled a black leather billfold embossed with the initials B.Y. from his breast pocket. He folded a twenty-dollar bill and dropped it down Baby Ruth's bodice. "Show this to your mama."

Yates made a stab at replacing the wallet but failed. In his drunken state, he didn't notice when the young butch relieved him of it. Luckily for the girl, only Désirée saw the theft.

The trio caught Young Miss's eye, and her upper lip curled in an involuntary sneer. She threw the bar rag on the counter before murmuring to Jim Dandy. "Damn it. I told Frankie not to bring johns here, but the kid has a head like a rock. That's just what I need with the flatfoots hanging around. Take that old bastard outside.

We don't need no trouble with the cops."

Jim Dandy worked his way through the revelers. Yates cast a watery eye at the burly man and extended his hand. "The name's Boyd Yates. In Memphis, they call me the 'Cadillac King.'"

Jim Dandy eased the drunken man up from the booth, glaring at Frankie all the while. "Mr. Yates, let's go outside to get some air."

Yates looked back at Baby Ruth. "What about my little gal?"

Jim Dandy helped the drunk to his feet. "New Orleans is full of little gals like that. Come on, chief."

Baby Ruth waited a moment, rose from her seat, and followed the two men to the rear of the club. She turned to blow a kiss in the masculine girl's direction before she slithered away.

Frankie, bristling with male swagger, left the booth and made her way to the bar. She shifted in place before taking the stool next to Désirée, who noticed the young woman sported a singularly masculine lump on the left side of her crotch and withheld a snicker. The girl was packing. Perhaps the young butch had convinced herself no one could tell the difference between a stuffed sock and a masculine package, but Désirée could.

Another butch joined Frankie at the bar. The other kid couldn't have been older than seventeen and lacked her companion's blustering masculinity. Désirée noticed a gentle refinement about her, a feminine quality, especially for a butch.

The girl gifted her with a sly smile and then averted her head. Désirée noted something familiar about her features, her dimples and her dark, unfathomable eyes. She'd seen her face before but couldn't quite place it.

The more masculine girl sat back on the stool, a lewd grin on her face. "Well, hey, sugar, you're looking awful sweet tonight. I'm Frankie, and my friend's name is Samantha, only I call her Sammy." Frankie turned to Young Miss. "Hey, Young Miss, how about Dixie beers for me and Sammy? Maybe you could mix up a Brandy Alexander for the young lady?"

Young Miss cast a wary eye on Frankie before speaking to Jim Dandy over her shoulder. "Two Dixie beers for Frankie and her friend. I already poured a Coke for the young lady."

Frankie arched an eyebrow. "Well, let me pay for her drink."

Young Miss smirked at the young butch. "You certainly will."

Chapter Five
The Cadillac King

A sweat-drenched Eddie and Gino doubled back through the alleyway behind the Starlight. Eddie wiped his face with his partner's handkerchief, ran his fingers through his dark hair, then straightened his tie.

"How the hell did Louie get away when we were right on his ass? We must have hit every rat hole on St. Marc and still missed him. Shit. Now I messed up the new shirt my cousin Angelo made special for me. I'll kill the bastard next time I see him."

A voice called out from the darkness. "God damn it. I need me another drink."

Eddie spotted a heavy-set, red-faced drunk in a tuxedo, hovering in the darkness. "Well, what have we here?"

The drunken man staggered over to them, his hand extended. "Hey, fellows. The name's Boyd Yates from Memphis. Come on inside and let me buy y'all a drink."

Eddie ignored the drunk's hand. "Chief, you don't hardly need another drink. You can barely walk as is. Go on now."

The drunken man took a wobbly step back. "You New Orleans folks ain't very sociable, are you? Do y'all know who I am?"

Eddie rolled his eyes. "No, I don't know who you

are and don't give a shit."

The older man puffed up his chest. "I'm the Cadillac King of Memphis."

Eddie sneered at Yates. "Well, we're the police, and you ain't in Memphis. Look, man, sober up and go back to Tennessee."

Yates shoved his hand into his pocket and felt around. "Where's my billfold? What's going on?" He felt his empty breast pocket and stumbled over to Eddie. "You took my money. Give me my wallet!"

Eddie pushed the drunk away. "Man, I told you, we're the police. We don't have your wallet. Who the hell you think you're talking to anyway?"

Yates glared at Eddie through watery eyes. "I'm talking to you, pretty boy." The drunk took a step forward and looked the young detective up and down. "Hey, fancy man, you a dago or something? I heard dagos run New Orleans. My daddy used to say dagos and Jews were one step from niggers."

The drunk followed up his words by spitting in Eddie's face. Eddie didn't change expression, but his eyes reddened with volcanic fury.

Gino circled Yates and pinned his arms behind his back.

All of a sudden, Yates's bourbon-drenched fog evaporated and fear emerged. Eddie, his anger seething to the surface, wiped away the spittle, pulled a set of brass knuckles from his belt, and slipped one over each hand. "Maybe you can do that mess in Memphis, you son-of-a-bitch, but not in New Orleans." Eddie glared at the drunk, his eyes two blue caldrons of rage. "My people were warriors and kings when your sorry-ass folks were still picking fleas out of their assholes."

Eddie connected a powerful right to the drunk's chin and let loose a barrage of blows to his face. When Yates's lower plate popped out, Gino pulled away and let the drunk's head slam against a brick wall. Yates slid to the ground, and Eddie delivered a few violent kicks to the prone man's side. "This is for what you said about my people. This is for messing up my new shirt, and this is for being an ugly peckerwood, you bag of dirt. Next time, keep your ass in Memphis."

When the young detective pulled his leg back to give Yates another kick, Gino stopped him. "Man, come on before you kill the bastard. We got business inside."

Eddie removed the brass knuckles and then looked down at the drunk. "Shit. First Louie Favre, and now because of this piece of shit, I'm too funky to go to the Mason-Dixon. Screw both of them." He pulled the ring from Yates's finger and placed it on his own pinkie. The ring flashed on Eddie's hand.

Gino took an angry step toward him. "Eddie, man, put it back."

The young man held the ring up in the dim light. "Hell no, I'm not putting it back. It's probably glass, but I'll have my cousin, the jeweler, look at it."

The two detectives walked away unaware someone had watched them from the shadows. Baby Ruth ambled over to Yates, gazed into his battered face and took off as fast as her stiletto pumps allowed. In her haste, she didn't notice when one of her rhinestone earrings dropped to the ground.

****

A minute later, Eddie and Gino strolled across the Starlight's threshold. Young Miss flashed the house lights on and off, the time-honored signal to let everyone know the law had entered the premises. Patrons crossed over to customers of the opposite sex. The Starlight changed from an animated bistro into a tomb.

Désirée sat at the bar, frozen in place.

The two detectives ambled through the bar, smirking at the boys in drag and the butch women. Eddie strolled up to the bar and leaned on the counter, smirking like the cock of the walk.

Young Miss gave him a wary look before placing an envelope on the counter. Eddie pocketed the envelope and fumbled around until he found a cigarette. Young Miss pulled a Zippo from under the counter and turned it up full blast. She nearly scorched Eddie's face when he bent over for a light.

His mouth twisted into a crooked smile at her show of defiance. He grabbed her lighter and fired the cigarette himself. Eddie took a leisurely drag as he scanned the bar, his boredom obvious until he caught sight of Désirée. He exchanged a look with Gino, broke into a wide grin, and slid next to her. "Well, hello, beautiful. Please don't tell me you're a queer."

Désirée sat motionless, her mouth tightening as Eddie amused himself by breathing into her ear. She glanced into his icy eyes and smelled his lavender aftershave. Being in such proximity chilled her more than seeing him at the Lucky 13.

Jim Dandy took a step forward, but Young Miss took his arm. "Let me handle this, darlin'." She tossed back her shoulders and sauntered over to Eddie, a scowl marring her lovely face. "Leave her alone, you prick. You got your money, so why don't you and your friend shove off?"

He looked from Young Miss to Désirée, ignoring the fury behind the bartender's words. Eddie's leer transformed to a knowing grin. "Oh, now I see it. Y'all favor each other. She's your sister, isn't she?" His attention returned to Désirée. "That means you're also related to that piece of shit Louie Favre. In case you didn't know it, he's back in town."

Désirée stared straight ahead without saying a word. Eddie shrugged his shoulders and scanned the bar. His gaze fell on Samantha, fixing her under a blue spotlight, and he circled the girl as he spoke to his partner. "Well, look at this, Gino. We found us a pretty boy; only look, he's got more. Girlie, you're too young to bother with this dagger mess. If I wasn't in a benevolent mood, I'd rush your ass straight to reform school."

Eddie rose and strolled over to the front door with Gino trailing behind him. He spun around, took one last look at Désirée, glanced at Samantha, snickered, and exited the bar.

In an instant, the Starlight became lively again. A furious Frankie marched over to Young Miss. "Well, ain't that some bullshit? I come here because I've never seen the law, until tonight that is. Shit, I thought they stayed away."

Young Miss glanced in Jim Dandy's direction, and the two of them snickered at the angry butch. "It's not your concern how me and my husband run our business. We've come to an understanding with Captain Vitale. I deal with him so some fat-ass bubba in a uniform won't barge in here and beat up my customers."

Frankie puffed out her chest like a bruiser aching for a fight. "Somebody needs to kick his ass."

Young Miss threw the bar rag down in disgust. "Kick his ass? Nobody kicks Eddie Vitale's ass. You think he's just another pretty wop punk, don't you? Well, he's not. I knew a fellow who went after a gal Vitale was screwing. Vitale didn't like it. Now the guy can't hardly walk no more. If you're looking for trouble, look somewhere else."

Samantha took her friend's arm. "You need to listen to what she's saying."

Frankie pulled away from her and stormed off with Samantha on her heels.

Young Miss sang out to the girls. "Remember what they say, a hard head makes a soft behind!" She focused her attention back on her daughter. "Désirée, I think you've had enough excitement for tonight. Go on home and call me tomorrow afternoon. We need to get you a nice frock and discuss your interview with Mr. Renaud. I've heard he's a fine young fellow."

If Young Miss only knew.

****

A blast of sultry night air welcomed Eddie and Gino when they left the Starlight. Eddie took his place behind the wheel of the '54 Ford police car emblazoned with the Star and Crescent of New Orleans. The stench of vomit hit his nostrils the moment he opened the door.

"Damn, Gino, I can still smell where that junkie puked. Crack the glass on your side, man."

Gino rolled down the passenger's window before popping a piece of gum into his mouth. "Aw, come on, Eddie. It ain't so bad."

The young detective glared at his partner. "You got

four kids, so you must be used to puke, but I'm not. And would you stop with the chewing, man?"

Gino pulled the half-chewed gum out of his mouth and folded it back in the foil wrapper. "I got to do something. Ophelia's pregnant again, and she gets sick when I smoke around her."

Eddie gave his partner a sideways glance. "Ophelia's pregnant? Again? Are you clowning me? Didn't she have a baby four months ago? Have you ever heard of rubbers?"

Gino shook his head. "The priest told Ophelia we can't use rubbers, got to use that rhythm thing."

Eddie pounded on the steering wheel, beating it like a bongo drum. "The rhythm thing? What the hell does a priest know about babies? Where is he when you need money for diapers and milk, or when the smell of the shit and piss stinks up the whole house? Man, don't you want something more?"

Just as Eddie turned the key in the ignition, a group of black teenagers tossed a cherry bomb at the police car and ran off. "Try and catch us, ofay!"

Eddie yelled out a half-hearted reply. "Kiss my ofay ass, you jiggaboo bastards." He turned back to Gino. "What was you saying, man?"

Gino remained glum. "You're right, Eddie. Ophelia hit the roof when I told her I didn't want no more kids. Damn, I got crappy luck."

Eddie fingered Yates's pinkie ring. "Listen, man, maybe your luck is about to change. If we play this right, we won't have to deal with the scum of the earth no more."

Gino stared at Eddie, his mouth tight, his eyes moistening.

Eddie's demeanor softened. "Congratulations on the new baby, man."

The police car roared down the street just as Désirée walked down St. Marc and made her way past the dark recesses of the Lucky 13. Had Patrick Renaud Junior roamed through the Lucky 13's dimly lit rooms? What did he make of the decadent acts, especially those of the strange woman in the leather bustier? She wondered if he'd joined in. The thought of him kneeling in front of that woman, his body taut with lust, stirred up feelings so strong she felt her panties dampen.

She rushed through the Quarter and turned onto Bourbon, a maze of gaudy neon signs. The brightest flashed from the roof of the Mason-Dixon Line, the older Patrick Renaud's pride and joy, an imposing nightclub with Grecian columns, the second-story encircled with wrought-iron balconies. In the magnolia-scented days of mint juleps and hooped skirts, the Mason-Dixon had been a plantation manor on a wealthy estate. Bonnie Blue flags celebrating the glory of the Old South still draped its walls. A banner ran across the entrance, welcoming one and all, that is, one and all with white skin and money to spend.

Ladies swathed in chic evening gowns and clouds of Joy perfume crossed its portal on the arms of gents in custom-tailored tuxes. *Gourmet Magazine* feted its cuisine and liquid refreshments as the finest in New Orleans, but food and drink alone didn't lure customers. A poster inside a glass kiosk displayed the charms of the current headliner, a ravishing platinum blonde ecdysiast, Lilly Thibodaux, the Bayou Volcano, the Queen of the Afro-Cuban Beat. Lilly's head tilted at a seductive angle, lips open in invitation, a fringed bikini barely concealing her curves.

She couldn't stop herself from scrutinizing Lilly's image, measuring the dancer's body against her own. They'd grown up together in the Quarter as best friends, yet Lilly had sparked an unspoken competition between the two girls. Désirée's bosom compared favorably to Miss Thibodaux's in shape and size, and some maintained that she possessed the curviest legs in the city. Her derriere surpassed Lilly's in roundness, and folks swore she must be part colored because of the plumpness of her ass.

She finally reached her home, where four white cottages with slanted roofs, the doors and shutters painted Chinese red, nestled behind a wrought iron gate. The little flats once ringed the courtyard of a great mansion and housed the master's mixed-blood concubines and children.

A small house with an inviting crimson door sat tucked at the rear of a cobblestone courtyard. Pink and red geraniums peeked from pots on the windowsills. Désirée unlocked the door and stepped into her little corner of the world.

The ceiling fan moved in a lazy drag. Still, it had cooled down the place so it no longer felt like the hot box on Devil Island. The incense she'd lit earlier made the flat smell like an Oriental spice shop. Her stomach growled, and she grabbed half of a po' boy sandwich from the icebox.

Works by Salinger, Faulkner, and Highsmith leaned against each other in pine bookshelves alongside copies of her short stories. Perhaps Désirée hoped some of the mojo from well-known authors would rub off on her writing, but except for two local literary anthologies, it hadn't worked. *Auntie Mame* sat open on her nightstand, but the evening had been a strange one. Mame Dennis's wild antics had nothing on hers.

The face of a dark youth stared out from a gilded frame. Désirée caressed the image of a boy who'd been as wild as a hurricane, kissed the glass that protected it, and placed it back on its perch. She'd kept the photo of Johnny, her lost love, nestled among her books for two agonizing years. After making short work of her sandwich, she stepped into the bathroom and filled the old clawfoot tub with hot water and bath salts. She stripped off her Capri pants, bra, and sodden panties, piled her hair on top of her head, and finally reclined in the soothing vapors.

No matter how much she fought it, she couldn't erase Mr. Renaud's beautiful face from her thoughts. Désirée wanted to crawl into those unfathomable pools he called eyes.

****

Young Miss carried a box loaded with empty liquor bottles through a side door leading to the rear. She lugged her load of jingling glass to the trash bin behind the Starlight and dumped it. The alley stench hit her nose, and she let out a curse. "Hell's bells!"

She traipsed around in the darkness, missed a step, and almost stumbled over a prone body.

"Damn it. Get up, bubba, and sleep it off somewhere else. Get up!" The fellow didn't move when she kicked his leg. Young Miss bent down closer. Yates's breathing was shallow. He stared back at her through open eyes, a pool of blood collecting around his head. She ran back into the bar.

Chapter Six
Maison Renaud

Désirée's phone rang at eleven in the evening. Still groggy from sleep, she let her hands scour the nightstand in the darkened chamber. No one ever called so late in the night. "Shit."

After a moment, she awakened in an instant and remembered her uncle. Her head throbbed, her pulse quickened, and her mind raced back to Louie's plight. Despite the heat, she shivered at the thought that he might have encountered the police. Désirée dreaded what horrible news might be lurking on the other end of the phone line. When she picked up the receiver, Young Miss's sobs greeted her.

"Mama?"

Silence. Then her mother's words spilled out from the phone. "Baby, I need you…here…now. I found that drunk from Memphis in the alley. Somebody beat the hell out of him. You should have seen the fellow, barely breathing, his dentures knocked out of his mouth. To make matters worse, the cops had the nerve to think one of my kids would hurt up some old guy like that."

Désirée threw on a blouse and a pair of Capris and rushed out into the night. By the time she arrived at the Starlight, a couple of uniformed officers still lingered in the alleyway, cooling their heels with smokes. The customers had deserted the place. Without the raucous pulse of youth, the Starlight was just another seedy, smoke-drenched dive.

Discovering the battered drunk had transformed Young Miss from a hard-edged beauty into a mascara-drenched pool of snot. She sat quaking from her ordeal, one hand in Jim Dandy's, her cigarette holder in the other.

Désirée poured a snifter full of brandy and set it in front of her mother. Young Miss placed her cigarette in an ashtray and swirled her glass before taking a healthy gulp. "Somebody knocked the shit out of that poor fellow. Who the hell would have done such a thing?"

Violence wasn't unknown on Rue St. Marc. "We're in New Orleans, Mama. Fellows get mugged all the time. Some thug probably tried to rob him."

Young Miss took another sip of brandy. "Not at the Starlight."

Jim Dandy kissed her hand. "Nasty stuff happens everywhere, darlin'."

The three sat in silence for an eternity, the quiet broken only by Young Miss's sobs.

Désirée had never seen her mother in such a state and exchanged a look with Jim Dandy. "Don't worry. I'll stay with you, Mama."

Her hands still trembled, but Young Miss managed a steady shake of her head. "No, baby. I shouldn't have called you in the first place, but I needed my little girl." She broke down, once again, and took another sip of brandy. They sat in silence until the liquor finally worked its magic. "Go on home, darling. I hope the old bastard will be okay. I'll call you in the morning, and we'll get you a new dress for your interview."

Désirée set her jaw at a determined angle and

didn't budge from her chair. "No, Mama, I'm staying."

Jim Dandy took his stepdaughter by the hand. "You need to get some sleep, baby. I'll take care of your mama. Let me drive you home."

She gave Young Miss a heartfelt hug before following Jim Dandy to the street.

****

By the next afternoon, Young Miss had banished Boyd Yates from her thoughts. Instead of wallowing in her predicament, she insisted on taking Désirée shopping for the proper interview ensemble. "You've got to look your best for Mr. Renaud."

Young Miss dragged her daughter from the Maison Blanche to D.H. Holmes as they purchased stockings, underwear, and stylish white blouses that she felt set a businesslike tone. Finally, her eyes lit on the right frock—a chic, bright-red shirtwaist with short sleeves and a white Peter Pan collar. "It'll look professional, Désirée, pretty without being prim, and not the least bit whorish."

No one on earth would describe the frock as "whorish." The dress gave her a pert secretarial look, perfect for a job interview, but not for her fantasies of Mr. Patrick Renaud. She'd planned to knock his eyes out, but that would have to wait.

****

The next morning, Désirée awoke to Lilly Thibodaux's orgasmic screams. "Oh, daddy! Do me good! Do me real good! That's it. Oh, daddy!"

Désirée had spent most of the previous night snoozing between the carnal wails emanating from the next cottage, an erotic frenzy. Lilly was captive to the lovemaking skills of her newest boyfriend, one Désirée had yet to meet. From the sheer volume of Lilly's groans, she figured the guy really knew how to get the business done. Since Désirée had lost her own husband, Lilly's sexual escapades had become her erotic release, but she'd made a desperate attempt to stop watching her friend's carnal adventures. She'd begged Lilly to close her windows and pull down the blinds during sex, but her friend ignored her. Lilly's noisy lovemaking kept her up at night. After a final, uncontrolled cry, another moan, this time from the man, the cottage went silent.

When Désirée opened her door to a scorching morning, the heat smacked her squarely in the face. As much as she wanted to shroud herself from her family's troubles, the urgency of their situation nixed hiding.

The kitchen clock read eight a.m., time for Désirée to ready herself for her appointment with Mr. Patrick Renaud.

After breakfast and a cool bath, she applied the Max Factor. People always remarked on her lively eyes, so she accented them with mascara, brown shadow, and pencil. A little face powder followed by rouge made her face glow, and then she coated her lips with coral lipstick. She didn't want to look like a B-girl from the Lucky 13, so she applied the cosmetics with a light touch. Désirée pulled her hair into a long ponytail fringed with curly wisps, then dabbed a bit of Shalimar on her pulse and neck. Before she dashed off, she grabbed her high school diploma, letters of recommendation, and a pair of white gloves.

Désirée feared arriving at Maison Renaud in a pool of sweat, so instead of rushing, she strolled through the Quarter at a leisurely pace. Unfortunately, dampness lingered in the air like a roaring drunk in a bar on a

Friday night. Everyone considered humidity a major curse of living in New Orleans, but on that July day, clothing stuck to skin as if glued on with Elmer's. Ladies with kinky hair knew it poofed like cotton candy. Others discovered hair lacquer was useless against wilting coiffures, so housewives did their early morning shopping with their locks in pin curls.

She turned onto Governor Nicholls, the street with the distinction of being the most exclusive enclave in the Quarter. In the city's past, wealthy Americans who refused to rub elbows with the French-speaking Creole elite had flocked to the Garden District. Governor Nicholls retained some of the European panache that made New Orleans unique.

By early morning, city workers had washed the grime from the cobblestones. The streets smelled of strawberries sold by street venders, the fragrance blending with the aroma of fresh-perked morning coffee and frying donuts.

Désirée strolled past an older gentleman garbed in an elegant ice cream suit, his Panama hat set at a jaunty angle. He observed the street scene from a perch encased in wrought iron. The gent sipped a mint julep from a crystal goblet. When Désirée sashayed past, he held up his glass in a gallant salute.

"Good morning, beautiful lady."

She embraced his greeting as a positive omen and returned his smile.

Her journey continued. A massive townhouse on the corner of Royal and Governor Nicholls loomed in the distance. She shivered, remembering the tales of the sadistic owner gleefully torturing and dismembering her slaves until the citizenry ran her out of New Orleans.

Désirée averted her face and moved on through the sultry mist.

The closer she got to the Maison Renaud, the more potent the perfume of French lavender scented the hot air.

When she finally reached her destination, the grandeur behind the gigantic stone fence forced her to catch her breath. An elaborate tower with huge arched windows peeked over the massive wall, which had been designed to protect the mansion from prying eyes. Désirée walked past interlocking blocks of terracotta-colored granite.

She approached an art nouveau wrought iron gate, the metal fashioned into intricate curlicues, interlocking leaves, and scrolls. Her heart pounded like a bass drum. Désirée looked through the elaborate twirls and helixes and glimpsed an enormous courtyard filled with marble statuary and flowering plants. An army of groundskeepers armed with clippers must have sculpted the verdant hedges, but that morning no one labored in the heat.

One glance at her watch, fifteen minutes to ten, calmed her, but Désirée's serenity disappeared when she pushed against the gate and found it impenetrable. "Shit." She searched for a secret lever or hidden lock but found nothing. Despite the high temperature, a chill overwhelmed her. Mr. Renaud had stressed promptness. Would being tardy, even if she couldn't help it, end the job before it started?

She ferreted around for a latch, a hidden panel, anything to allow entry, but found nothing. Sherlock Holmes couldn't have opened the gate. Desperate, she called out, "Hello, is anybody there?"

Silence greeted her. Désirée searched the massive wrought-iron affair, scouring the gate for another opening. Then something glinted from a decorative recess—a buzzer cut into one of the stone corners surrounding the gate.

Désirée took a deep breath before she pressed it. Nothing happened. She stewed in silence, glanced at her watch: ten minutes to ten. She called out once again, "Excuse me, but I have an appointment."

Finally, she heard footsteps sauntering toward the gate and sighed in relief. Through a space in the elaborate swirls, she glimpsed a figure garbed in a butler's white coat ambling toward her. The gate opened, and a smiling fellow greeted her. He appeared to be in his forties, his skin the color of pale honey. "What can I do for you, ma'am?"

She relaxed, relief flooding her body. "I'm expected. I have an interview with Mr. Patrick Renaud. My name is Désirée Broussard."

He opened the gate wider. "Mr. Renaud told me to expect a young lady at ten o'clock. My name is Remy. Please follow me."

Désirée moved behind him, past flowerbeds of peonies, roses, and daffodils. Crates of Sweet William and pansies awaited planting between the clumps of lilac, whose potent fragrance impregnated the air. Remy led her to an imposing three-story Italianate structure with massive arched windows, balconies, and balustrades. They approached the piazza, and Désirée stopped dead in her tracks, awestruck at the magnificence surrounding her. "This place belongs in Venice or Rome."

The butler nodded in agreement. "There's nothing

like it anywhere in the city."

Massive portals swept open, as if by their own volition, and she entered a world of Persian carpets, coffered ceilings, and mahogany panels.

He pointed to a large oak door, turned back, and spoke over his shoulder. "Mr. Renaud is waiting for you in his office, miss." He gave her a reassuring smile before disappearing down the corridor.

Désirée took a tentative step into the room. Someone had decorated the chamber with contemporary flourishes. The modern styling was a respite from the overwhelming formality of the rest of the place, yet the arrogance of wealth flowed throughout Maison Renaud. Massive windows released sheets of light into the airy gray-and-beige room filled with first editions and entitlement.

Patrick Renaud stood next to a steel desk, perusing a document, just as he had the night they'd met. Désirée made quick notes of his literary collection—plays by Tennessee Williams, novels by Faulkner, Hemingway, and Flannery O'Connor. She took a deep breath before speaking. "Hello, Mr. Renaud."

He'd dressed casually in chinos and a pale gray polo shirt that showed off his muscular body to perfection. His loafers probably cost more than her entire wardrobe. Mr. Renaud looked up from the paperwork, his face unreadable, and his dimples not in evidence. He stared in her direction for what seemed an eternity before pointing to a chair positioned across from the desk.

"Please sit, Miss Broussard."

She slid onto the chair and crossed her legs. He frowned. Without warning, the air turned icy. Désirée, fearing she'd displeased him, quickly uncrossed them.

He turned his head from side to side before checking his wristwatch. "Promptness is an admirable quality in an employee. I must say you look quite fetching, Miss Broussard, or should I say, Mrs. Broussard?"

A chill worked its way down her spine. "How did you know?"

His eyes revealed nothing. "I like to learn as much as possible about my employees. Your marriage is part of the public record. At age eighteen, you wed Johnny Lee Broussard on January 5, 1953. I'm afraid it didn't last very long. He passed away on July fourth of the same year."

Désirée felt violated. Mr. Renaud's minions had unearthed something private and quite painful. She thanked Providence she'd learned to hold her temper. "Yes, sir, we were married for six months before Johnny died."

He gave her a dispassionate smile. "You have my condolences," but his words had an icy emptiness.

"Thank you, Mr. Renaud." Désirée fiddled with her handkerchief. She wanted to dismiss him as a son-of-a-bitch, but something in his voice told her not to. She looked up, her gaze fixed on his face. The moment she looked into those unfathomable eyes, Désirée glimpsed the unbearable sadness that lived there. The deeper she looked, the more sorrow she saw. She wanted to turn away, but his pain held her captive. They continued staring at each other in silence, the tension building, the air suddenly unendurable. One of them had to break, so Désirée ended it.

She unfastened her portfolio and placed the papers

on his desk. "Mr. Renaud, I brought my high school diploma and my certificate from the business school, along with letters of recommendation."

"I won't need them."

For a moment, his words confused her. Her heart pumped, and she felt her face flush. The bastard had summarily dismissed her. "Oh."

She stood to leave, but in a flash, he planted himself squarely in front of her. "I'm afraid you've misunderstood me, Mrs. Broussard." His voice softened. "Mrs. Broussard seems awfully formal. May I call you Désirée?"

"Yes, sir."

"Let's not stand on ceremony. Call me Patrick, and please, do sit down."

She did as ordered.

He grinned and the heavenly dimples emerged, but his smile never reached his eyes. "I've already checked your wonderful qualifications. To be honest, I could have hired a thousand other stenographers, but I wanted you; despite that fact, I find your looks distracting."

He moved nearer, so close Désirée smelled his cologne. She recognized the fragrance from the men's section of D.H. Holmes—*Pour un Homme, de Caron*, the scent of men of wealth.

His smile disappeared. "You see, Désirée, you have something I need, something I value more than your skills with a typewriter."

Without warning, the door swung open. A dark-haired girl, dressed in dungarees and a white blouse with a Peter Pan collar, bounced into the office. "Pat...oh, you have a guest. I—" The girl froze in place the moment she spied Désirée. "Uh, uh—"

Mr. Renaud looked from the girl to Désirée as his lips spread in a grim line. He signaled for her to enter. "Samantha, allow me to introduce you to Miss Désirée Broussard. Désirée will be working here and, hopefully, will become a great friend to you."

Samantha mumbled a half-hearted, "Pleased to meet you," before flying from the room.

Dumbfounded, Patrick stared at the door and then turned his gaze to Désirée. "Now you see my problem, my little sister, Samantha. She's almost of age, seventeen, six years younger than I am, but with my parents currently in Europe, she's my responsibility."

He kept his gaze on Désirée. "I'm afraid Samantha is attracted to a deviant way of life. I can't keep her chained in her room, but her choices could bring great dishonor to my family, and I won't have it."

Her shoulders slumped in disappointment. "I should have figured getting a job with you was too good to be true. Look, Mr. Renaud…uh, Patrick, I've known girls like your sister all my life. I swear to you, she can't help the way she is, and you can't do a thing about it. What did you want with me anyway?"

He threw a copy of the *Times Picayune* atop the desk. The blazing headline read: "Memphis Auto King Attacked Behind a Quarter Bistro!"

He paused. "I know my sister was at the Starlight Bistro two nights ago. Samantha recognized you, didn't she?"

She refused to lie. "Yes, she did."

Patrick clenched his right hand into a fist and pounded the desktop. "I thought so. Please, I need you to ask your mother to watch out for her."

Désirée stared at him and sighed in resignation.

"My mother? Do you know everything about me?"

He chuckled, his laugh as frosty as a daiquiri. "Not yet, but I hope to. I could tell Samantha recognized you from her visit to your mother's establishment." He picked up the document he'd been perusing when she entered. "Shall I tell you what it says? Désirée Girard was born to Yolanda Girard on October 31, 1934."

Patrick placed the paper back on the desk. "Your mother was a child of fifteen when she had you. This information turned up a while ago when I checked on the Starlight."

He gazed into Désirée's face. "You see Samantha is a beautiful girl, a gifted scholar, who's attracted to degeneracy. I've done everything, even locked her in her room, but she still seeks it out."

Désirée rankled at his words, her pulse rising, and her ears ringing. She stood and took a step toward him, her face blazing with rage. "How dare you call your sister a degenerate? Do you really think she wants to be the butt of jokes, abused, tormented, only to have her own brother call her a pervert? I'll ask my mother to watch over her, but I don't think I can work for a man like you. Good day, Mr. Renaud."

She turned to storm out the door, but Patrick grabbed her by her wrist and pulled her back to him, the façade of calm destroyed. Once again, Désirée saw agony in his beautiful eyes.

"I'm sorry if I spoke out of turn. I'm not the man you think I am. I'm not heartless, but I don't understand my sister. I need your help. Please, Désirée, forgive my words. You see, all I have is Samantha. If anything happens to her…" His voice drifted away. "Please, let me make it up to you tonight. I'd like to take you to

61

dinner at the Mason-Dixon Line." He paused, as if waiting for her to respond.

A part of her wanted to say no, but she couldn't. "Very well, but please, no more talk of Samantha. What time?"

"I'll pick you up at seven-thirty. Don't worry. I know where you live."

She couldn't stop a sigh from escaping her lips. "Of course you do. I'll see you at seven-thirty, Mr. Renaud."

His face was barely an inch from hers. "I'll make it worth your while, Miss Broussard."

She couldn't stop herself from smiling. "Yes, sir, I'll see that you do."

Désirée wrenched her hand away and moved to the door. He stopped her with his words, but she didn't turn back.

"And do you have strong self-control, Miss Broussard?"

"Yes, sir, I do."

"Good."

Chapter Seven
Mistress Adele

The Duck Girl, a plain-faced creature with a marked overbite, floated past Désirée, down Royal Street, on a pair of ancient roller skates. A Quarter fixture, she wore her customary garb, a gossamer gown, and hair coiffed into the long ringlets of a silent-screen ingénue. A flock of quacking ducklings followed her when she turned onto St. Marc.

She rolled on, oblivious to everything around her, another eccentric in a city that embraced the quirky. Désirée couldn't contain her anger with Patrick Renaud, especially after learning that the son-of-a-bitch had investigated her mother like a common criminal. Despite her fury, she managed to give the Duck Girl a friendly wave.

An unknown force pushed her to the Lucky 13, and she knew fighting it was fruitless. She took a tentative step toward the smoky threshold, but then turned away. Rather than enter the bar from the front and be mistaken for a B-girl, Désirée maneuvered through a refuse-strewn alley and walked in from the kitchen. Eddie Vitale had mentioned the filthy room that first night, but Désirée soon discovered he hadn't begun to describe the concentrated foulness that lay there. The stench hit her square in the gut, and her stomach lurched.

Molten Crisco and lard had painted the white walls amber and left the floor slippery with grease. Two watery-eyed cooks, stripped to their undershirts, greasy Schwegmann's paper bags covering their hair, worked at a lackadaisical pace. One fellow slid a tray of piping hot cornbread onto a grease-encrusted countertop. The other man tossed battered oysters into sizzling fat. Both ignored a dead mouse trapped in a corner near an ancient icebox.

Pots filled with rice and bubbled-over red beans sat atop a stove laced with caked-on gumbo dripping. A vat of butter on the countertop had trapped a flying cockroach, the bane of New Orleans. The cook flicked the pest into the trash with a dirty fingernail before he rolled the butter into tiny paper cups. She remembered Patrick's comment about the lack of sanitation not mattering. As he'd said, people didn't visit the Lucky 13 for the food. She certainly hadn't.

Besides, no one except the cooks and those who worked at the Lucky 13 knew about the filth. Sprinkle Tabasco sauce on the fried oysters, serve enough Bourbon or rum to wash them down, and germs ceased to be a problem.

She moved through the smelly gloom until a thug in draped pants and two-toned shoes stopped her. "What you doing here, girlie?"

Désirée handed Patrick's card to the fellow.

"Excuse me, sir. I'm…uh, not a client. I just wanted to have a short word with the lady who…uh…disciplines her clients."

He grinned, revealing a mouthful of sparkling gold teeth, then gave her a slow, lewd once-over. The guy checked his watch. "So you're the new girl Miss Adele is training."

She felt her face flush. "No, sir."

He shook his head, grunting in disapproval as he handed the card back. "Too bad. You could make a pile of money in that little outfit." The man loped off in the darkness. "Since you're here now, you might as well look around. Mistress Adele is occupied with a client and might be a while."

Désirée had turned to leave when a door yawned open. She neared it and heard the swat of a paddle followed by a masculine groan of pleasure. "Thank you, Mistress Adele. I know I've been bad. One more, please."

Désirée peeked through the doorway.

A man lay across a padded table, his underwear lowered to his ankles, his rosy-red ass facing her. Mistress Adele had swaddled his testicles in cotton to protect them from an errant blow. Another smack and he moaned again, his satisfaction evident. Heat surged through Désirée's body, but not from the temperature in the club. She had to speak to the woman.

Mistress Adele stood over the fellow, a smirk across her ruby lips. She was dressed in stiletto pumps and black pedal pushers, her abundant bosom confined in a bustier. She drew her arm back and gave the man another healthy whack.

Désirée cleared her throat and whispered, "Excuse me, Mistress Adele. May I please have a word with you?"

When Désirée looked past her heavy makeup and flame-red hair, Mistress Adele had the round face of a kindly librarian, replete with twinkling blue eyes and chubby cheeks.

"Well, hey, sweetness, I always have time for a lovely young lady. What is it?"

Désirée glimpsed the gentleman's bare ass and felt heat come to her face.

Mistress Adele took a step toward her. "Ignore that fellow. I'm disciplining him for being naughty. What's ailing you?"

She whispered in response. "Do you know Mr. Renaud, Mr. Patrick Renaud? I believe he's your employer."

The older woman moved her head from side to side as she examined the girl's face. Something crawled up Désirée's spine. The woman had seen through her. Miss Adele smirked at Désirée. "Hmmm. I can guess why a beautiful young lady would want to know about a handsome gent like Patrick Renaud, but I need to hear it from your lips. Tell the truth. I'll know if you're fibbing. You like to watch, don't you?"

The jig was up. "I, uh, well, I, you see, I'm a writer, and—"

The older woman ran her crimson talons through her hair. "Girl, you can't write about nothing that goes on here without getting arrested. Don't be shy, little lady. Most folks like to watch, but they'd never admit it." She took another step toward Désirée, a dark smile crossing her lips. "Want to know why Patrick Renaud bought into this place? Because his daddy, Mr. Renaud Senior, used to be a regular client."

The girl took a step back, too shocked to speak.

Mistress Adele grinned once again, but Désirée saw no mirth in her face. "The older Mr. Renaud was once my best customer, but he went and had a heart attack on me, right here in this very room. He liked watching, too, anything involving degradation. Junior bought the Lucky 13 so no one would learn about his daddy."

She moved close enough for Désirée to smell her musk. "Junior isn't like his daddy. Maybe you like the thought of him crawling on his hands and knees, but it ain't going to happen, not with that one. His daddy needed a strong hand, but not the son. Patrick Renaud will be a challenge for a gal like you."

Her lips spread into a dark grin. "You're mad at Junior, ain't you? You'd like to slap his butt around for being arrogant, but like I said, it won't happen. Folks should stay away from fetish when they're angry. You've got to be cool. A fellow I knew who called himself a master got pissed off one night and killed a gal who forgot to call him 'sir.' The bastard is in Angola, waiting for the hot seat. Good riddance, too. You don't never need to hurt them, at least, not most of them."

Mistress Adele took a step back to the room, but instead of entering, she swiveled around to face her. "Little lady, I have a suggestion for you. Stay away from this place. It's dangerous for a pretty thing like you. There's death here. Leave."

Her customer groaned. "Mistress Adele, I've been very bad. Please punish me again." Mistress Adele nodded in the man's direction. "Excuse me. Someone needs me."

The older woman went back to business without saying another word.

****

Mistress Adele's words followed Désirée all the way down St. Marc. *"You like to watch, don't you?"*

Although it shamed her to admit the truth, Désirée had lurked in hallways and corners since childhood. She didn't *like* to watch; she *loved* to watch. She'd once deluded herself into believing writers were observers, after all, not voyeurs, but she'd learned the truth. She had to know what lurked behind the closed door, especially when wails of passion shrieked from the other side. Over the years, she and Lilly had become conspirators in her dark obsession, a perfect marriage of voyeur and exhibitionist. When they were teens, Désirée had watched Lilly eagerly servicing a former love, an over-endowed Marine. Lilly couldn't contain her enthusiasm; her paramour wouldn't stop groaning and writhing in pleasure.

Willpower never mattered. Désirée couldn't stop herself from looking, and when her guilt got the better of her, she confessed her naughty secret. Lilly giggled and said, "But I knew you were watching. Maybe you learned something."

Lilly always kept her windows open, as if flaunting her oversized libido, and that afternoon was no exception. Désirée tiptoed past her friend's cottage, willing herself not to look for fear she'd see something that would lure her in.

She didn't make it.

The boom of a plate crashing against a wall propelled Désirée to peek into Lilly's living room window. As she did, Lilly screamed, "You lousy prick," at eardrum-shattering decibels. Her friend was at it again. She and her new lover were in the middle of a knock-down, drag-out fight.

Désirée watched as Lilly stormed into her bedroom and tossed down that day's newspaper. In the dim light, she could see the form of Lilly's new amour as he reclined on her bed.

"When were you going to tell me about her?"

Lilly's new lover sat up and rubbed the sleep out of his eyes. A trail of ice ran down Désirée's spine, and her stomach lurched when she looked through the slats in the wooden blinds. Eddie Vitale lay across Lilly's bed, a confused expression muddling his handsome face.

"What you talkin' about, baby doll?"

Lilly stood over him, waving the society page of the paper. "You got some nerve, you slick bastard, laying with me and messing with another girl all the while."

Lilly must have been "the girl on the side" Vitale had bragged to his partner about. Her friend, the Bayou Volcano, had picked some prizes in the past, but Eddie Vitale took the cake. Despite her dislike of him, Désirée couldn't stop from admiring his muscular body.

Vitale shot Lilly a hungry look and reached for her breasts. His whisper sounded warm and buttery. "Come here."

Désirée stood in place, transfixed.

Lilly tossed the paper to the floor. "The society section of the *New Orleans Times Picayune* says, 'Captain Edward Vitale of the New Orleans Police Department and Miss Bianca Corolla are engaged to be married.'"

He glanced down at the paper before flashing his pearly whites at Lilly. His insolent grin reminded Désirée of Louie's, and for the first time, she pitied her friend. "Oh, yeah, well, I'd planned on telling you."

His indifference appeared to stoke Lilly's fury.

"Oh, you were planning to tell me? Before or after the honeymoon?"

Eddie's blue eyes sparkled, his skin flushed. "I understand, baby, you're a little jealous, and it's okay. I told you before you don't need worry about Bianca."

In an instant, Lilly transformed into a red-faced harridan. "What? Lord, Eddie, you…you bastard. You said you were seeing her to further your career. You didn't say you were going to marry her."

He ignored her protestations and patted a place on the bed. "How about you plop your beautiful ass down here? I'm horny, baby. I feel like playing."

She turned her head from side to side, unable to comprehend his words. "Huh? You want to lay with me, but you're going to marry another girl? What's wrong with you?"

Eddie's smile vanished. "Nothing's wrong with me. You're the one who said you didn't want to be tied down with no wedding ring."

Lilly paced in front of the bed. "You have your nerve throwing it in my face. A girl can change her mind, can't she?"

His skin reddened, rage finally showing in his face. "Well, she better change it back. I love you, baby, but I can't marry a stripper."

When Lilly's eyes flooded with angry tears, Désirée wanted to storm into the room and stop her friend's torment but knew enough to watch instead.

"But you can screw one? Where does it leave me, you prick? Maybe you'll learn how to suck your own, because I won't be doing it. I should've listened when Opal told me about you."

Désirée had no idea who this Opal person was, but

uttering her name caused Vitale to hit the pillow with his fist, his blue eyes blazing in his handsome face. "Opal? I told you she's a man-hating bitch." His voice softened. "Baby, why are you doing me like this? Haven't I been good to you? Got you a television and a hi-fi?"

"So you can watch *Superman* and listen to Frank Sinatra."

Eddie pulled her down on the bed and placed his lips to her neck. "Come to daddy. You know I love you, don't you?"

She tried to pull away from his grasp. "If you loved me, you wouldn't be marrying another girl. Why don't you stab me in the heart while you're at it? I guess I'll just find me another fellow, not some mama's boy living at home. Get out of my house, you lowlife dago! Get out!"

Eddie grabbed her shoulders with such force she cried out in pain. His service revolver hanging across the chair stopped Désirée from coming to her friend's aid. He tossed Lilly on the bed like a rag doll before throwing himself on top of her and crash landing on her stomach. Eddie spoke in a placid voice, but Désirée found his rage frightening. "Don't you ever talk to me like that again! I'm not a dago, a wop, a guinea, or a gumba. I'm Sicilian, like the great Frank Sinatra. You got some nerve, asking me why we're not getting married, when half of New Orleans has seen your titties." He pressed his face to hers. "Don't ever call me a mama's boy or talk about no other man, ever. Nobody puts horns on Eddie Vitale. I'll kill you if you do somebody else!"

"Eddie, I, please, don't—"

His body relaxed. He pressed his lips to her neck, whispering as he unfastened her robe. "I said I'd kill you, baby. I mean it. You're mine. I love you, you crazy bitch."

A single tear rolled down her cheek. "Then why do you treat me so bad?"

"Because I love you. Say it, baby, say you belong to me."

Lilly stumbled over the words. "I belong to you."

"Tell me you love me."

"I love you, Eddie."

Eddie spoke in a husky whisper. "I love you, too, Lilly. I love you."

His lips moved to hers, and his tongue appeared to ravage her mouth. He moved southward, first resting his lips on her neck, then moving to her breasts.

Désirée walked away, a nasty feeling gnawing at the pit of her stomach. She knew Lilly loved wildness in her men and would later crow about their afternoon of passion. Lilly would toss her head back, smiling all the while, as she bragged that the bastard loved her enough to kill her. Lilly would find the thought thrilling.

Chapter Eight
A Night to Remember

When Eddie left Lilly's flat a couple of hours later, she fled to her friend's cottage. Lilly pounded on Désirée's door with such ferocity that Désirée rushed to open it before it was battered in.

The moment she unlocked the crimson portal, Lilly barged into the living room, her face still flushed from her encounter with her lover. She'd draped her curves in a flesh-covered negligee. Lilly carried the society page of the *Picayune* in one hand and clutched an ancient deck of tarot cards wrapped in a frayed silk scarf in the other. When Lilly flounced into the kitchen and plopped down at her dinette, Désirée knew she'd spit out a litany of Vitale's sins.

Lilly threw the paper onto Désirée's dinette table before breaking into a torrent of tears. "That son-of-a-bitch. Look." Her sobs escalated into gasping breaths. There, in crisp black-and-white print, was a photo of Eddie Vitale embracing a plain-faced girl at a Brotherhood of St. Joseph's gala.

"What am I going to do, Désirée? He's going to marry the bitch."

Désirée folded the paper and handed it back to her. "Lilly, I hate to be the bearer of bad news, but Mama has had dealings with Eddie Vitale. He's a no-good, rotten snake. If you were honest, you'd admit you know it too. You told me you did one of your tarot readings on yourself and it came up bad."

Lilly wiped her tears away and set her jaw at a defiant angle as she shuffled the tarot cards. "Sometimes the cards are wrong."

Désirée shook her head at her friend's words. "Lilly, you've sworn to me on many occasions that the tarot is never wrong."

Lilly sat back in the chair, refusing to move. "Please don't lecture me. Even my own mama is against me being with Eddie. Opal Jordan, the older Mr. Renaud's lady friend, warned me, too. Everybody said Opal is on the queer side, so I didn't listen to her like I should have." Lilly's façade of self-assurance suddenly disappeared when she dealt the Lovers in reverse. "Shit!" She broke down once again. "I can't help it if I love the no-good bastard."

Désirée jumped from her chair and pulled Lilly up to envelope her in a hug. No matter how volatile and foolish her relationships were, Lilly was the closest thing Désirée had to a sister.

"Oh, c'mon, Lilly. We've been through a lot worse. No girls would play with us when we were kids because we didn't have daddies and our mamas were loose women. They called us 'white trash,' but we were having too much fun to give it a thought. Besides, weren't our mothers the most beautiful ladies in New Orleans? Then, when you turned fourteen, you took up exotic dancing and got a fox fur. Boy, weren't you something!" An errant tear grazed Lilly's cheek, and Désirée felt her own eyes moisten. "Darlin', you never told me how you met Eddie."

When Lilly planted a sisterly kiss on Désirée's

forehead, Désirée knew the worst had passed. "Do you remember when I shot that no-good peckerwood on Valentine's Day?"

Désirée would never forget the "no-good peckerwood," another bastard Lilly had picked up during an erotic escapade. Lilly fixed her lips in an obstinate pout and plopped back down onto a kitchen chair. "The sucker tried to beat me up when I told him to get the hell out of my house. You should've seen the look on his face when I pulled out my gun and shot him in the leg. I should have shot his wiener off while I was at it. Of course, I didn't really need a gun. I probably could've kicked his ass real good without one."

Lilly had managed to beat the rap. Until that afternoon, Désirée never knew how Lilly had done it.

Lilly sat back, a smile on her beautiful face as if a memory of rosier times had entrapped her. "That's how me and Eddie became acquainted. He helped me out of that mess, even got the lowlife prick arrested, though he was the one that got shot. Afterward, he asked if I'd step out with him. Hell, why not? He was good-looking, wore nice clothes, and had manners—at least, I thought he did. We even had a few laughs together."

Désirée couldn't stop herself from rolling her eyes. "Yeah, he's a real funny guy."

Lilly blew her nose. "Yes, funny, good-looking, and, girl, what a lover. He's got the prettiest, biggest package and really knows how to please a girl." Her grin broadened. "He always has money to spend, and, Lord, the boy has a gilded tongue."

She broke down into a puddle of tears and snot once again. She adored handsome men who flashed wads of bills and who were well endowed—yes, money and large penises made Lilly's world go round. Désirée swore her friend must have had radar; she could always sense when a fellow was packing. "Well, anyway, he just got himself engaged and thinks he's getting married. I'm putting an end to it. I'll fix his little red wagon. He might be a bastard, but I have my reasons to love him."

Désirée grasped her hand. "Lilly, please, be careful with him. He's not like the guys you usually mess around with."

Her friend shrugged her shoulders. "I can take care of myself, thank you very much. You got to be tough to be an exotic dancer. The girls duke it out all the time, put ground glass in your face powder, slip razor blades in your G-string and shoe polish in your eyeliner."

Désirée had a momentary respite from Lilly's anger and decided to mention her good news before her friend brought up her paramour again. "Lilly, can we change the subject, please?" She took a pause. "You'll be happy to know I'm now employed by Mr. Patrick Renaud...Junior."

From Lilly's shocked expression, the news appeared to take her by surprise. "What?"

"You heard me. I got a job with Mr. Patrick Renaud Junior, and he's taking me to dinner tonight at the Mason-Dixon Line. I guess I better dig up something to wear."

Lilly quickly jumbled the tarot deck. The World card flew from her hands and landed on the table. She jumped up from her chair. "Désirée Josephine Broussard, this card means you hold the world in your hands. Every gal I know has tried to turn Junior's head, but he never was interested." She arched an eyebrow. "I can tell by looking at him that the boy has a swinging thing and knows just what to do with it. The most eligible fellow in New Orleans is taking you out, and you want to 'dig up something'? Uh-uh, that won't do, not at all. I have a dress that'll knock his eyes out of their sockets, and it'll fit you just perfect. Come on."

****

The filigreed ceiling fan in Lilly's flat made a lazy rotation. Désirée's simple taste in furnishings contrasted greatly with her friend's adoration of everything flashy. Cheesy French furniture, mirrored and enameled in shades of gold, packed the living room. Lilly rushed into her bedroom and ran back a minute later with a black cocktail dress, stiletto pumps, and gold hoop earrings. She laid out the jewelry and heels on her sofa, then held up the dress.

"Remember when you read to me about Coco Chanel and her little black dress? Well, I bought one off a drag queen, but black isn't my color. Besides, it was awful tight. Try it on."

Désirée unfastened her robe and stood naked as a jaybird before slipping on the dress. The designer had cut the bodice low in the back and front and wired it so the wearer wouldn't need a bra. The thought of something so daring thrilled her. She couldn't wait for Mr. Patrick Renaud to take a gander.

Lilly sauntered over to the sofa and picked up a pair of black ankle-strap stiletto pumps, the sort of shoes Young Miss labeled "whore boots." They were the type of foot apparel favored by the ladies from the Lucky 13.

Désirée gave them a look and said, "I'm not sure I can walk in those things."

"Walk? Hell, you need to be able to dance in these shoes, or else you're screwed. I've heard Junior is a dancing fiend. Don't be scared. I've even taught fellows how to maneuver around in them. It's not hard."

Désirée slipped on the pumps and fastened them around her ankles. They felt like stilts. "Heck, I wear heels all the time, but nothing this high."

She took a few tentative steps around the living room before breaking into a broad smile. "Look. I'm walking."

Lilly snorted. "You stepped in them, but you didn't really walk in them. You've got to get those hips swaying and put some effort into it. Watch me."

She tossed her head back and opened her mouth in a half-smile as she slithered around the flat, her hips moving as if to the beat of a silent drummer.

"They call this the 'stripper strut.' Keep your head up, your shoulders back, and lead with your breasts. You need to keep the weight on your heels and let your hips sway."

Désirée watched her without saying a word and then imitated what she'd seen. She undulated her hips, stopped, pivoted, and then turned to Lilly. "How was that?"

Her friend's expression said it all, but she added, "We got us some work to do."

****

Désirée emerged in a fog of Chanel No. 5 a few hours later, the mistress of the stripper strut. She'd piled her hair into an upswept do, fringed with bangs, made her face up like a movie star, and hung the golden hoops from her ears. The black dress sheathed her body like a glove, the black stockings infused the look with naughtiness, and the pumps showed off the curve of her legs.

At seven on the dot, she heard a rap at the door. Her pulse quickened.

She found a smiling Patrick standing in the doorway. He'd dressed in an elegant tuxedo, smelled of fine cologne, and looked every inch like a crown prince. He carried a huge bouquet of roses.

They stood at the threshold without talking, gazing into each other's eyes, filled with questions, like explorers seeing a new world for the first time.

The minutes ticked by until Patrick finally handed her the bouquet. "I didn't know what kind of flowers you like, but these came from our hothouse."

The flowers looked as though a master gardener had grown them from fuchsia velvet. Their fragrance overpowered the incense she'd burned to perfume her flat. "Thank you. You're the first person to ever bring me flowers."

He smiled, his dimples deepened, and her heart gave a flutter. "Really? Now that I know, I'll send them regularly."

She looked up at him. Their eyes locked once again. Her hand trembled as she gestured for him to enter. "Please, come in."

He crossed her threshold, then handed her the flowers. Désirée rushed into her kitchenette. "Let me get these beauties in water."

Patrick circled her living room, checking every nook and cranny. Her tiny library appeared to captivate him, especially her copy of *Catcher in the Rye*. He thumbed it, a mischievous grin on his handsome face. "I really enjoyed this book. Holden Caulfield reminded me of all the rich kids I met in New York."

At the words "New York," Désirée's face lit up like a toddler on Christmas morning. "You've been to New York? For true?"

His grin deepened. "I went to college there. Columbia."

"Wow, I've never met anybody who went to Columbia, let alone graduated from it. You must be a real smart fellow. My husband, Johnny, played the jazz trumpet. He sounded a lot like his idol, Miles Davis. Johnny wanted us to move to New York, to Greenwich Village, so he could play music at night while I wrote my stories by day. Of course, it was just a kid's fantasy, but I loved every moment of the dream."

Patrick brushed his hand over her manuscripts. He perused one, and then grinned at her, his eyebrow cocked. "You write? New York is certainly the place for writers, but so is New Orleans."

She felt a blush come to her face and averted her head. "Being an author is something I aspire to…one day. I've written a bunch of short stories set here. I call them my *New Orleans Suite*."

He placed the pages back in place. "Perhaps you'll trust me with your writing sometime in the future."

She giggled nervously. "Well, maybe. I've published a couple of short stories in small journals, but I'm afraid I'm no J. D. Salinger."

"Doesn't matter. I like to read." When Patrick swiveled around, Johnny's photo caught his eye. His smile disappeared, and they exchanged another look before Désirée floated into her kitchen with her cherished gift. The floral fragrance wafted through the little flat. She arranged them in an ancient, gold-etched porcelain vase once belonging to her grandmother. Without warning, the scent of fine aftershave cut through the rose's fragrance and minty breath warmed her cheek. "Your place is charming, Désirée, almost as lovely as its mistress. I'm glad the roses pleased you. You looked at them as if they were the rarest jewels on earth."

Once again, they stood stock still, Désirée at the sink, Patrick behind her. Her heart pounded so fiercely she was sure he heard it. Her voice quivered, and she croaked out a whisper. "I have spirits, Mr. Renaud, anything you want—bourbon, scotch, whiskey. It comes from having a mother who owns a bar."

He shook his head. "No, darlin', one drink and I'll never leave. We better be on our way."

Instead of moving, they remained rooted in the tiny kitchen, unable to leave. The moment didn't last forever, however. Patrick turned her around, placed his hand in hers, and off they went.

Chapter Nine
The Mason-Dixon Line

Désirée and Patrick strolled into an evening as dense with moisture as a Turkish bath.

A gleaming black Cadillac limousine sat in front of the wrought-iron gate, and a driver garbed in full chauffeur's livery stood at attention and opened the passenger door. Désirée slid onto the seat and inhaled the delicious fragrance of the luxury automobile—the metallic whiff of fresh lacquer, chrome polish, and window cleaner. She relished the feel of buttery leather on her behind.

Patrick slipped in next to her. "Never ridden in a limousine before?"

"No, sir, never before."

He greeted her answer with a chuckle, then gave her hand a tight squeeze. "You'll get used to it."

The driver started the engine, and the Caddie's motor purred. The limousine sailed through the streets, gliding over the concrete like a fine vessel cutting through placid waters. Bourbon blazed, a maze of flashing neon, bodies packed together, barkers hawking decadence from every doorway, and music blaring at eardrum-blasting decibels.

Désirée sat in silence, her eyes staring straight ahead despite the sweet fragrance of Patrick's breath on the side of her face. She fought to ignore her elevated pulse and the quiver deep in the pit of her stomach but lost the battle.

Without warning, the driver called out to Patrick. "Mr. Renaud, sir, isn't that Miss Renaud walking with a young man?"

Patrick whipped his head around and looked out into the street. Désirée felt his body tense as he pulled his hand away. She followed his gaze. Two youths, one darkly handsome, the other, strapping and muscular, strode down Bourbon. Both boys wore draped pants with silk dress shirts. The darker kid wore a red satin Korean jacket embroidered with a roaring tiger motif.

A closer look at the "boys" revealed their true genders: Samantha and her friend Frankie. The girls ignored the curious stares as they engaged in a spirited conversation. They skirted puddles of puke and treaded around the horse turds that littered the street, oblivious to the pandemonium surrounding them. They stared upward at the flashing neon sign on the roof: *Bourbon Street's Classiest Bistro, The Mason-Dixon Line*.

Désirée looked out from the limo's window. The Mason-Dixon's barker, a rough mug with slicked back hair and a hatchet face, paced in front of the entrance. When he grinned, a diamond-stud drilled into his front tooth sparkled in the garish light. He looked like a vicious thug but, in a nod to gentility, wore a tuxedo.

Frankie strode past him with Samantha at her heels. Samantha caught sight of a poster trapped inside the kiosk. Lilly Thibodaux, the Bayou Volcano, posed in all her naked glory. The image stopped Samantha in her tracks. An impatient Frankie grabbed the girl by the arm and pulled her inside the club.

Patrick's body was as rigid as an oak plank. His

face reddened, but he managed to control his anger. "What the hell is my sister doing with that dagger?" He turned back to the chauffeur. "Please stop the car, Henri." Instead of waiting for the driver to escort them from the auto, Patrick threw the door open, jumped from his seat, took Désirée's hand, and abandoned his confused chauffeur without a word.

They moved from the air-conditioned limo into the oppressive heat of the street. They crossed the Mason-Dixon Line threshold and entered rooms cool enough for ladies to wear their summer furs.

The collection of Civil War paraphernalia had brought the Mason-Dixon Line as much renown as the beauty of its performers. The lobby displayed every manner of artifact from the War of Northern Aggression: rifles, uniforms, and even a chamber pot from the occupation of New Orleans embellished with the face of the notorious Yankee Major General Benjamin Butler.

Désirée and Patrick entered a world of polite chatter, expensive cigars, and rustling crinoline. Every eye in the place focused on New Orleans's most current golden couple, Patrick Renaud Jr. and the stunning but nameless young lady on his arm. Désirée should have been elated to be the date of the most eligible fellow in the city; instead, she felt a prickly sense of foreboding.

They waded through a crowd of well-wishers, and he managed a smile, even when people called out, "Hey, Junior!" He endured the incessant backslapping by business associates and nodded to acquaintances, the picture of gentility. Désirée knew seeing his sister had put the kibosh on an evening that had begun with such promise.

Patrick kept his hand on the small of Désirée's back, a sneer on his beautiful lips. "God, I hate being called 'Junior.' Daddy pulled me out of law school because he couldn't hack doing business anymore. Then his heart gave out from all his fried oysters, cigars, and sundry perversions. I've been running the family business for two years, made it a success, but I'm still 'Junior' to most of New Orleans."

As they entered the club, the pong of a bongo drum drove couples onto the dance floor for a cha-cha-cha. The *crème de la crème* of New Orleans' society packed the Mason-Dixon, and the place smelled of gourmet food, fine bourbon, and Chanel No. 5. Tuxedoed waiters hauled trays crowded with steaming bowls of the Mason-Dixon's signature turtle soup, Oysters Rockefeller, Shrimp Remoulade, crystal dishes of Beluga caviar, and chilled bottles of Taittinger's Champagne to wash it down.

They followed a smiling maître d' to a ringside table glittering with fine china and crystal. As soon as he seated Désirée, Patrick gave the fellow a chilly command. "Jim Beam for me, neat, Champagne for the lady."

He cut her off before she could request ginger ale instead of Champagne. Désirée watched as his eyes searched the room. He focused on two girls in boyish attire who huddled together in a dark corner near the stage entrance, then dismissed the waiter with a polite wave of his hand.

He turned to Désirée, an angry flush on his face. "How could Samantha walk around dressed like some bulldagger?"

She struggled against lashing out at him for his

nasty words. "I'm sure no one's looking at them. Even if they did, in this light, they'd think they were two boys. Forget about it, Patrick."

He shook his head. "I can't. Samantha can't drag my family's name through the mud." Patrick turned his gaze back to Frankie and Samantha. The girls laughed and roughhoused with each other, unaware of Patrick's scrutiny.

The waiter returned with his order. Patrick downed it on the spot. "Bring me another."

The cha-cha ended with a loud volley from the bongo, and the gents escorted their partners to their seats.

An oily master of ceremonies loped onto the stage and French-kissed the microphone.

"Ladies and gentlemen, it's my pleasure to present the most beautiful girl in the city of New Orleans, the Queen of the Afro-Cuban Love Dance, Miss Lilly Thibodaux, the Bayou Volcano!"

A percussionist pounded the bongos like a mad man. Then a trumpeter blared out a melody first heard in the casinos and bordellos of Havana. The spotlight fell on a shapely leg as it emerged from behind a massive *papier mache* conga drum. A hand materialized, followed by an arm. Finally, Lilly Thibodaux appeared, clad in a rhinestone bra, jeweled panties, and matching pumps. The spotlight flashed from garish orange to scarlet as Lilly moved one hip, then the other, to the drummer's rim shots.

Every pair of eyes in the room remained fixated on the goddess dominating the stage: every pair except for one. Patrick ignored Lilly and kept his focus on Samantha and Frankie.

Désirée watched the girls, too, and noticed that the floorshow appeared to consume Samantha. It held no interest for Frankie, who tugged at Samantha's sleeve, as if exhorting her to leave. Samantha remained rooted to the floor and ignored Frankie when she whispered into her ear.

Frankie gave a shoulder shrug and walked away. She approached a raven-haired beauty garbed in a revealing amethyst-colored gown. The woman sat at a secluded table, sipping Champagne from a flute of the finest crystal.

When Patrick caught sight of Frankie and the woman in the jewel-toned dress, his body stiffened once again. Désirée touched his cuff, but then pulled her hand away, as if fearing his proximity would scorch her.

"What's wrong, Patrick?"

"Nothing, really. That girl in purple is my father's, uh, special friend. She used to dance here, but Daddy made her his hostess. She, uh, has an affinity for a certain type of woman."

His words confused her. "But why?"

"Daddy doesn't care. He's attracted to the…uh… unusual."

"Oh." Mistress Adele's words about Patrick Sr. danced in Désirée's head.

The dark beauty in the amethyst gown signaled Frankie with a wave of the hand, then slithered away from the table. The two women disappeared behind a red velvet curtain.

Lilly gyrated across the stage, undulating to the primitive rhythm, her tiny feet moving at lightning speed. She swung her head around, tossing her platinum hair in a frenzy of passion. After a series of bumps and grinds, the dance ended. Lilly turned her back to the audience, unhooked her bra, and flung it across her shoulder. She swiveled her head toward the crowd and gave the gents an over-the-shoulder wink. Then the stage went black. Thunderous applause, shrill whistles, and catcalls from the cruder members of the audience filled the room.

Samantha stood transfixed, unaware until the dance ended and the dancer disappeared that Frankie had abandoned her.

Patrick watched as his sister frantically searched for her friend. The girl's gaze fell on a souvenir card placed on a tabletop. Samantha snagged the card, parted a pair of red-velvet curtains near the stage, and entered.

Désirée picked up an identical souvenir from their table, a cardboard image of a nearly nude Lilly with pasties covering her nipples and a marabou fringe concealing her private parts. A furious Patrick tossed back his bourbon and slammed the glass down on the table as he rose from his chair.

The sense of foreboding, once again, reared its head, and Désirée took his arm. "Patrick, no scenes, please. I know where Samantha is heading. I've known Lilly Thibodaux since we were kids. She told me strippers often get entangled with young butches. The girl with her, Frankie, is probably seeing one of the dancers. Let me find Samantha."

She found his face unreadable. "Very well, Désirée. I trust you to be discreet."

"I promise, Patrick. I'll be the soul of discretion, sir."

He attempted to smile, but couldn't. "I'll give you

ten minutes."

****

Désirée rose and strolled toward the dressing rooms, swiveling her hips as Lilly had shown her. Men grinned in her direction, some gentlemanly, others definitely not.

When she parted the crimson drapes, a sordid mingling of perfume, cold cream, and perspiration enveloped her. Three exotic dancers chatting in the corridor parted when she passed. They'd caked their skin with Pan-Cake makeup that barely covered their battle scars, stretch marks, bruises, and black eyes.

A voluptuous redhead spun away from her companions and moved toward Désirée, a snarl on her face as she coolly appraised her. "What are you doing here, little girl?"

Désirée smiled with all the brightness she could muster. "How are all y'all ladies doing tonight? I'm here to visit Miss Lilly Thibodaux."

The sneering dancer pointed to a closed door. "There's her dressing room. I think she has company, but I'm sure she'll be overjoyed to see you." The other dancers joined in when the woman cackled.

Désirée muttered a quick, "Thank you," then walked past, hoping no one noticed the nervous shake beneath her stripper's strut.

Dinah Washington's bluesy voice wafted down the corridor. Désirée heard an explosion of laughter from behind the closed door and knocked. Lilly called out, "Whoever you are, come on in. The gang's all here."

Désirée poked her head inside the room and took in the ratty surroundings, faded rose-colored walls, and all the rickety faux antiques her mama had given her. The sweet smell of Shalimar perfume permeated every inch of the tiny space. Lilly had declared Shalimar her favorite and drenched herself in it.

Frankie opened the door all the way, and Désirée entered the cramped room, a counterfeit smile on her face. "Good evening, ladies. My name is Désirée. I'm here to say 'hey' to my friend Lilly."

The young butch's lips spread in a grin of recognition. "Well, hey, beautiful lady. Didn't I see you at the Starlight? I remember Young Miss saying you ain't queer, you're a regular gal. Some of the kids at the Starlight told me Young Miss and you are kin. You sure favor each other."

"Yes, we're relations." She'd never admit to the depth of her relationship to Young Miss.

Everyone stared at Désirée, except for Samantha, whose gaze remained fixed on Lilly.

She took a step toward the girl. "Hey, Samantha."

It appeared to take a Herculean effort for the young butch to pull her eyes away from Lilly, but she managed to. From the scowl on her face, she seemed annoyed at the interruption.

Désirée ignored the girl's glare and whispered, "Somebody's waiting for you, and he's getting hot under the collar. I suggest you make it a short visit."

Samantha's nostrils flared. "My brother followed me? Who does he think he is? J. Edgar Hoover? He can drop dead."

The girl stepped away from Désirée and inched closer to Lilly, who sponged her skin with a damp rag. Lilly appeared amused and made a deliberate show of ignoring Samantha.

The ravishing green-eyed brunette broke away

from Frankie's embrace. She appraised Désirée before extending her hand in greeting. "Well, hey. I'm Opal Jordan."

Lilly hadn't lied about Opal Jordan loving women. Opal tossed a mop of black hair over her shoulder while Frankie kneaded away at her neck and shoulders. She moaned as if the young woman's grip held her prisoner in an erotic odyssey.

"Make it a little harder, daddy. My neck is in a knot tonight. Got golden hands, don't you?"

Opal continued moaning but fixed her gaze on Désirée as if taking in her features. "I've known Young Miss for years. Y'all certainly do favor each other."

Frankie nuzzled Opal's neck and blew in her ear. Opal's carnal growls of pleasure filled the room. "Daddy, you've got to control your passion."

The young butch snorted, "Baby, you know I can't control myself when I'm around you." Frankie moved her lips upward from Opal's throat to her face. She eased her tongue into the beautiful femme's mouth, and they kissed for an eternity.

Samantha's face turned bright scarlet at their show of affection.

The lovers parted. Opal smirked in Samantha's direction. "So, you're the Sammy my Frankie's always talking about. She never said you were bashful. Don't worry, nobody's going to bite you…unless you want them to."

The room erupted into laughter once again. Samantha's blush started at her hairline and continued to her toes. She managed a nervous twitter.

Désirée murmured a quick "Samantha, let's leave. Your brother is outside."

Samantha turned her back on Désirée with an angry grimace, and then mustered the courage to address Lilly. "Excuse me, but is that Shalimar perfume you're wearing?"

Lilly nodded. "Uh-huh, I love Shalimar. I'd bathe in it if I could."

She dropped the washcloth, revealing two perfectly symmetrical breasts. Samantha's face flared like a firecracker. She looked away. Lilly smirked at the girl before slipping behind the dressing screen.

Opal freed herself from Frankie's embrace and extended her wrist to Samantha. "I'm wearing Jungle Gardenia. You didn't say how good I smell."

Samantha sniffed Opal's perfume. "You smell wonderful, too." She turned her gaze toward Lilly. "Were you playing Dinah Washington?"

Lilly called out from behind the screen, "No, not Opal. It was me. The way I figure, Dinah Washington sure beats Patti Page."

Samantha remained fixated on the screen, her face as forlorn as a lovesick puppy. She appeared enthralled by the marvels going on behind it. "Uh, excuse me, Miss Thibodaux. Did anyone ever tell you that you favor Miss Marilyn Monroe?"

Lilly's husky voice answered back. "Just every single day of my life."

Désirée hissed in the Renaud girl's ear, "Samantha, I'm not kidding. Your brother is in the club. He's pissed you're at the Mason-Dixon and swore he'd come and get you. He'll be here any minute now. You don't want a scene, do you? Please, go home."

Before Samantha could reply, Lilly emerged from behind the screen, clad in a G-string and garter belt.

Désirée took one look at Samantha's love-struck face and knew instantly her words of warning had no power.

Lilly leered at the smitten girl without bothering to conceal her partially exposed breasts. She clutched a black satin bra to her bare chest as she brushed against Samantha.

"How about you make yourself useful?" Lilly pulled her platinum hair to one side and exposed more skin. She looked over her shoulder and grinned at Samantha. "I need more help, baby. Do up my bra, will you?"

Samantha's hands trembled so badly she could barely connect the hooks to the eyes. Lilly seemed amused by her clumsiness. When she backed into the girl, her proximity seemed to intensify Samantha's nervousness.

Lilly sniggered at the butterfingered teen. "This your first time helping a lady get dressed, is it?"

Samantha stuttered an answer. "Uh, yes, ma'am."

Lilly tossed her mane like a sulky mare. "You called me 'ma'am' like I'm an old lady."

"No, ma'am, I mean, Miss Thibodaux, I'd never mistake you for an old lady."

Lilly grinned at her, a seductive pout on her face. "Well, thank you, since I'm only twenty, a mere babe in the woods."

Désirée watched the two without saying a word. She decided it would be best to have a private chat with Lilly about practicing her feminine wiles on her employer's sister.

The tension disappeared in an instant, and once more, the place rocked with laughter.

Suddenly the door swung open. Eddie Vitale

walked in.

The air left the room.

Opal turned off the record player, and everyone stared at the new visitor.

Chapter Ten
Collision

Eddie had dressed to the nines—black suit, pale blue shirt, an orange pocket handkerchief—and he'd scented himself with lavender cologne, one that screamed expensive. Still, despite his elegant appearance, his presence was as oppressive as the humidity outside. Lilly glared at him. Frankie shifted nervously in place. Samantha and Désirée averted their faces. Only Opal appeared unperturbed.

"It's the police, y'all. Mr. Silky, you checking the premises for B-drinking?"

Eddie flashed an icy smile. "Nah." He nodded at Désirée, his teeth glinting in the light like a panther. "Oh, how lovely to see you again, Miss…"

Although she knew better than to mess with the police, Désirée steeled her shoulders and replied, "It's Broussard. Miss Broussard."

Eddie appeared unfazed by her formality. "Well, then, how lovely to see you again, Miss Broussard." He glanced at Frankie before turning his attention to Samantha, his eyes never leaving her face. "This is just a social call."

"Mr. Silky." A wicked cackle escaped Opal's lips. "That's what the gals used to call Eddie when we were kids. He had a line that worked just like magic. Lord, drawers dropped all over the place, didn't they, Eddie?"

He gave Opal a sideways glance. "I guess my 'line,' as you call it, worked on some young ladies, not all of them. I remember one little gal who never bought into it, and for the longest time I just couldn't figure out why."

Opal dismissed his remark with a cackle. "Shucks, I guess you can't win 'em all, can you, baby?" She looked down at his hands, and pulled back the sleeve of his jacket to reveal a gleaming I.D. bracelet and cufflinks glinting in the light. "Very nice."

His lips spread into a cagey grin. "They should be. I got a cousin who's a jeweler."

Opal fondled his lapels. "Sharkskin suit, too."

He pushed her hand away. "My uncle's a tailor."

Eddie ignored Opal, sauntered over to Lilly, gave her a peck on the cheek, and then made a show of sniffing the air. He sidled up to Frankie, a vile grin on his face. "You're stinking up the room with that loud mess. You need to get you something besides Aqua Velva, kid. I'm wearing the finest made, Agua Lavenda Puig, Frank Sinatra's favorite."

The young butch grinned at him. "I don't wear Aqua Velva or any other 'loud mess.' You'll be happy to know my mama named me 'Frankie' after Frank Sinatra."

Opal grabbed a cigarette from Lilly's dressing table and took a light from Frankie's Zippo. "I remember how much Mr. Silky loved Frank Sinatra."

Eddie tossed his head back and snorted a raucous laugh. "Frank Sinatra is the greatest singer in the whole world. We even have the same birthday, December twelfth, only he's fifteen years older than me. Did you know his daddy was Sicilian?"

He took a step toward Samantha, and circled her as he did in the Starlight. No one spoke for a long moment, and the tension in the room felt as stifling as the heat outside. The only two people smiling were Eddie and Opal. Lilly folded her arms with an angry huff, swiveling toward Frankie and Samantha, her seductive façade gone. "I think you girls better leave now."

The door opened.

Patrick stood in the doorway, taking in the room. He noted Eddie's proximity to his sister and shot her a furious grin. "Hello, everybody."

Eddie ambled up to him, and the two men exchanged chilly smiles and handshakes. "Patrick. I didn't think I'd run into you so soon."

Patrick spoke through clenched teeth. "Since I'm my daddy's partner and he owns the Mason-Dixon, I've been known to frequent the place."

His tone sounded cordial, but Désirée remembered his words to her uncle about needing the bastard. Patrick spun around and faced Samantha, an expression of disgust marring his handsome features. He whispered *sotto voce*, "Darlin', I think it's time for you and your friend to leave. Go on home."

Samantha fixed her lips in a pout and moved to the door. She called out to her companion, "C'mon, Frankie."

Eddie looked from Patrick to Samantha, his eyes narrowing. He barred her way. "I won't hear of it. Why don't you let the little lady and her friend stay and have a drink? You, too, Patrick."

Lilly took his arm. "Eddie, can we call it a night, please?"

He shrugged her off with a grunt, then pulled a whiskey bottle and shot glasses from beneath the vanity table. "The evening's young, and the more the merrier. Won't you ladies share some libation with me? Jack Daniels, Frank Sinatra's favorite."

He passed a shot glass to Samantha, who shook her head. "No? Oh, well. Nobody can say my mama didn't raise Eddie Vitale right."

Eddie gulped down the Jack Daniels, his attention still on Samantha. "We haven't had a proper introduction, have we? When I saw you the other night at the Starlight Lounge, I couldn't help wondering why this lamb was treading the primrose path with a pack of wolves." The young police officer gave Patrick a brief sideways glance before smirking. "Patrick, I noticed how much y'all favor each other. Are you and this little gal relations?"

Patrick wrapped an arm around Samantha's shoulder. "Yes, indeed, Samantha is my sister. She's on her way home, aren't you, sugar?"

Eddie laughed as if to himself. "Don't that beat all, a Renaud in the Starlight?" He now sipped the Jack Daniels instead of guzzling it. "Are you aware your sister visited that den of vice? I personally think it's a shame to see a genteel young thing waste her time in trashy dives where homosexuals indulge in their sundry perversions."

Patrick's sniggering erupted into a loud belly laugh. "A youthful indiscretion, Eddie. Haven't you ever walked on the wild side?"

Eddie ignored his words and turned his attention back to Samantha. "Kind of young to be hanging out in those places, aren't you? Little lady, I don't want to be a scold, but you could end up in the Good Shepherd with those nasty, old nuns."

Frankie grabbed Samantha by the arm, pushing her to the door. "Let's split."

Samantha's face flushed hot pink once again. She gave Lilly a plaintive look before crossing the threshold. "Sure was a pleasure to meet you ladies."

Eddie's smile returned. "And it wasn't a pleasure to meet me? Girl, you cut me to the quick."

Opal grinned like the cat who ate the canary. She followed the two girls, moving toward the door, a swash of purple satin. "Well, my friends are gone, so I guess it's time to say *au revoir*."

Patrick bowed to Lilly. "I enjoyed your dance immensely, Miss Thibodaux, but it's time for us to say our goodbyes, too. Désirée and I haven't had dinner yet." He extended his hand to Eddie. "Lovely to see you, Eddie. I'm sure our paths will cross again soon."

He opened the door for Désirée. The moment it shut, they heard arguing from the dressing room; instead of turning back, Patrick pushed her down the corridor. "C'mon, darlin'. I'm hungry. Time for some supper."

****

Lilly crossed her arms in anger, then fixed her glare on Eddie. "What was that all about? Those girls weren't doing nothing."

He snorted in response. "Girls? Those were girls? I believe the correct term is 'baritone babes.'"

Furious, she snatched up a leopard-print cocktail dress and slipped it on. "You know something? You can be a real bastard sometimes."

He spun her around and zipped up her gown. "Me?

I was just being sociable with Opal's friends. I can't help it if she pals around with bulldaggers."

Lilly pulled away from him and began fiddling with her hair. "Why do you always have to be so nasty?"

Eddie stepped behind her and placed his lips on her neck. "'Cause I'm a big, old, nasty man. Can't I get me some sugar? Please?"

His words appeared to infuriate her. Lilly inched past him and opened the door. "You're not funny, Eddie. I don't even know what I was doing with you. Guess I was a fool in love, but no more. You need to go. Bianca must be waiting."

He slammed the door with his foot. "You know you're the only girl for me. I just want my baby to stay away from Opal's friends."

She took a step away from him, a pout on her face. "She's free, white, and twenty-one. She can have any friends that she wants. If Mr. Renaud Senior doesn't care, why should you?"

Before she could move farther from him, Eddie trapped her in an embrace. "Because I prefer my lady friend not to associate with sexual deviants, that's why. I saw the way that kid looked at you, probably thinking of all the nasty mess she'd do to you if she got you alone. I won't have it, baby."

Lilly stiffened. "Won't have it? You can kiss my ass, Eddie Vitale."

He swiveled her around and planted a kiss on her derriere. "Your wish is my command, baby."

She laughed despite herself and threw her arms around him.

Chapter Eleven
Shall We Cha-Cha, Miss Broussard?

Trumpets blared as the band started the popular dance number "Cherry Pink and Apple Blossom White." Couples moved onto the dance floor, captive to the cha-cha's peppery beat.

Désirée watched the dancers from a ringside table, paying scant attention to the food placed in front of her. She stabbed her fork into the plate and speared a bit of creamed asparagus. "I had no idea so many folks liked dancing."

Patrick bent over the table until his face almost met hers. "How about us taking a spin on the floor?"

She couldn't suppress a giggle. "I'm afraid I've never been much of a dancer. In fact, I possess the two most left feet in New Orleans, and these heels will probably make it worse. Besides, I don't know how to dance the mambo or the cha-cha-cha."

He examined Désirée, turning her head to the side, a randy smirk on his face. "What do you mean, you can't dance? Everybody in New Orleans is a dancer, even if they have to learn. I bet I could teach you. We'll have a lesson later tonight."

Her nerves got the better of her, and she dropped her fork onto her plate. Patrick slid his chair closer, his breath against her cheek. "Is something wrong with the food?"

The fare tasted delicious, but seeing Eddie Vitale had robbed her of any hope of enjoying the evening. Instead of confessing the truth, she averted her face and sipped her Champagne.

Patrick placed his mouth next to her ear. A current of electricity raced down her spine. "Don't tell me Vitale upset you?"

She looked down at Patrick's plate. He seemed infected by the same affliction as Désirée. He'd barely sampled his vegetables or nibbled on his steak. The sumptuous cuisine hadn't ignited his appetite any more than it had hers.

She sighed and managed a weak smile. "Yes, he did, and I know he bothered you, too. I saw the way that bastard looked at Samantha. He's out to destroy my uncle. Of course, after what happened to his brother, maybe I can't blame him. My uncle is a snake, poison on two legs, but still, as bad as Uncle Louie is, I have a feeling that Vitale is a hundred times worse. Lilly sure knows how to pick 'em."

His laugh sounded empty. "Yes, she certainly does."

The bouncy cha-cha ended to raucous applause. The piano player gave a nod to the musicians. The band seamlessly transitioned into a slow and easy rumba, the languid rhythm as unhurried as palms swaying in the Havana breeze—or at least how Désirée imagined they'd sway. The dancers moved in time with the unhurried pacing. Patrick stood, his hand outreached to hers. "It's almost eleven, and my driver will be here soon. Just one dance, please, before Cinderella rushes from the ball. Consider it on-the-job training."

Désirée followed him onto the dance floor, aware

every eye in the place was watching them. Patrick held her close, his hips slowly rolling to the music, hers answering them back. They danced hip to hip, and it took a Herculean effort for Désirée not to grind herself into his crotch. She'd craved his touch since she'd met him, but she knew disaster loomed if she stepped into a liaison. Dinner and small talk masked what some would consider an inevitable coupling. She refused to let their provocative movements become previews of coming attractions.

Désirée felt a hard bulge against her thigh and pulled away. "Perhaps we'd better leave the dancing to others."

He shifted his trousers and gazed at her. "I guess you're right. If we stay any longer, I'm afraid we might give them a better floorshow than the one on the stage."

They strolled off the dance floor, their unhurried movements masking the desire that threatened to boil over. By the time Patrick and Désirée arrived at their table, the smiling maître d' greeted them. "Your driver is waiting, Mr. Renaud. Everything has been handled, sir."

When Patrick extended his hand to Désirée, her stomach lurched. Despite the real hunger that gnawed at both of them, she knew she couldn't chance a liaison with a man she barely knew. They left the club and found the driver standing in front of the Caddie, the passenger door open. Désirée slid in, but Patrick was not right behind her. Instead, he whispered to the chauffeur, "Take Miss Broussard home."

She smiled, barely able to conceal her disappointment. There'd be no late-night cocktail. "What time do you need me tomorrow?"

"I'll be spending the day with Samantha. Why don't you plan on showing up Friday at ten? Of course, I'll pay you for tomorrow."

She laughed. "But I haven't done a lick of work yet."

"Don't worry. There'll be plenty for you to do on Friday." His mouth tightened. "Désirée, I need you to talk to your mother about my sister. She's not quite of age yet and has threatened to leave when she turns eighteen. I can't keep her locked in at night, despite her unsavory friends. I've had her watched. She's running with a rough crowd—that kid Frankie and a morphodite they call Baby Ruth."

"Yes, Frankie is a bullshitter of the first order and Baby Ruth, young as she is, has strolled down a dark path." She decided not to mention them or their connection with Boyd Yates. "Do you want my mother to bar Samantha from the Starlight? Think about it before you say 'yes.' If she does, your sister is more likely to get in trouble with the police. Mama pays the law to stay away so she doesn't have to worry about the cops raiding the place."

He ruminated on her words. "No, I want your mother to watch her and report back to you. Tell her I'll pay for it. Hopefully, things will return to normal when Samantha starts Barnard in the fall, but until then, I'll need your help." Patrick extended his hand. "Are we agreed?"

She placed her hand in his. "I'll see you on Friday."

****

The next day, Désirée sat behind the wheel of her mother's 1955 azure-blue Cadillac. Jim Dandy had bought it as a birthday present and named it My Blue Heaven. The Caddie cruised away from the Quarter toward Gentilly, the streets packed with cars. Désirée gritted her teeth, wondering if the drive would end.

"Mama, there's a perfectly good Schwegmann's near you."

Young Miss rolled her eyes at her daughter. "Baby, I already told you, the one in Gentilly is newer, bigger, and has okra on sale. I promised Jim Dandy I'd make him some gumbo, and I hear their shrimp is really fresh."

After a few attempts to dissuade her mother from the trip, and receiving hostile glares for her efforts, Désirée gave up. When the bright red Schwegmann's sign came into view, a sigh of relief escaped from Désirée's lips. She slowed My Blue Heaven down to a roll and drove into the parking lot, mindful of tipsy shoppers dressed in their robes and housecoats.

Young Miss flounced out of the car, a goddess in a peasant blouse and form-fitting hot-pink Capri pants with matching heels. She ignored the lolling tongues of male admirers and crossed the threshold, Désirée right behind her. Once inside the supermarket, a disquieting mess of sights, smells, and sounds greeted them. The store manager added to the din by bellowing into the loudspeaker nonstop, "Discounts today on red beans, okra, and dill pickles."

Young Miss turned to her daughter. "Hear that? I told you okra was on sale."

Although the calendar read July seventh, many of the shoppers hadn't recovered from their Independence Day excesses and had continued them into the week. Matrons bedecked in bright housedresses and hair curlers guzzled cups of sugary coffee to rid themselves of hangovers. Others sampled the hair of the dog, sipping highballs as they pushed their carts through the market. Men sopped up the remnants of their Fourth of July benders with a mess of raw oysters or one of Schwegmann's famed chilidogs washed down with cold beer.

The market's hypnotic lure once caused a baby to be born in the produce department: An expectant mother's water broke as she picked through the green beans. She continued shopping despite the pleas of her family and ended up giving birth in the store.

Désirée found the aroma of cooked food, blended with cigarettes, booze, and fresh fish, overwhelming. Still, her desire to please her mother trumped nausea. She pushed the shopping cart in silence while Young Miss filled it with Wonder Bread, Cuban sugar, and coffee, along with bottles of the market's own line of cheap vodka, rum, and beer.

Young Miss ignored admiring looks from male patrons as she examined the array of vegetables and fruit, glossy red peppers, ripe peaches, bananas, and melons. She threw onions, celery, and tomatoes into the cart, then gave a joyous yelp when she spied the green bounty she'd been searching for. "Fresh okra. Now Jim Dandy's getting his gumbo."

Désirée called out, "I'll go get the fish." She was careful not to call her "Mama."

Young Miss answered with a preoccupied grunt as Désirée followed her nose to the seafood counter.

Those who liked their frog legs fresh chose from a selection of live frogs. Before Désirée could make a selection of fish, the male voice boomed from the loudspeaker once again. "Will Floyd Saint-Just please see the manager? Your father had a heart attack in the parking lot."

The counterman exhorted a group of plump matrons in brightly colored housedresses, "New catch from Lake Pontchartrain brought in this morning. Some of them are still fighting the hooks in their mouths!"

He could have saved his voice, the fresh trout, snapper, and whiskered catfish lying on beds of ice sold themselves.

Two matrons eyed the same sea bass, and one made it quite clear she'd already set her cap on it. "Darlin', I'm fixing to buy this fish, so if I was you, I'd look for another one."

Désirée eased her way closer to the counter, past the two women who were engaged in a glaring contest. She called out to the counterman, "I need a pound of crab, a jar of oysters, a pound of your white fish, and two pounds of jumbo shrimp."

The latest edition of the newspaper lay on the countertop. Désirée scanned it while she waited for the fellow to fill her order. The front-page photograph caught her short. The image showed a heavy-set fellow standing next to a spanking new Cadillac. She pulled the page off the counter.

An unknown assailant robbed and murdered Mr. Boyd Yates of Memphis, Tennessee, sometime during the Independence Day celebration. The crime occurred in an alley outside a bistro on the Rue St. Marc. The owner of a local tavern, Mrs. Yolanda Pierre, discovered Mr. Yates at 10:30 P.M., shortly after the attack had taken place. The perpetrator is still at large.

Désirée looked up from the page to the face behind

the counter. "Excuse me, but could I have this?"

He grinned, displaying a mouth full of broken teeth. "Sure, pretty lady. Go on. Take it. Hope it ain't too stinky."

She read the blurb again, cursing to herself all the while. Damn, the day just kept getting worse.

Chapter Twelve
Ode to the Dead

The Criminal Courts Building on Tulane and Broad Street was a soulless granite block with the charm of a sarcophagus. Decades of grime covered the Beaux Arts edifice, the home of the courthouse, the coroner's office, and the city lockup.

Eddie and Gino marched into the police headquarters that occupied one funky floor, its walls, dingy with tan paint and cigarette smoke. Overworked and overweight street cops hauled in the petty criminals and deadbeats who cluttered the Quarter. Grumbling and cursing drowned out the clatter of ancient Underwood typewriters as harried sergeants hunted and pecked out reports.

A once-upon-a-time Adonis trailed blood as he limped through the office in handcuffs. An overzealous peace officer had bashed-in his mug and left him a battered mess.

"Y'all screwed up my face!"

An obese officer in a grease-stained uniform looked up from a half-eaten po-boy. He winked at Vitale and Gino as they walked past, but then growled at the young man, "Hell, you've been on a bender since July the second. Today is the seventh, you donkey. I guess your hell-raising finally caught up with you. You should thank us, boy. Maybe you looking all raggedy will keep your ass in one piece in the lockup."

Eddie and Gino walked into a bleak office, the walls painted institutional tan, ratty venetian blinds concealing the barred windows. Once inside, they watched the new superintendent of police lean back in his chair and light his pipe. The smoke, vanilla-scented Captain Black, rose to the ceiling, curling around an old fan.

He was a plain fellow with a lined face, his wavy black hair pomaded into place, his feet plopped on the desk. His photo, from the front page of the *Picayune*, sat atop his desk.

Although he always greeted Eddie cordially and had recently given him a commendation, the stiffness of the older man's manner made it apparent that the young detective rubbed him the wrong way. The new superintendent of police had crawled through the ranks, his career trajectory as slow as a glacier, while Eddie's star began rising the moment he got his badge. Eddie's ambition had made the older man uncomfortable until he heard the son-of-a-bitch planned to leave the force for politics.

The chief, his intelligent eyes hidden behind horned-rimmed glasses, ignored Gino, since the beefy young man held no interest for him, but Eddie did. He perused the young detective's face, chuckling when he noted a purplish bruise on Eddie's neck.

"Fellows, I want to thank you both for your work. I've got to applaud y'all on that narcotics haul at the docks. I'm planning on another commendation for you, Eddie, one for DeLuca, and your men, too."

Gino could barely contain himself and grinned at his partner. "Ain't that some hot shit, Eddie? Thank you, sir."

Eddie flashed a dazzling smile. "Sir, the fellows are going to be happy about having their dedication to the force noticed."

Though his grin brightened, the older man's voice turned chilly. "I'm sure they will. We have some real hardworking officers. By the way, there's a rumor out that a sizable amount of cash turned up missing from that heroin bust you made the week before."

Gino looked down at his two-toned shoes. Eddie folded his manicured hands, and the ring flashed from the little finger of his right hand.

"Sir, we heard the same bullshit. As you well know, criminals lie."

The superintendent relit his pipe, puffed away, his eyes never leaving Eddie's handsome face. "Well, we'll discuss it later. I got an earful from the mayor this morning about the car dealer who got beat up outside that queer bar on the Fourth of July."

Eddie sat back in his chair, his hands pyramided. "Sir, johns get rolled in New Orleans all the time. Don't tell me the mayor's shedding salty tears over some cracker, a fruit at that?"

The chief nodded. "Yeah, he is. That poor son-of-a-bitch is dead."

Gino coughed so violently that the chief grabbed a pitcher and poured him a glass of water. "Drink up, DeLuca." He didn't notice when Eddie slipped the pinkie ring from his finger and pocketed it.

Gino took a generous gulp. "Sir, I uh, swallowed my gum!"

The older man turned his attention back to Eddie. "Tourists are big business in New Orleans. This guy was a big mucky-muck in Memphis and a pal of Patrick Renaud, Sr. The mayor raised all kinds of Cain, even brought up that mess from five years ago when some big cheese from Tennessee died after a bartender slipped him a mickey. Estes Kefauver himself came down and threatened to call in the army."

The chief tapped his pipe on the ashtray. "Thank God that bastard Kefauver is staying out of New Orleans. Look, boys, the mayor wants to prove we're on top of it. Give the public a show. Raid some queer joints and run in a few cross-dressers."

Neither detective said a word. The only sounds were the faint whirring of the ceiling fan and the muted clicking of typewriters. Eddie flashed his thousand-watt smile and looked the superintendent square in the eyes.

"Sir, I think I know who might have done in the fellow. Me and Gino saw Louie Favre on the St. Marc last night, hanging around the Starlight. Isn't that where the fellow got killed?"

Gino had recovered enough from his coughing fit to chime in. "Yeah. Hey. Wait a minute. We—"

The chief spoke over him. "Louie Favre? That reefer-selling pimp?"

Eddie straightened his tie. "Yes, sir. He got out of Angola a little while ago and probably needed money. Besides peddling pussy and narcotics, his stock in trade was rolling johns in morphadite bars. I bet he's our man."

The superintendent pulled the pipe from his mouth and dropped it into the ashtray. "Favre is one stupid son-of-a-bitch, or he never would have come back to New Orleans. Somebody must know where he's staying. Ask around, and as long as you're searching the gutter, pick up the nasty bull-bitch he used to work with. What's her name?"

Eddie gave Gino a sideways smirk. "Tinkerbelle."

The older man nodded in agreement. "Yeah, that's her. Tinkerbelle. A drunken deviant like her shouldn't be too hard to find. Try the docks first." He fiddled with his pipe, went silent for a moment, but then spoke. "There's one problem with Louie. I saw the body before they brought it to the morgue. How could a scrawny bastard like Louie Favre have worked over that big cracker?"

Gino shifted in his seat. "Well, sir, uh, regarding Louie—"

A smiling Eddie cut his partner off. "Sir, who knows what Favre learned in the penitentiary? I wouldn't put anything past that bastard or his friend Tinkerbelle. She may be female, but she's tougher than most men. Maybe they used knucks when they kicked his ass."

He paused, waiting for the inner fury that always erupted when he thought of Louie to subside. "Favre's got a sister in the Quarter called Young Miss. Me and Gino could make a call on her."

The superintendent turned his attention back to the bruise on Eddie's neck.

"Lord, Vitale, is your lady friend a cannibal or something? She really got you, didn't she?"

Eddie touched the love bite. "Uh, no, sir, I cut myself shaving."

The older man smirked at the younger man, chortling as he placed his feet back on the floor. "Well, be more careful next time. Put some ice on it. When y'all start raiding the fluff bars and making statements

113

to the newspapers, Vitale, you do the talking."

Eddie nodded to the superintendent, a pleased grin plastered across his face.

****

The dregs of New Orleans society milled around the Criminal Courts Building, moving in slow motion through the corridors, as if beaten down by the oppressive humidity. The city had located the morgue in the bowels of the building. Thankfully, the cooling system worked that day. When it didn't, the sickening stench of rotting corpses permeated the building.

The young detectives walked through the smoke of countless unfiltered cigarettes.

Eddie didn't utter a word until they were out of earshot. "Why the hell did the chief bring up that money from that dope deal? He'll get his taste."

Perspiration rolled down Gino's face and onto his seersucker suit. "Money? Man, we got other things to worry about besides the money. We're in deep shit over that cracker."

Eddie glowered at Gino, incredulous at his words. "What you talking about, Gino? Don't you see? We're home free. That peckerwood is going to make us famous."

"Huh?"

Eddie popped a spearmint Lifesaver into his mouth. "Man, this could change everything. No more chasing junkies, fairies, and jungle bunnies. This could put us on the television, just like Jack Webb."

"Jack Webb? Eddie, are you crazy?"

Eddie grabbed Gino by his lapels. "Don't you never call me crazy!"

"Sorry, man."

A plump woman approached. Eddie released his hold on Gino, grinned, and waited for her to pass before he straightened Gino's jacket. "Remember, you were there, too, so don't get any bright ideas about rolling on me."

"I said I was sorry!"

Eddie straightened his cuffs. "All right. We was only doing the job they pay us to do. How d'you think we keep the streets clean with all the drunks, hopheads, and morphadites that crawl out of the sewers like cockroaches? Besides, that prick had it coming. Just don't let nobody catch you is all."

"What about that ring?"

Eddie pulled it from his pocket and held it up to a light. "Don't worry, Gino. I got plans for this."

If Eddie or Gino had bothered to look around the smoky corridor, they might have noticed a shapely beauty in black toreador pants making her way down the hallway. Désirée, imprisoned by her thoughts, descended the stairs to the basement without seeing the two detectives.

When Désirée arrived at the morgue, she found a somber Patrick waiting. He'd dressed casually in a sports shirt and chinos. "Thanks for calling me. Daddy had planned on making a deal with Yates, even though he hated him. I guess it's over now."

She looked around at the grim surroundings. "I have something to tell you. Samantha was in the club when that fellow got beat up. When my stepfather walked him out, Mr. Yates was just fine. It's like I said over the phone, I know somebody who works here, and she'll tell us what she's found out."

Désirée tapped the shoulder of a *diener*, a morgue

worker, who rolled a corpse down the hall. "Excuse me, but can you tell me where Miss Claudine De Ville is? I'm her relation."

The fellow stared at her for a moment, shook his head in disbelief, then pointed to a double door. "Claude's in there."

Désirée glanced at Patrick and took a deep breath before entering. She spied the old woman standing over a table, a black apron covering her skirt. Désirée had never seen Claude off a barstool and vertical, but here she was, in the light of day, sober, mobile, and animated.

Claude greeted Désirée with a friendly, "Well, howdy, Miss Désirée. Is this handsome young fellow your gentleman friend?"

The younger woman's face flashed bright red. Patrick stepped in front of Désirée, his hand extended. "The name is Patrick. Miss Broussard works for me."

Claude gave a loud snort. "Really? Well, I know what y'all want to see. Follow me."

Désirée shivered involuntary. "I appreciate you doing this, Claude. I called Ma…Young Miss. She's real upset about this fellow being killed in the Starlight's alley."

Claude grunted her words in a throaty alto. "Young Miss should've come herself or sent Jim Dandy. A young lady like you don't need to see a body as banged up as this one. Believe me, he ain't pretty."

Patrick placed a hand on Désirée's shoulder. "Perhaps you should wait here."

Désirée gave a toss of her head. "No, I promised I'd learn as much as I could. Besides, I've seen dead folks before. I live in New Orleans, after all."

Claude cackled, then pointed a finger at her. "Yeah, but the stiffs you've seen are all painted and pumped up with embalming fluid. This guy just came straight over, and he's a real mess."

Patrick shot Désirée a wary look. "Are you sure you want to see this?"

She bit her lip. "Yes. As I said, he's not my first dead body. I saw a man after he got shot in the head on Canal Street. I even wrote about it, and they published my account in the *Picayune*."

The older woman looked at Désirée through watery eyes and smiled, her teeth stained deep brown from years of cigarettes and bourbon. "I guess that makes you an expert on corpses. Well, if anybody asks what y'all are doing here, just say the deceased was your uncle."

Patrick and Désirée followed her into a dank, mold-encrusted chamber smelling of chemicals and decomposition. A large roach crawled around a baseboard, but not for long. A janitor mopping the floor crunched it beneath his work boots.

Troughs adjoining the slabs that held the bodies for dissection carried the fluids of the dead to the sewer. Blood-encrusted scales, used to weigh organs, hung from the ceiling. Vaults occupied by toe-tagged cadavers lined one wall. Désirée surveyed the room, then looked back at Claude. She understood the drunk for the first time. Perhaps the old woman survived her days here by drinking at night.

Claude rolled out a shelf in the refrigeration chamber. She pulled back the sheet and revealed the battered face with its puffy, discolored skin, a broken nose, and a dislocated jaw.

Désirée didn't move a muscle. Patrick placed an arm around her shoulder. "Who could have done this?"

"Don't know, sir, but they worked him over real good. It looks like brass knuckles to me. A sissy didn't kick his ass."

Claude pointed to a pale band of skin on his pinky finger. "They never found his wallet or his ring. Who knows what happened to them?"

She rolled the shelf out a bit farther before pulling the sheet down to Yates's ankles. "Hate to show this to the young lady, sir, but I think she's seen a johnson before."

Désirée gave Patrick a wry smile. "I've had plenty pointed in my direction." Although she'd steeled herself for an afternoon of horrors, nothing could have prepared her for the dark purple bruises all over his body. She didn't turn away, but gasped in shock at the sight. "He looks awful."

Claude pulled the sheet up and rolled the shelf back in place. "I told y'all it was rough. If it makes you feel better, the coroner said he didn't feel much. Being drunk has its uses. He was out like a light before he hit the ground and never regained consciousness. Fellow was in dreamland the entire time."

Patrick nodded to her. "We've seen enough. C'mon, Désirée."

Maybe Désirée would forget the smell of the liquor, cigarettes, and Quarter rot on the dead man, but she wondered if she'd ever erase Boyd Yates's ruined face from her memory.

Chapter Thirteen
Shiny Earrings

Désirée and Patrick, their eyes masked by dark glasses, meandered down Rue St. Marc, their lazy pace belying the anxiety both felt. Accordion music drifted from an archway adjoining a bakery. A Cajun two-step wafted through air perfumed by the fragrance of fried chicken and fresh cornbread.

Désirée took Patrick by the arm. "Madame Ruby knows everything that goes on in the city. Let me talk to her."

Patrick gave a hearty chuckle. "Désirée, I've known her since I was in diapers. C'mon."

He approached the street singer, a broad grin spreading across his face. "Madame Ruby, it's me, Patrick Renaud. How you doing, darlin'?"

The old gal let loose with a wild cackle. "Patrick, you rascal." Without warning, she turned her sightless eyes toward Désirée. "I smell some real good perfume. You're with a lady, ain't you?"

Désirée stepped toward her. "It's Désirée, Madame Ruby. I'm working for Mr. Renaud now. We need to ask you about that fellow who got killed behind the Starlight."

Madame Ruby waved them closer and whispered in conspiratorial tones. "I heard a heap of mess, baby, all of it bad. He was a rich fellow, and somebody rolled him. Tell your mama to be careful. Things is nasty. Louie's in a mess of trouble."

Désirée gasped. "Louie? My uncle Louie? But he didn't have anything to do with it."

The blind woman gave a shake of her head. "Doesn't matter to the police. A cop told me they're after him for killing that dead peckerwood your mama found behind the Starlight."

Désirée felt the blood drain from her face. "He wasn't at the Starlight." She spun around to Patrick, her face filled with confusion. "This is worse than I thought." She remembered her uncle's last words, turned back to Madame Ruby, her lips near the old woman's ear. "Have you seen Tinkerbelle lately?"

The old singer answered with a wild cackle. "Big Tinkerbelle? Ain't seen her, but I hear the cops are looking for her, too. She'll be laying low—at least until the liquor gets in her. Then, she'll feel like raising hell."

Désirée gave the woman a gentle pat on the shoulder. "If you see her, tell her I need to talk to her really bad. Goodbye."

Patrick dug into his wallet, retrieved a sawbuck, and stuffed it into Madame Ruby's hand. "Madame Ruby, this is important. If you hear anything, get in touch with me at the house."

The blind woman tucked the folded bill into her bodice. "Yes, sir, if I hear anything, you'll be the first to know."

Patrick bussed Madame Ruby on the forehead. "I'm holding you to it, dear."

The two tromped off in the direction of the Starlight. A few people cast admiring looks on the young couple, possibly wondering why such a glamorous young couple had moseyed to the rear of a club with a queer clientele.

"Mama said the cops didn't even bother to search, just put Mr. Yates in an ambulance and drove off."

He pursed his mouth. "Everyone knows the police are notoriously inept."

They ignored the stench and the maze of the flies feasting on the refuse in the battered tin garbage cans behind the bar. Désirée waded through broken bottles, cigarette butts, candy wrappers, even a used rubber, until she saw a flash in a clump of weeds that had broken through the asphalt. "Over there. I see something."

She knelt and picked up a gaudy rhinestone earring. When she stood, she held the piece of costume jewelry up to the light. "Baby Ruth was wearing this that night when she arrived with Mr. Yates and Samantha's friend, Frankie."

Patrick opened his mouth as if to speak, then appeared to think the better of it. He didn't say a word. Désirée placed the earring into her pocketbook and snapped it shut. "We need to find Baby Ruth, but I have no idea where she lives."

He shot her a wily look. "Baby Ruth used to work at the Lucky 13. I might have an address for her. C'mon."

****

A chubby stripper undulated atop the bar at the Lucky 13. The club was empty, except for a drunken quartet soaking up the local color by chugalugging rum daiquiris and gobbling down the greasy fare. Patrick led Désirée through the afternoon funk and walked through the wooden curtains that separated the bar from the mischief going on in the rear.

They walked through the darkness, past a fleshy blonde seated in a glass booth. She had a broad grin on her face as she masturbated before two sailors who'd dropped their own trousers to the ground. She giggled, then let a scarlet curtain descend, blocking their view. The gobs rushed to deposit silver dollars into a slot. The red drape ascended once again.

Patrick placed his palm on the small of Désirée's back and pushed her into the sultry air scented by carnal desire. They moved past Mistress Adele as she worked over a nude customer with a chamois whip. The fellow had shackled himself to an apparatus that resembled a medieval torture rack. Madame Adele had a bright smile on her librarian's face as she gently flicked the fellow with her whip. She ran it up and down his thighs before she tickled his balls. The fellow gave a loud groan, his pleasure spurting up from a dark place.

They plodded down the corridor, past two naked, giggling girls rubbing pelvises on a bare mattress as six men watched in silence. Patrick placed a protective arm around her shoulder. "Désirée, I'm sorry to expose you to this filth. I promise to make it up to you."

She whispered in the darkness. "Don't worry, Patrick. I'm not shocked." In truth, she found the blatant carnality so arousing that she feared she'd have to change her sodden panties.

The two journeyed through the dark passageway at a leisurely pace. It seemed like eons before they reached the closed office door. With Désirée at his heels, Patrick unlocked the newly painted portal.

A tropical ceiling fan circled, banishing the overwhelming heat. Someone had scrubbed the place with lemon soap and erased the once-fetid air. Unfortunately, except for an elaborately carved buffet covered with bottles of fine liquor that sat against a wall, the office looked just as tacky as before, only cleaner.

Patrick poured himself a glass of Blanton's fine bourbon, then swiveled around to Désirée. "Excuse me. I need a drink. You want one, darlin'? I can order a champagne cocktail."

Désirée shook her head. "No, I'm not much of a drinker, maybe because I was raised around drunks. Besides, I need to be sober to talk about this mess." Désirée took a nervous step toward Patrick. "You remember when I came to the Lucky 13 with Uncle Louie, the night we met? When we were leaving the place, I saw Mr. Yates."

He took a gulp of bourbon. "Yeah, I wined and dined the bastard at Antoine's, but he dragged his drunk, hillbilly ass here."

"Yes, he was quite soused. Baby Ruth and Frankie could have messed him up, but they didn't do anything to him. I swear the only thing Frankie touched on Boyd Yates was his wallet. Luckily, Samantha wasn't there."

He swallowed a gulp of bourbon. "Thank God."

She unfastened her pocketbook and plopped the gaudy rhinestone earring on the desk. "Baby Ruth followed Mr. Yates out the door. She was probably going to take his ring or something, but I know she didn't touch him. Shucks, I'd have had better luck beating up Mr. Yates than Baby Ruth. No, I'd swear she never laid a finger on that man, at least, not with violence. I think she saw something that scared her off, maybe whoever beat up Mr. Yates. Can you talk to her,

Patrick? After all, my mother's involved in this horrible situation."

Patrick dug through a small strongbox containing slips of paper and grease-stained index cards. "Here it is. Baby Ruth Watkins. I don't know if she's still living there, but it used to be Baby Ruth's address, and it's just a hop, skip, and a jump from here. If she's moved, I have an employee at my club, a cigarette girl, who had, shall we say, a special relationship with Baby Ruth and might know how to contact her. Like I said before, Boyd Yates was a skunk who couldn't hold his liquor, but he had business with Daddy, so I guess I'm the one who has to clean up this mess."

****

Désirée and Patrick strolled to St. Peter Street, both calm, despite the specter of impending doom. He remained silent through much of their walk, finally opening his mouth when they approached a small Sicilian delicatessen.

"Daddy is much more understanding of this type of, uh, activity than I am. I knew homosexuals in college. I didn't like it, but it happens with fellows, but I'll never understand it with ladies, never. Why would a beautiful girl like my sister want to be a boy?"

Désirée stopped on a dime. "Samantha doesn't want to be a man."

He snapped at her. "Then why does she dress like one?"

She gave a shrug, wondering how such a brilliant man could be so dense. "Could it be that she just wants to be herself?"

Patrick didn't reply.

The place smelled of salami, parsley, and fresh-baked Italian bread, the delicious fixings for muffaletta sandwiches, one of Sicily's many gifts to New Orleans. The spicy aromas hit Désirée like a punch in the nose, reminding her she hadn't eaten since breakfast. She ignored her empty stomach and took the card from Patrick. She pointed to a flight of stairs that led up to a small flat above the market. "That's where Baby Ruth lived. Let me go up."

She'd climbed halfway up the stairway when a man's voice stopped her. "Hey, girlie, where you think you're going?"

A chunky, mustached fellow in a white apron and undershirt stained with oil walked out of the little market on the ground floor. Even from a distance, Désirée could smell garlic, pickles, and Old Spice on the man.

Patrick greeted the guy with a faux smile. "Sir, the young lady was looking for Baby Ruth. Nobody's seen her lately."

The fellow looked him up and down, a sour expression on his face. "Don't know what y'all are doing with the likes of Baby Ruth, but I ain't seen her either. That bulldagger she lives with might know something, only she ain't been around either. I'd kick both their asses out, only they paid their rent up to the end of the month."

Désirée ran down the steps. She managed to give a polite nod to the grocer. They moved on down the street, Patrick silent, Désirée still upset by the landlord's words.

Patrick must have sensed her confusion. He smiled, revealing his dimples for the first time that day. "We've seen a lot of strange sights, Désirée. Would you to care to join me for lunch?"

Despite the ghastly sight of Boyd Yates's battered corpse, her stomach growled loud enough for Patrick to hear. "Yes, sir."

****

That afternoon, it appeared that everyone in the city chose to lunch at Collette's on St. Charles, a favorite of the city's elite. Signed photographs of celebrities covered the pale-yellow walls. The black-and-white images of Orson Welles, Zachary Scott, Tennessee Williams, and even the great Frank Sinatra were one of the two reasons denizens of New Orleans visited Collette's establishment. It afforded folks a chance encounter with a person of note, and in a town renowned for world-class cuisine, Collette served the best Creole dishes in the city.

The moment Patrick and Désirée strolled to the entrance, an enthused greeter moved them past customers queued in wait. The fragrance of fried chicken, crawfish étouffée, and spicy gumbo assailed Désirée's nostrils. The tinkle of glasses filled with sweet tea and forks scraping against fine china nearly overpowered the progressive jazz wafting from a neighboring club.

Colette, a plump, middle-aged woman in chef's drag, her skin the color of amber, took time from her kitchen duties to greet her patrons. She moved from customer to customer, past tables covered in white linen and her signature yellow dishware. Her eyes lit on the corner table where Patrick Renaud and his lovely guest devoured smothered pork chops, rice, and ham-spiced green beans.

Patrick bounced up from his chair and threw his

arms around the older woman. "Collette, if you weren't already married, I'd run off with you. Those pork chops make me want to slap my mama!"

Collette gave a hearty laugh before turning in Désirée's direction. "Patrick, I thought I taught you better. You haven't introduced me to your lady friend."

His face flared bright red at Collette's admonition. When he turned to Désirée, his gaze was so intense the girl averted her face. "Collette, please forgive my rudeness. May I present Miss Désirée Broussard? She's working for me, and I have to say, she's a jewel."

Désirée wondered how Patrick could call her a jewel when she'd never typed a letter or taken a minute's dictation. She extended her hand anyway. "It's lovely to meet you, ma'am. This is the best food I've had since my Maw Maw died."

Collette took her hand. "Yeah, well, I learned to cook from my own grandmother." The older woman placed Désirée's hand in Patrick's. "You be good to my boy. Hold his hand, sweet pea. He'll be good to you."

Without warning, Collette's sunny smile deserted her face, and a look of great longing replaced it. Désirée feared that the older woman might break into tears. "Patrick, tell Samantha to come to me. I haven't seen her in a while. I don't care about her friends or the way she dresses. I just need my baby."

A waiter flagged her. Collette slapped on another wide smile and sauntered off to another table. She called out as she strolled away, "Y'all eat real good now. It's on the house. Patrick knows his money is no good here."

He released Désirée's hand with a nervous laugh. "You must excuse her. She's always looking out for me. Collette once worked for my family; in fact, she pretty much raised me. Mama was too involved in bridge and canasta or her latest attack of the vapors to pay us much mind. Daddy had his business interests and couldn't spare a moment to be with his kids. Samantha and I had nannies and tutors aplenty, so the staff brought us up, not our parents. Things fell apart when Samantha started calling Collette 'Mama.' She was only four, but she knew her mind, even then."

He sopped up some of the rich gravy swimming on his plate with a piece of crusty French bread. "Samantha struck a pose, her hands on her little hips, and told Mama she was a silly lady and she didn't love her."

A flashbulb popped as a waiter took the chef's photograph with a local radio celebrity. Collette beamed the entire time.

"Mama wanted Collette dismissed immediately, but wiser heads prevailed. Daddy set her up here and insisted that his friends frequent the place. Her cooking did the rest."

Patrick moved so close she felt his body warmth as he spoke in a conspiratorial whisper. "People are under the impression Daddy owns this place, but it really belongs to Collette. Of course, it doesn't matter what anyone thinks as long as they pay for her cooking. She said she's always cooked for white people, and until the law changes, she always will."

He grinned, his dimples emerged, and Désirée's heart skipped. "Collette loves Samantha like a real mother. She'd die for my sister. Will you please ask your mother to look out for Samantha? She's really a wonderful girl when you get to know her."

"Yes, Patrick, of course I will."

They gazed at each other in silence. For once, Désirée didn't look away. Her pulse throbbed, and she stared at his lips, wanting to devour them. Even a deaf and dumb man could have felt the passion between them.

Finally, Patrick spoke, and his words cut through their unspoken ardor. "Désirée, you must try Collette's banana pudding, *par excellence*. You'll never taste better."

Chapter Fourteen
The Best Brandy Alexander in New Orleans

The July moon lit the sky, illuminating the Duck Girl's silhouette as she sailed down St. Marc. Thoughts of Patrick and their afternoon together so consumed Désirée that she didn't notice when the bizarre young woman in a gossamer gown roller-skated past her.

Désirée had never met a fellow like Patrick, and most likely he'd never met a girl like her. The two of them talked for hours at Collette's, ruminating about music, politics, and books. They finished each other's sentences, shared the same thoughts, and locked each other in smoldering gazes. Their attraction had been both immediate and combustible. She feared how dangerously high it flamed.

After they'd each devoured a bowl of Collette's wonderful banana pudding, Patrick sat in silence. "Désirée, I have another request, one which you can certainly refuse."

Her pulse quickened at his words. "What is it?"

"I know you'll ask your mother to watch out for my sister, but will you, could you, watch over Samantha, too?"

She breathed in relief. This was a request she couldn't refuse. "Of course. Samantha needs a friend, and so do I. I'll go there tonight."

He smiled, his alluring dimples revealing

themselves. "Can we shake on it?"

Désirée extended her hand. He took it in his and caressed it for the longest time. She feared she'd faint dead away.

****

Désirée crossed the Starlight's threshold. Rowdy patrons packed the club, the raucous crowd lined up at the bar. A rough butch and a petite femme danced pelvis to pelvis on the postage-stamp-sized dance floor.

Young Miss and Jim Dandy worked like mad, barely able to keep up with the requests.

Désirée scooted under the counter and joined her mother at the tap. "Ma, uh, Young Miss, you handle the mixed drinks, and I'll take care of the beer."

Young Miss angrily wiped up a spilled beer on the counter. "Girl, I told you I don't want you working here."

Désirée shrugged her shoulders and continued to fill mugs with frosty lager. "Maybe we should have this conversation when you're not so busy."

Her mother raised an eyebrow at her daughter but seemed to think the better of ordering her from the bar. She shouted to her husband, "Baby, we're low on bourbon."

Jim Dandy gave her a nod, opened a trap door leading to the basement, and descended the stairs.

A female voice managed to punctuate the hubbub. "I told you, I don't want to talk about him."

Désirée looked into the smoky void. Samantha and Frankie fought their way through the crowd as they made their way to the counter. Their conversation so engrossed them that neither girl noticed Désirée on the other side of the bar. They strode up to the bar and plopped down on the stools, ignoring Claude, who sat at her usual perch, calmly sipping bourbon and branch.

Désirée watched the two girls from the corner of her eye. Frankie couldn't keep her voice down even when she hissed at her friend. "I'm tired of talking about that dead peckerwood. Folks in New Orleans have short memories. They'll forget about him in a couple days."

Samantha grabbed her friend by the arm and spoke in a breathy whisper. "Lower your voice. The police don't have short memories, you donkey. My brother's breathing down my neck, that Désirée girl is hanging around, and you still haven't told me where Baby Ruth is."

Frankie yanked her arm from Samantha's grasp. "If I knew where she was, don't you think I'd tell you? Why do you care anyway? She's probably fooling with one of those nasty old men who like playing with that big thing of hers. You need to stop asking me questions. Forget about Lilly Thibodaux, too. Get a girl of your own, not some stripper who's fucking a cop." Frankie dug into her pocket and flashed the image of a ravishing brunette gowned in violet with a fringe of deep purple marabou across her shoulders. "Opal is the reason I needed some extra money. Got to buy things for my baby."

Samantha picked up the souvenir card from the Mason-Dixon Line and perused it for a moment. "My brother told me Opal is spending time with my daddy."

Frankie's face turned bright crimson and snatched the card back from her friend. "Aw, that's just for show. My baby loves me." The young butch stared at the card as if it was an object of religious veneration.

"Have you ever seen anything so beautiful before? She's mine." Frankie sneered at her friend. "I know you're thinking about Lilly Thibodaux, but she's a regular gal. She ain't interested in dykes, no matter what their last name is."

Samantha's lips twisted in a pout.

"You gone over that girl, and she doesn't know you're alive. Just for once, don't you want a lady to call you 'daddy'?" She batted her eyelashes at Samantha and lightened her voice, mimicking a femme. "Buy me a Brandy Alexander, daddy."

The two friends laughed, the tension broken.

A plump blonde sashayed through the crowd and sidled onto the stool next to Frankie. The girl had styled her hair in a fashionable poodle-cut with spit curls framing her face. A pointy brassiere barely contained her ample breasts. The young woman tossed back her shoulders, crossing her shapely legs as she applied a coat of Fire and Ice lipstick.

Désirée exchanged an amused look with her mother as Frankie went into action. She gave the plump femme the once-over and then nudged Samantha. "Watch and learn." Frankie turned to the girl, a salacious grin on her face.

"Ain't that what they call gilding the lily? My name is Frankie. What's yours, sugar?"

"Rose."

Young Miss smirked at the show before whispering to Désirée, "Doesn't that dumb kid know Rose is Tinkerbelle's woman? She's lucky Tinkerbelle isn't allowed in here."

Frankie placed an elbow on the counter, her gaze on the busty femme. "Guess what, baby? Rose is my favorite name in the whole world. You look like a lovely pink rose and smell as sweet as one, too."

Samantha averted her eyes, barely able to keep a straight face. Rose, however, appeared touched by the flattery and simpered, "Thank you." She swiveled on the barstool, arched an eyebrow like Lana Turner and tapped a Lucky Strike on the counter. "I bet you say that to all the gals. You gonna buy me a drink, daddy-o?"

Rose held her cigarette up for a light. Frankie snapped to attention, pulled out her Zippo, and obliged. The girl inhaled. The young butch looked up at Young Miss.

"A Brandy Alexander for the young lady. Put it on my tab."

Young Miss tossed her rag on the countertop. "What tab?"

Frankie's face reddened, and she tossed a dollar on the counter.

Désirée's heart pounded like a bass drum the moment she saw the letters B.Y. embossed on the leather wallet. Frankie hadn't gotten rid of it.

Samantha, however, didn't see the wallet. The girl couldn't contain a chuckle over her friend's antics. When she averted her head, she looked straight into Désirée's solemn face. Her smile disappeared, and she elbowed Frankie. "Look who's here. We need to go."

Frankie swiveled closer to Rose. "We ain't going nowhere."

Young Miss ignored the two girls, her attention on Rose. "You'll like this, little lady. I make the best in the city—one part cream, one part Courvoisier, and one part crème de cacao."

She poured the concoction into a cocktail glass, dusted it with nutmeg, and placed it before the girl. Young Miss stepped back, waiting for a reaction, her arms crossed in expectation.

Rose took a sip, savoring it as she licked the froth from her voluptuous lips. "You ain't kidding. This is the best Brandy Alexander I've ever tasted."

Young Miss folded her arms, her lips spread in a satisfied grin. "It better be."

The girl lapped up the cocktail. Young Miss's reputation for making the finest Brandy Alexanders in New Orleans remained intact. Frankie puffed up like a Bantam rooster. Laughter filled the place until a deep voice growled out from the rear of the club.

"I knew I'd find you here, you bitch!"

Tinkerbelle rammed her way through the throng. When she reached the bar, her face was scarlet with rage, her anger at a fevered pitch. "You frigging whore, always messing around behind my back!"

Young Miss screamed out, "Dammit, I told you to stay away from here."

Tinkerbelle ignored Young Miss, grabbed Rose by her hair, and tossed her into the crowd as if she were a rag doll. Before anyone could react, the furious butch balled her right hand into a fist, knocked Frankie off the barstool, and then yelled at the prone girl. "What you doing with my woman?"

Samantha knelt next to her prone friend and discovered Tinkerbelle had knocked her out cold. "C'mon, Frankie. Get up. C'mon!"

Désirée screamed out at Tinkerbelle from behind the bar. "Why did you hit her? Those girls weren't doing anything."

A boozy smell emitted from Tinkerbelle's every pore as Tinkerbelle turned in Désirée's direction. "Shut up, bitch."

Young Miss yelled through the open trap door, "Jim Dandy! Jim Dandy! Where the hell are you? Get up here! The dykes are at it again!"

She pulled her pistol from beneath the counter and pointed it at the angry woman.

"Tinkerbelle, I warned you once before. Get out of here, or I'll use this. I swear I will!"

Jim Dandy emerged from the cellar door, a bottle of bourbon in each hand. He slapped them on the counter and rushed from behind the bar. Tinkerbelle greeted him with a fist to the face. The powerful man joined Frankie on the floor.

Samantha stood in front of Young Miss, spoiling her aim. The older butch reared back and took a swing. The girl jumped away, and Tinkerbelle missed her face by mere inches.

Samantha called out to her. "Hey. Wait a minute. I wasn't doing anything to you. Somebody help me."

"Shut up, you kiki bitch! Nobody talks to my woman but me!"

Everyone knew the term "kiki" was a pejorative for a queer who wasn't butch or femme; instead they were half-assed and in between. The word usually guaranteed a fight, certainly among butches. Samantha whipped around, as if searching for an escape, but the sudden throng of cheering youths wanting a brawl ringed her in. The crowd wanted a battle.

Young Miss threw her revolver down in disgust. The crowd hooted and crowed in delight as the girl danced around the drunken brawler. Désirée grabbed a small baseball bat her mother kept behind the counter. If she reached Tinkerbelle before she hit the younger girl, Samantha might leave the Starlight in one piece.

The one-sided fight continued. Samantha managed to bob and weave like a professional, barely escaping the older woman's bruising fists. Each time Tinkerbelle took a swing and struck empty air, a cheer went up. The hooting started in earnest, further maddening the enraged butch.

"Hey, y'all. That baby butch is a regular Sugar Ray Robinson!"

"Ain't nothing better than two dykes duking it out!"

Samantha continued ducking, bouncing up, down, and around, somehow evading Tinkerbelle's bruising fists. The older woman growled, lunged at the girl, but couldn't connect. The more times she jabbed air, the more she screamed in frustration, "C'mon! Fight me, bitch!"

No one noticed when Désirée pushed her way between two cheering boys. She leapt over a table and drove the bat into Tinkerbelle's stomach. The woman bent over in pain and looked up just as Désirée smashed it over her head. Tinkerbelle dropped to the floor, and a cheer went up.

Jim Dandy had regained consciousness. He pulled a bloodied Tinkerbelle up to her feet and twisted her arm behind her back before pushing her toward the door.

Young Miss rushed from the bar, the pistol in her hand pointed at the large woman's head. "You see this? Show your ugly face in here again, and I promise I'll shoot you between the eyes the moment you walk in the door."

Désirée stopped Jim Dandy before he hauled Tinkerbelle to the street. "Where is Louie Favre?"

The bruised and bloodied woman glared at her. "Wouldn't you like to know?"

Désirée waved the baseball bat in her face. "People are going to laugh like crazy when they hear a feminine young lady kicked your ass. Don't make me have to beat the shit out of you with this bat. I'm going to ask you real nice again. Where is he?"

It appeared the threat of another ass-kicking by a femme sobered Tinkerbelle up. She whispered, "Tremé. He's been staying at Buster Garnier's place."

Jim Dandy pushed Tinkerbelle out the door, to the cheers of the assembled patrons. A young fellow placed an arm around Désirée's shoulder. "Tinkerbelle won't show her ugly face around here soon."

Désirée grunted a reply. "Uh, uh, I bet we never see that bitch again."

She propped up the overturned chair, then headed for the bar, where her mother had a Coke waiting for her.

As the dust settled, people turned to Samantha. Frankie gave her shoulder a brotherly pat. "I watched your moves. I couldn't have done better myself."

Rose, the cause of the conflict, thrust her ample bosom in Samantha's face, as if offering the spoils to the victor.

Neither the cheers from the crowd nor the enticement of Rose's ample bosom appeared to cheer the young warrior.

Young Miss placed two beers on the counter in front of Frankie and Samantha. "Don't get too comfortable, girls. After you finish your drink, you need to go on home."

It took a moment for Young Miss's words to register. Frankie looked back at her, shocked. "Why you doing us like that, Young Miss? We didn't start the fight."

Young Miss ignored Frankie and focused her eyes on Samantha. "The fight isn't the reason. The cops have been nosing around, and word is out that they're going to start raiding queer bars, maybe even mine. Frankie and the other kids are used to it, but, little lady, you don't need to be part of that mess. Now drink up and get out."

Tears rolled down Samantha's face. "But how am I going to see anybody? Who am I going to talk to? I come here to meet my friends, my only friends. Everybody else makes fun of me. Please."

Young Miss passed her a handkerchief. "It don't look good to see the conquering hero cry. The raids won't last long. You can come back then. Now drink your beer and go on home."

Frankie drained her mug, chugalugging the icy brew, but Samantha took a dainty sip. The two girls made their way out through a crowd still hyped from the fight.

Young Miss glared at Rose. "You, with the big bosoms. You can get out, too."

A tearful Rose grabbed her pocketbook and rushed out of the club.

Désirée took tentative steps to the bar. She spoke in soft murmurs, so faint Young Miss could barely hear her words over the cries of the frenzied crowd. "Mama, that girl, the one called Sammy, is a Renaud."

Young Miss's eyes widened. "What?"

Her daughter nodded. "Yes, a Renaud. One of the reasons Mr. Renaud hired me was because of you. He knows you own a queer bar. Mr. Renaud wants you to watch out for his little sister. Mama, I have to go after her."

Young Miss went to the tap and squirted one beer after another. She positioned mugs of the frosty brew on the counter. "You need your job, baby. Tell Mr. Renaud I'll keep an eye on her if she comes back, but I can't do nothing about her choice in friends. Frankie will get her in a lot of trouble." She fixed her gaze on her daughter. "What did Tinkerbelle tell you about Louie?"

"He's hiding in Tremé."

Young Miss rolled her eyes to the heavens. "I knew Louie was stupid, but not that stupid. How the hell can a scrawny white guy hide there?"

Désirée slipped from behind the bar. "I'll have to go to Tremé to look for him."

Young Miss shook her head. "Oh, no, not you. Leave him alone."

Désirée didn't relish the thought of searching for her uncle in a part of New Orleans filled with people of color, trudging around Tremé in the late summer heat, but if she had to, she would. At that moment, however, she had one concern—Samantha.

Chapter Fifteen
Street-Fighting Gal

Samantha waved goodbye to Frankie. Then, she made her way down Bourbon to the Mason-Dixon Line. She pulled the lobby card from her pocket and was overjoyed the scuffle hadn't damaged it. The scent of the Shalimar wafted from the image. She put it to her nose and inhaled deeply.

Samantha stood in the shadows, across from the alley behind the Mason-Dixon Line. Lilly leaned indolently against the side of a shiny limousine and waited for one of two goons in tuxedos to light her cigarette. She followed a raucous cackle by uttering the lines from a Mae West movie, "Cigarette me, big boy."

Samantha continued watching until Lilly slithered back into the club.

Instead of going home, however, the young butch took St. Peter Street to Hy's, a queer bar that catered to the female trade. A paddy wagon ringed with uniformed cops waited outside. Samantha spun around, walked a couple of paces, and felt a hand on her shoulder. She shuddered, thinking perhaps the law had caught up with her, but turned and came face to face with Désirée instead.

Samantha exhaled, her relief palpable. "I thought you were the police."

Désirée looked around. "Be glad I'm not. Let's get

out of here."

Samantha shifted in place, her eyes cast down to her high-top sneakers. "Are you following me?"

Désirée gave an enthusiastic nod. "Yes."

Samantha's mouth tightened. "Well, don't. I can take care of myself."

Désirée couldn't stop a chuckle. "I wouldn't say you did very well with Tinkerbelle. I promised your brother I'd look after you. Come on. It's late. Let me walk you home."

Samantha puffed up her chest. "Since I'm a butch, I should be walking you home."

Désirée hooted. "We'll talk about that later, when we're away from the cops."

The two girls hotfooted away from the police and moved on. A passing couple glared at them.

Désirée glared back and slipped her arm through Samantha's. "Your brother told me you're going to college in New York."

"I'm supposed to go to Barnard, but maybe I'll stay here instead."

Désirée stopped on a dime. "You want to stay here, so you can hide from the law with your friend? I don't think that's a good idea. In fact, it's a lousy one. Frankie is used to living on the streets. She's rough trade, but not you. By the way, I saw her at the Lucky 13 with that Yates fellow."

The girls moved on. Then Samantha gave her a sideways glance and tossed her head back. "So what? My brother owns the Lucky 13." She turned to Désirée with a smirk. "Want to know why Patrick bought the place? Daddy had a heart attack there when he was doing nasty stuff with Mistress Adele, the whip lady."

She smirked as if pleased with herself. "No one thinks I know, but I do."

Désirée came to another dead stop. Dealing with Samantha would be harder than she first thought. She took the girl by the arm.

"Listen, I saw Frankie in the Lucky 13 with Baby Ruth and Mr. Yates. Mr. Yates is dead, and Frankie has his wallet. Maybe she didn't have anything to do with his death, but this whole mess stinks like week-old garbage. She'll be in a lot of trouble if the cops catch her with something belonging to a dead man, and so will anyone who hangs around with her."

Samantha shrugged her shoulders. "I've told her to get rid of it a million times, but she won't do it."

"She's stupid like my uncle Louie. Oh, well. Have you seen Baby Ruth?"

Samantha's lips narrowed. "No. She hasn't been around. Seems I'm losing all my friends, and it's not fair."

The girls caught the attention of a drunken boy and his less-intoxicated friend. The drunker of the two, his hair styled in a slick pomp, ambled up to Désirée. "Ooh-ee, baby, you sure look good to me!"

The not-so-drunk boy grabbed his drunken friend's shoulder. "Come on, man. Leave her alone."

Mr. Pompadour pulled away, ignoring his companion's suggestion. "What's a fine girl like you doing with that friggin' bull bitch?"

The other boy pulled at the drunken boy's arm. "Shut your mouth, man."

Désirée took Samantha's arm. "You'd blush at some of the things fellows call me. We better be on our way."

Before Désirée could move on, the pompadoured boy blocked her way, and she hissed at him under her breath, "Leave me alone."

Mr. Pompadour appraised her through bloodshot eyes. "What you doing with that bulldagger?"

The boy's less-intoxicated friend interceded once again. "Man, come on. Let them be."

The drunken kid shoved his friend away and glared at Samantha, his face florid from booze and rage. "What the hell are you anyway? You look like a boy, but you got titties? A boy with titties."

He turned and took a wobbly step toward Désirée. "*Cher*, you need to get you a real man."

Désirée pushed Samantha toward the curb. She turned back to the drunken boy and kneed him in the groin with all her might. When he keeled over, screaming in agony, she stood over him, blazing with anger. "Somebody sure did a piss-poor job of teaching you manners. Didn't your mama train you to respect ladies?" Désirée turned to the other boy. "Do you want to know if my friend is a girl or a boy?"

The kid backed away. "No, no, miss, I don't want no trouble."

Désirée and Samantha walked away, arm in arm, and turned onto Dauphine Street just as Mr. Pompadour recovered his voice. "I'm dead, man! Dead!"

His friend looked down at him, no pity in his youthful face. "Well, that's what you get for messing with them. I told you to leave those gals alone."

Samantha turned to her new friend, her eyes glowing with admiration. "Where did you learn to fight like that?"

Désirée strutted on with a shrug of her shoulders.

"My stepfather showed me a few things after I got my period. The boys were tittie mad then. A girl has to know how to protect herself against fellows when they don't know how to behave."

Samantha gave a knowing snort. "Aww! I know about fellows. I can't tell you how many guys have offered to pay me for a hand job." Her face beamed as bright as a summer moon. "Golly, I've never seen a girl fight like that before. Would you show me how to take care of myself the way you do?"

"Sure." They walked on. "Uh, Samantha, I didn't want to bring this up. I've known Lilly Thibodaux for years. We went to kindergarten together and grew up in the Quarter. I love her like a sister, but she's a terrible flirt. She's got that crazy bastard of a boyfriend, and I don't know what he'd do if he caught the two of you together, no matter how innocent it was."

Samantha's eyes misted, and she looked away. "I just thought, well, maybe she could be my friend. We wouldn't have to do anything, just be friends."

"Lilly isn't one to just stop with friendship. You'd be better off leaving her alone."

The two girls walked in silence until they arrived at Maison Renaud. Samantha unlocked a side gate. "Well, I guess we should say goodnight."

Samantha extended her hand in friendship, but Désirée ignored it and gave her a hug instead. "Good night, Samantha. My offer still stands."

With that, Désirée turned and walked off into the night. Her breath quickened, and she felt clammy. She knew Samantha hadn't heard a word she'd said about Lilly.

Chapter Sixteen
The Jewel

Désirée arrived at Maison Renaud at ten a.m. sharp. She'd dressed in a simple black skirt and white blouse. Faux pearls encircled her neck—the very picture of a crackerjack secretary. Désirée carried her lunch, a chicken sandwich and an apple, in a Schwegmann's paper bag. Her pulse raced, and her hands shook uncontrollably. She feared she'd leave a ring of armpit perspiration on her new blouse. She took a deep breath and moved on. When she arrived at the front gate, a smiling Remy stood in wait.

"Mr. Renaud said you'd be prompt, and you are. He's not here, but he made sure to set up your office with everything you'll need. Please follow me."

Désirée took an intake of air before she stepped into a beehive of housekeepers, gardeners, and housemen. Groundsmen transported fragrant bouquets for maids to arrange in massive vases, while others dusted the vast chandeliers and squeegeed oversized windows with vinegar and water. The drone of the workers filled the vast rooms as they polished, scrubbed, and swept Maison Renaud. Very soon, it would be shipshape.

They walked past the army of laborers and into Maison Renaud's massive foyer. When Remy opened the portal to a small chamber adjoining Patrick's office, she followed him.

Someone had taken great pains to create a comfortable, modern space. Stacks of stationery embossed with the Renaud watermark sat atop a walnut pedestal desk next to a Smith Corona electric typewriter, carbon paper, and a Dictaphone machine. Her day had begun.

****

By one o'clock, Désirée had waded through the mass of documents and contracts, many yellowed with time, some in French and others in Spanish, all testaments to New Orleans's vibrant history. The parchment deed to Maison Renaud dropped into her lap, the French scroll faded with time.

Before she could read on, Remy rapped the open door. "You haven't eaten yet, miss. Would you like a tray brought up?"

Désirée smiled up at him, her face bright and cheery. "I brought my lunch, but I'm sure anything you have would be better. Where does the staff eat?"

"In the kitchen, miss."

"Would y'all mind if I join you?"

Her question appeared to take Remy aback, and he deliberated for a moment. "No, not at all. The last secretary refused to set foot there. She told Mr. Renaud she didn't care for...uh, Negroes." Remy's chuckles filled the room. "He fired her prejudiced ass. You should have seen the look on her face. Guess she didn't know Mr. Renaud spent a great deal of his childhood in the kitchen. It's the hub of this place. Follow me, please."

Désirée bit her lip to keep from joining Remy in his laughter. Mr. Patrick Renaud was an interesting

147

fellow.

****

A sweet strawberry fragrance assaulted Désirée's senses the moment she walked into the kitchen. The oversized windows revealed a kitchen that surpassed her entire apartment in size. The snowy tile gleamed pristine white, along with floor-to-ceiling cabinets with leaded glass. The sheen from polished brass pots and pans suspended from iron ceiling racks above a huge stove nearly blinded her. Brown faces looked up at her from an enormous kitchen table. The huge room retained whiffs of the crimson-colored berries, ripe bananas, and freshly perked coffee.

A platter of sandwiches sat in the middle of the table. The place went silent the moment Désirée entered. "Hey, everybody. My name is Désirée Broussard. I'm working for Mr. Renaud. It's a pleasure to meet you, and I hope to join you for lunch every day, if you'll have me."

The staff went silent for a moment. Then one of the maids clasped her hands together and giggled. "Ain't you the nicest lady? We welcome you."

The room broke into applause. Remy pulled out a chair for Désirée. "Time to eat, y'all."

****

An hour later, a satiated Désirée returned to her desk and set to work putting the papers in alphabetical order. One suddenly dropped to the floor with a plop. Désirée glanced at the document, titled Lucky 13 Bistro. Her interest piqued, she unfolded the copy of the deed for the Lucky 13.

Désirée perused the document but didn't get beyond the square footage when warm, perfumed breath grazed her cheek. She looked up into her employer's handsome face. Her pulse quickened once again, first hot, then cold, while she prayed he couldn't hear the pounding of her heart.

Patrick's beautiful lips spread into a wide grin, revealing his glorious dimples. "It's quite an interesting document, Désirée. When you read further, you'll notice we didn't pay a plugged nickel for the Lucky 13. The owner wanted to wash his hands of the place."

"Uh…" flew out of Désirée's mouth. Then she went silent. She feared his proximity might bring on a fit of giggles, so she bit her tongue instead of her lip.

"What is it, Désirée?"

"I…uh…saw Samantha yesterday."

Patrick couldn't hold back a chortle. "Yes, she told me. I must say, I'm impressed, two battles in one night. You're Samantha's Joan of Arc."

She shook her head. "I don't think I'm anyone's Joan of Arc. I just dealt with two drunks, and I don't know what I would have done if they'd been sober." She took a deep breath. "Patrick, maybe I'm speaking out of turn, but Samantha said your father had a heart attack in the Lucky 13."

Patrick took a step away, his face unreadable. "I won't deny it. Everybody has eccentricities. My daddy likes getting beat up by naked ladies. I assure you, Mr. Tennessee Williams would have a field day writing about my father's epic fornications, Opal Jordan being the main one."

Patrick's outward calm might have deceived someone who didn't know him, but Désirée saw the tension in his jaw. "Does it bother you that your father finds a bit of comfort with Miss Jordan? From what you've told me, your parents are cold toward each other. I've only met her the one time. I don't know her, but I think there's more to Opal Jordan than just beauty."

He shot her a wry smile. "I can't comment. I try to stay out of Daddy's private affairs, but I think Mama's holding onto him by a thread, a frayed one. By the way, if you're free on Sunday, I have to go to an engagement celebration, and I'd like you to accompany me."

His words took her aback. They barely had begun working together, and he had already asked her out on another date. "Well, I don't have plans on Sunday. I'm honored you asked, but are you sure you want to go with me?"

Patrick's mouth tightened. "Yes, you're the only girl I would plan to take." His mood changed on a dime. Tension permeated the room, and his words only worsened it. "Of course, maybe you won't want to go with me. You see, the celebration is for Eddie Vitale's engagement to Bianca Corolla. Her father is a business partner of ours, and she's my daddy's goddaughter. Although I dislike Vitale, it's a business obligation, and I have to attend. If you want to say no, I'll understand, but I'd like to have you with me."

The invitation robbed Désirée of speech for a moment, but she found her tongue. "Lilly Thibodaux told me he'd gotten engaged to that poor girl. Patrick, if you care about her, you'll do everything you can to kill it. He's involved with Lilly, and I assure you, it won't end well. He thinks he can control Lilly, but no one can." She paused for moment, unsure if she should continue.

They gazed at each other in the stillness, the

tension still palpable. "I'll go with you, Patrick, but I'm warning you, that man is dangerous. He'll do everything he can to destroy anyone who stands in his way."

Patrick gave her nod. "I know."

With that, he walked from the room.

Chapter Seventeen
Love's Labors Lost

The alley behind the Mason-Dixon reeked from the remains of lobster and shrimp, the dregs from liquor, and the butts of a million smokes. Samantha stood in the shadows, waiting. A rear door opened, and her heart thumped in her chest.

Lilly took a dainty step into the foul-smelling passageway, pulled a cigarette from her pocketbook, and then rummaged around in her purse, as if searching for a match. A flame appeared from the darkness, and Samantha emerged, silver Zippo in hand. "Miss Thibodaux, don't you know smoking is bad for your health?"

Lilly steadied Samantha's trembling hand. "So I've heard." Lilly grinned at the girl. "Are you going to light me or lecture me?" Samantha held the Zippo steady enough for Lilly to light up. She inhaled deeply. "Thanks. What are you doing here anyway?"

A nervous Samantha shifted in place, then looked down at her high-top sneakers. It suddenly occurred to her that perhaps it wasn't the opportune time to tell Lilly she'd been thinking about her day and night. "Well, it's kind of late. I was hoping maybe you'd let me walk you home."

Lilly took another drag and silently appraised her. From the set of Lilly's jaw, Samantha knew the blonde beauty wanted nothing to do with her.

"I'm sorry, I won't bother you anymore. Just wanted to talk."

She turned and walked toward the street, but Lilly's voice stopped her in her tracks.

"Come back. Maybe I can use an escort after all."

Samantha swiveled around, her face lit in a thousand-watt smile. "Then it's my honor to accompany a lady."

Lilly threw her cigarette onto the damp cobblestones. "Lady? You really think I'm a lady?"

When they moved out of the alley onto Bourbon, Samantha crossed in front of Lilly to walk close to the curb.

"Yes, ma'am. First time I saw you, I thought, 'Now that is a real lady, the most beautiful one I have ever seen." She handed Lilly a flat paper bag. "I hope you don't have this one. It's Dinah Washington singing 'I Concentrate on You.'"

Lilly's beautiful mouth twisted into a smirk. "Is the title a suggestion or something? You don't beat around the bush, do you?"

Samantha's face flared bright red, but her color returned when she noted Lilly's smile. "No, it's just the name of the song. I've been thinking about you a whole lot since the last time we saw each other, though. Are you, uh, in love with that police fellow?"

Lilly made an abrupt stop. "Now who's not beating around the bush? Yes, I guess I am."

Samantha couldn't conceal her disappointment. "Oh."

Lilly resumed walking, her jaw in a defiant pout. "The bastard just got himself engaged and thinks he's getting married, but I'm putting an end to it. I'll fix his little red wagon. He can be a son-of-a-bitch, but I have reasons to care about him." She turned her face to Samantha, her eyebrow raised. "You still think I'm a lady?"

Samantha nodded her head. "Yes, ma'am."

She tossed her hair back. "Don't 'ma'am' me. You make it sound like I'm a million years old. I'm twenty. You're eighteen, aren't you?"

Samantha walked on, her face flaming even brighter. "Yes, ma'am, I'll be eighteen in a few months—uh, darn it, I mean, Lilly—and I'm about to go to college in New York."

A few people turned and stared at the two of them as they made their jaunt through the Quarter. Samantha was so involved in the conversation she didn't notice the unfriendly looks following them. Lilly ignored them.

"You finished high school? Of course, you did. So did Désirée. She was a real scholar, not like me. I dropped out after the eighth grade, but I read all the time—*Redbook*, *Reader's Digest*, *The Saturday Evening Post*, cultural magazines like that. Eddie laughs at me for trying to better myself, but to hell with him."

Samantha answered, with a chuckle, "A beautiful lady who likes reading is a wondrous thing. I read *National Geographic* and *Scientific America*. You can learn a lot from *Scientific America*."

A passing couple glared at them. Lilly glared back, gave a defiant headshake, and slipped her arm through Samantha's. "Maybe I'll pick up a copy of *Scientific America* and show it to you-know-who."

The girls walked a bit farther in the sultry darkness. Lilly stopped at a wrought iron gate and unlocked it before entering a flagstone courtyard. "Here we are at the family manse." She pointed to a tiny cottage behind hers, a light glowing from the window. "Désirée lives in that place next door. She must be reading or writing."

Samantha shifted from one foot to the other in her nervous jig. "Oh, didn't know y'all were neighbors. Uh, well, good night. Thank you for letting me walk you home." The young butch made a curt bow before turning around. She'd unlatched the gate when Lilly called out to her. "Hey, why don't you come in for a drink?"

The teen stared at Lilly, incredulous at the invitation. "Me?"

Lilly placed the key in the lock, then swung the screen door all the way open, a seductive smirk on her beautiful face. "You see anybody else?"

Samantha walked through the court, stepped over the threshold, and followed Lilly into a darkened living room. The light flicked on, illuminating the flashy furnishings. The girl whistled in appreciation.

"Wow, you sure got a pretty place."

Lilly shrugged her delicate shoulders. "Yeah, I guess it's okay." She sauntered into the kitchenette and opened the refrigerator. "Heck, I'm out of Coke. Is root beer okay?"

"Fine, ma'am, uh, I mean Lilly." Samantha gazed at Lilly, unable to look away, her body a mass of nervous energy. "Nobody's taken care of me like this since school. The nuns were very nice."

Lilly turned her head to one side with a smirk. "In case you haven't noticed, I'm not a nun." She slithered over to the hi-fi, slipped on Prez Prado's "Mambo No. 5," and, seduced by the beat, undulated her hips to the music. Lilly shook her behind up and down, giggling all the while. "Come on, Samantha. Dance with me!"

Samantha shook her head. "Sorry. I'm not a dancer."

Lilly opened her arms wide, beckoning Samantha to join her. "Your daddy and your brother are dancing fiends. Oh, hell, anybody can dance. Come on. Dance with me!"

Samantha didn't move. "I can't dance like that."

Lilly arched an eyebrow and slithered over to her. "Don't be a chicken. I'll show you how. It's easy. I even taught Eddie how to mambo." Samantha shook her head again, amusing Lilly. "Are you afraid to move your hips? Eddie isn't."

The two faced each other, a nervous Samantha standing in place as Lilly's carnality flared as hot as an oven. She turned off Prez Prado and placed Samantha's gift on the record player. "I know how to get you to dance. Come on, baby. I want to dance with you."

Dinah Washington's voice sounded sweeter than melted pralines. Samantha slid her arm around Lilly's waist and pulled her close. She shut her eyes and inhaled Lilly's perfumed skin. The girl caressed Lilly's platinum tresses. "You have the hair of an angel."

Lilly put her head on Samantha's chest. "Would you believe I'm not a natural blonde?"

They swayed in each other's arms until Samantha mustered the courage to ask the question that had tortured her all evening. "Uh, Lilly, I was hoping, well, maybe you'd step out with me sometimes."

Lilly stopped dancing. "No."

Samantha pulled her back. "But why not? Why can't we be friends? You think I'm ugly, don't you?"

Lilly placed her hands on her shoulders. "Nobody thinks you're ugly. Come on. Let's dance some more."

Samantha pulled her closer and attempted to kiss her neck and face. "I love you, Lilly."

Lilly's sweetness evaporated, and she pulled away. "Don't say things like that."

Samantha pressed her. "But why not? It's the truth."

Lilly took her hand and led her to the faux-French sofa. "Samantha, I don't want to hear that love stuff! I saw the way people looked at us tonight. I could never live like that. I'm guessing Opal can't neither."

"What do you mean?"

"She's fixing to leave New Orleans with your daddy."

"What?" Samantha appeared confused by Lilly's words.

Lilly sighed and continued speaking. "I said, she's fixing to leave New Orleans with your daddy. I'm sorry, but they've been planning it for a while. I guess Opal is going to break it to Frankie soon. He's planning on divorcing your mama for her. She swears your daddy doesn't care about his lady love sleeping with a woman, but I don't believe it, do you? It would make any man go crazy—at least, one fellow I know."

Samantha felt as if someone had walloped her. Lilly held her captive, body and soul. Samantha could barely restrain herself from taking Lilly in her arms and devouring the lips that promised so much but denied everything.

"I don't care if Daddy leaves my mother. They hate

each other, and they both make me want to puke. Well, I guess it's time I shoved off. Thank you for the hospitality and the dancing lesson."

Just as Samantha took a step to the door, a knock and a familiar male voice stopped her from turning the latch. "Lilly, baby, come on. Open up. It's Eddie."

Chapter Eighteen
Beauties and the Beast

Lilly yelled through the closed portal, an impish grin on her lovely face. "Go away, Eddie. I have a guest, you son-of-a-bitch."

A scream from the other side broke through the evening calm. "Girl, open this friggin' door, or I'll break it down!"

A leering Lilly crossed her arms in defiance. "You just do that, you bastard!" When Lilly grinned again, Samantha had the frightening suspicion that Lilly was enjoying herself.

The pounding stopped. Then the young butch heard a loud thud as if Eddie had thrown his weight against the portal. "Girl, don't pull this shit on me! Let me in!"

Samantha jumped away from the door. Although an overhead fan cooled the room, perspiration rolled down the girl's face, her fear palpable. "I need to get out of here. Please."

Lilly ignored Samantha, her smirk widening as the door pummeling continued. Finally, she called out, "You know what my landlady said last time, Eddie. She was fixing to kick me out after you messed up her property, and she don't care if you are the police."

Eddie yelled from the other side of the door, "Screw that bitch!"

Lilly screamed in faux indignation, "I told you not

to use that sort a language around me, you friggin' bastard."

When the door clonking became more frenzied, Lilly grasped Samantha's hand and led her to the back door. "You better leave now."

The teen summoned every ounce of courage she possessed. "What about you? Maybe I should stay."

Lilly gloated like the cat who'd swallowed the canary. Her attention remained on the closed portal Eddie kept pounding on like a battering ram. "No. Don't worry about me. I can take care of him. He ain't nothing."

The girl stood frozen. An impatient Lilly opened the rear door and pushed her through. "We don't have time for you to get all gooey. Go on to Désirée's. Goodbye."

Samantha appeared hesitant, her fear obvious. "I'm going, only don't forget I love you."

****

Her pulse racing, adrenaline surging through her veins, Samantha rushed from the kitchen to the adjoining cottage. She rapped on the door but didn't yell out into the night. Instead, she hissed, *sotto voce*, "Open up, Désirée, please, open up."

When Désirée flung the door open, Samantha flew straight into her arms. "What are you doing here?"

The girl hung onto Désirée for dear life. "It's Vitale. He's come after Lilly. I think he broke down the door to her place, and he's going to kill her. We've got to get the police."

Désirée wrenched away from the girl. "He *is* the police. Lilly knows how to handle that bastard. She's an expert at it." Her gaze remained on Samantha, who stood rooted in place. "Go home, Samantha. There's nothing you can do." She took the girl by the shoulders, led her from the cottage, and pushed her onto the street. "Good night, Samantha, and don't worry about Lilly. Like I said, she can take care of herself."

Désirée waited until the girl rushed off into the night, then tiptoed to Lilly's place. She eased herself to the side of the cottage and watched the drama through an open window.

Lilly ran into the living room and appraised the damage before screaming to the voice behind the battered door. "That's the third lock you've busted. I'm tired of calling the locksmith. You're going to pay for that, Eddie Vitale! Anyway, what do you think you are doing here? We broke up." Lilly's grin disappeared, replaced by a sulk as she swung the front door open.

Désirée looked on as Eddie stormed into the apartment, his face flaming. "Broke up? How many times do I have to tell you I decide when we break up, not you?" He threw his hat on the sofa, uttered a quick, "Sorry, baby," then looked back at the pulverized door. Eddie pulled Lilly close and buried his face in her neck.

When Lilly turned her back to Eddie, Désirée made out her gloating visage in the dim light.

Eddie's voice softened. "What's wrong? You know I'm gone on you, baby."

When he turned her to face him, Lilly's smirk had transformed into a seductive pout again. "Maybe I don't care if you're gone on me, Eddie. Maybe I'm looking for something different."

Eddie picked up the half-empty root beer bottle on the coffee table. "When did you start drinking root beer?"

He moved closer, his expression menacing enough for Lilly to back away. "Has that muff diver been here? You let her put her hands on you, didn't you? Was that dyke licking on something that belongs to me?"

"Son-of-a-bitch. I know I didn't hear you say that. Get out."

Eddie took an angry step toward her and grabbed her crotch. "This is mine, and I'm not sharing it!"

Désirée lunged toward the door, but suddenly remembered Eddie carried a gun. She backed away and stayed in place.

Lilly pulled away from Eddie and grabbed a vase from an end table. "Touch me like that again, and I'll knock the shit out of you."

Eddie's demeanor softened, his voice gentled, and his smile returned. "Put that down, baby. I'm just trying to watch out for my little girl. Don't you love me no more?"

Lilly's body shook with rage. "No, you bastard, I hate you! Get out!"

She stomped into her bedroom with Eddie at her heels.

Désirée moved toward the bedroom window at the rear of the cottage. Her addiction to voyeurism reared its head; unable to control herself, she watched the lovers, a self-loathing Peeping Tom.

Eddie grabbed Lilly's arm, pulled her to him, then rubbed his crotch on her hip. "You're getting me hot. Feel how hard I am. Come on, baby. Let's play."

Lilly didn't look as if she wanted to play. "Screw you!" She pulled away, and they struggled, knocking over a lamp. Lilly thrust her long nails at Eddie, clawing at his face.

Eddie managed to grab her wrists and pushed the struggling woman onto the bed. "No bitch is going to put horns on me! Did you let that little dyke do that nasty stuff to you? What did y'all do?"

Lilly broke free of him and jumped off the bed. "Nothing. I didn't do nothing with her, you fool!"

Eddie made a move toward Lilly, angering her even more. Without thinking, she hauled off and slapped him soundly in the face.

"Bitch!" Enraged, he hit her with so much force she landed back on the bed.

Désirée looked around for something, anything she could use to pummel him. She grabbed a flowerpot, ready to storm the flat, but her friend's action stopped her.

Lilly rolled over to her nightstand, opened a drawer, and pulled out a small-caliber pistol. She jumped up from the bed and aimed the gun at his head. "You've gone too far this time, Eddie. I'll kill you if you don't get out of here. You know I will."

The gun in one hand, she opened her closet door and threw a sharkskin suit and some silk shirts at him. "Take this crap with you. I'm tired of it stinking up my locker!"

The room went silent.

From the darkness of her hiding place, Désirée saw tears in Eddie's eyes. "Don't you love me no more, baby? I love you so much. I can't handle the thought of you being with someone else."

Lilly stood in the silence, fuming. "You prick."

When his sobs started, Lilly appeared moved by his pain. She took a tentative step toward him, then moved closer. She ran her fingers through his dark hair and caressed his face. "That girl didn't mean anything to me, Eddie, just a silly little puppy, but you wouldn't let me explain. Maybe you should go. We can talk later."

At that point, Désirée breathed a sigh of relief and thanked the Lord Samantha hadn't seen it. Lilly couldn't help the way she was. Men were the world to her.

Lilly placed the gun back in her night table drawer. Then she turned back to Eddie.

He held a velvet box in his outstretched palm. "I brought you something, *cher*, one of those ankle bracelets you wanted. It's real gold. My cousin made it. I thought it would look pretty on you."

Instead of tiptoeing away, Désirée watched Eddie kneel at Lilly's feet, fasten the golden bauble to her right leg, then kiss it. "You've got the most beautiful legs, skin like velvet."

His lips slowly worked their way up to her thighs, moved up to her stomach, to her breasts, and finally, to her face. "I can do you real good, darlin'."

Lilly winced when Eddie's lips touched her cheek. He pulled back. "Did I hurt my baby? Did I? I swear I didn't mean to. You just made me mad because I love you. Tell me you love me."

Lilly turned her face to his. "I love you, Eddie."

He held her with his eyes. "Tell me there's nobody else."

"There's nobody but you."

Lilly's dress fell to the floor, followed by her bra. Eddie lifted her onto the bed and then slowly pulled down her panties. "Let me kiss you all over, baby."

Eddie flicked the bedroom light off.

Moonlight barely illuminated the bedroom.

Désirée shrugged her shoulders, turned away, and walked back to her apartment.

Chapter Nineteen
Cherry Pink and Apple Blossom White

The Roosevelt Hotel's Blue Room thundered with applause and robust backslapping. A grotesque Plaster of Paris seashell surrounded the bandstand where Monte and His Society Boys sat in pristine white dinner jackets. Monte gave the command, "Hit it, fellows!" and the band roared out into a raucous version of "Love and Marriage."

Monte took a bow before speaking over the rhythmic din of the music. "Ladies and gentlemen, please give a hand to the loving couple, Captain Edward Vitale of the New Orleans Police and his beautiful fiancée, Miss Bianca Corolla."

Eddie swept up a sweet-faced young thing from a near-by table and positioned her under the grand chandelier. As the guests cheered, he planted a big smooch on her closed lips. The bride-to-be's father, Willie Corolla, looked every bit the dapper mobster in his black suit. His hair slicked back, his English loafers polished, his beautiful, patrician wife by his side, he beamed all the while.

The smiling faces packing the grand ballroom whispered among themselves. Some questioned how a shy gal like Bianca Corolla could have snared such a good-looking beau. Others suggested her wealthy father bought a fiancé for her, while those who knew the prospective groom kept mum about the machinations that had brought Eddie and Bianca together. Ladies murmured, their hands shielding their lips as they swore Lula Vitale had orchestrated the whole thing.

If the charmed couple heard any of the gossip, they didn't give a sign.

Every Sicilian family in New Orleans had received an invitation to the festivities, and all the familiar names—Mercante, Maceo, Ferruggio, and Lentini—showed up. Grocers, tradesmen, and taxi-drivers attended, gold-toothed men in ill-fitting suits with gossipy wives, surly sons, and fleshy daughters. Laughing children darted around the room's elaborate flowered pillars.

A few of the guests murmured about how the famed gangster, Carlos Marcello, had sent emissaries, fancy men who took pains not to wrinkle their flashy suits on the plush red chairs.

Guests piled the tribute table until it groaned with linens, towels, toasters, irons, and MixMasters. Patrick Renaud sent the engaged couple a color television, while a washer and dryer had arrived at the hotel that morning, sporting a shiny red ribbon and a card of congratulations from his parents.

A group of giggling young ladies encircled Bianca as she showed off an engagement ring specially designed by Eddie's cousin.

Waiters carried in platters of traditional New Orleans cuisine along with the lasagna, sausage, and cannelloni that the guests consumed with gusto and washed down with gallons of red wine. Some of the older folk spoke a smattering of Italian, but most chatted in plain New Orleans English. The din nearly obliterated the music until the band broke into the Prez Prado hit "Cherry Pink and Apple Blossom White."

Lula stood in the reception line next to Eddie, a radiant smile across her face. "Eddie, I'm so proud of my boy. Everybody's here for my baby. The mayor and his wife will be here soon, along with the archbishop. The way I figure it, first you become a councilman and then, in five years, mayor."

"It's all for you, Mama."

A cheer went up when Eddie took Lula Vitale's plump hand and led her to the dance floor for a mother and son cha-cha-cha. Everyone marveled at how light on her feet Lula was, considering she weighed nearly two hundred pounds. The crowd went berserk after her perfect execution of a cha-cha turn.

When Eddie and his mother performed an effortless sidestep, a roar erupted in the room. "Mama, with you in my corner, make it three years. Now come on, I'm going to spin you again."

Lula's pink satin pumps turned on a dime, and once again, the crowd broke out into cheers. She and Eddie sauntered arm in arm through the throng, their lips spread in wide smiles when they took their places at the door to greet new arrivals.

Eddie's white teeth gleamed, wolf-like. "Patrick Renaud hasn't shown up."

His mother gave a friendly nod to a passing couple, then spoke out the side of her mouth. "Yes, but he sent that lovely color television. You watch, Junior will be here eventually."

Eddie snorted, his face blazing with anger. "Hell, a color television ain't shit when you're rich. He's pissed off over some bullshit, and there's nothing I can do.

Bianca *would* have to be his daddy's goddaughter."

Lula hissed a reply through clenched teeth. "I don't want to hear talk like that."

Without warning, the place went silent. Patrick Renaud strode into the Blue Room with Désirée on his arm.

Lula gave a cackle of victory. "I told you he'd come!"

Patrick Renaud had dressed to the nines in a black tuxedo, but all eyes were on the brown-eyed goddess, in pale aqua chiffon, who clutched his arm. Désirée fixed a tense smile on her lips and spoke to her escort in sideways whispers.

"I'm so nervous, Patrick. Do I really have to talk to that horrible man?"

Patrick held her close. "You don't have to do anything you don't want to, but showing fear to a bully won't help. You're with me, Désirée. Vitale won't do anything in front of all these folks."

Eddie nodded at the newcomers, a feral grin on his face, steel in his eyes when he spied Désirée. "Why the hell did he bring that bitch?"

Lula nudged her son. "Behave yourself. I've known Patrick's family for years. That girl looks like a sweet young lady, at least to me. She's a beauty, whoever she is."

Eddie fixed the smile on his face. "Young Miss, the owner of that queer bar on St. Marc Street, is her mama."

Lula's eyes remained on Désirée. "They do favor each other. Bleach her hair, and she could be her mother's twin."

He snorted angrily, remembered himself, and

stretched his lips back into a wide grin. "She's related to Louie Favre. He's her brother."

His mother took a deep breath. "No, he's her uncle. Young Miss is her mama. We can't help who's in our family. Look at the difference between you and Sal."

"I'd take bets that she's as big a whore as her mother was."

Lula scowled at her son. "I never raised you to talk about ladies like that."

Eddie waved at Patrick, who slowly made his way up to the host. When Patrick and Désirée approached, Lula's face beamed even brighter than Eddie's. She sauntered over to the new guests, her plump arms open in welcome.

"Junior, darlin', who is this lovely creature?"

Patrick thrust Désirée forward; she found herself enveloped in a haze of perfume and pink flesh. "May I present Miss Désirée Broussard. Désirée is working with me now on several projects, aren't you, sweet pea?"

Désirée flashed a nervous smile. "I'm pleased to meet you, Mrs. Vitale."

Lula threw her head back in a loud guffaw. "Aw, sugar, call me Lula like everybody else in New Orleans does. Eddie mentioned that you are relations with Young Miss. I've known her for years, since she was a beautiful little baby crawling around Bywater, and I must say you are her spit and image, especially in her youth. May I speak for Eddie and Bianca and thank you for coming to our little party? Junior, I'm so sorry your daddy can't be here. I've heard he and your mother are still in Europe, trying to get him stronger. I sure would have loved seeing—"

Suddenly, every head in the ballroom turned in the direction of the newest guest. An attractive, suntanned fellow with a receding hairline entered before Lula finished her sentence. "Lord, Mayor Morrison just arrived. Sorry, y'all, but I need to have a word with him. Eddie, take care of Patrick and Miss Broussard."

As Lula rushed off to the newly arrived dignitary, Eddie turned to Patrick and Désirée, his grin frightening in its lupine ferocity. "Well, hello, Patrick."

Désirée noticed that Patrick's smile never disappeared. He focused his gaze on Eddie. "Eddie, you are one lucky guy. It isn't every day a fellow gets a prize like Bianca. I don't want to rain on such a festive occasion, but we have a couple of problems to discuss."

Désirée turned to leave, a tentative smile on her face. "Well, I guess I'll go mingle with the other guests."

Before she took a step, Patrick grabbed her by the arm, holding her fast. "We have no secrets, Désirée. This involves you, too." Patrick's gaze fell back on Eddie, a grim expression on his face now. "I know boys will be boys and need their little amusements, but once you're married, Bianca's daddy is not going to take kindly to you two-timing his little girl with Lilly Thibodaux."

Eddie's chin dropped. "How do you—"

Désirée could barely contain her discomfort and pulled away from Patrick. "Please, perhaps I should leave you two to speak in private."

Patrick grasped her wrist so hard she winced. His grin matched Eddie's in feral ferocity. "Désirée, I'm sure Eddie understands that, as my employee, you need to be aware of everything."

Eddie snorted derisively as he gave Désirée a lewd appraisal. "'Employee?' Is that what they're calling it now?"

Désirée gasped at the naked insinuation. Patrick's grin widened, but he wasn't happy. "If we weren't at your engagement party, I'd knock your block off for insulting this young lady. Since Willie Corolla and my father are in business together, I know everything that goes on in that club." His smile chilled. "Willie knows about Lilly. She's a beautiful girl, and I'm sure a passionate one, too, but you've got to end it. My partner might ignore your little dalliance for now, but Bianca is his heart. She's my daddy's godchild, and that makes her a sister to me."

Patrick took in Eddie's shocked expression and moved in closer, dragging Désirée with him. "We'll get Lilly a job in Miami or Las Vegas, but she won't be messing with you anymore. That's for damn sure. Remember this, we're helping you with your political aspirations for only one reason—gaming. Willie and Daddy's other business partners and I have interests in Las Vegas and Havana. I believe Cuba's going to blow up, so we're getting out. Got to plant our casinos somewhere else. New Orleans is just as good a place as any other."

Patrick leaned over, whispering in conspiratorial tones, "Daddy has heavenly dreams of roulette wheels and slot machines in the Mason-Dixon. With the new highways bringing folks into town, he wants to make New Orleans the Las Vegas of the South. Our current mayor is eyeing the governor's chair, so we need a mayor who's friendly to gambling, but there's one caveat. He's got to be happily married, to get the women's vote."

Patrick's smile returned. He released Désirée and placed a brotherly hand on Eddie's shoulder. "Now, the other thing is trickier, that Yates mess. His partners are calling Willie and me every single day wanting to know who killed the bastard."

Eddie shook his head and looked Patrick dead in the eye. "Gosh, Patrick, I wish to hell I knew, but I'm working with Homicide on this one." He turned his icy stare on Désirée, then fixed it with an equally chilly smile. "I'll tell you one thing—if I had a million dollars, I'd be betting that Louie Favre was involved." He pivoted in Patrick's direction. "You might could ask Miss Broussard about it, since she and Louie are relations."

"Hmmm, Louie Favre?" Patrick's chilly smile made Eddie step back to avoid frostbite. "Funny, your superintendent mentioned his name to Willie the other day." Patrick stared into the young detective's face, his gaze intent, his eyes dark. "I don't think Louie had anything to do with it."

The two men gazed at each other for one deadly moment. Patrick chuckled, breaking the lethal tension. "Eddie, will you excuse us? I'm going to sample some of that cannoli at the dessert table and then dance the night away with Miss Broussard."

He wrapped an arm around Désirée's waist and walked away, leaving a furious Eddie standing alone.

Désirée's eyes flashed the moment they were out of earshot. "Patrick Renaud, you are a real bastard. You dragged me to the engagement party of a man we both know to be dangerous and crazy, and then you let him insult me."

Patrick waved to a well-wisher before murmuring from the side of his mouth, "I had to see his reaction. He's blamed your uncle for Yates's untimely demise, but now he knows I have something on him. We have to get Louie out of New Orleans. Do you have any idea where he's staying?"

Her shoulders relaxed when she looked into his face. The vulnerability she'd glimpsed before had returned. "Tremé."

His mouth twisted as he digested her news. "Hmmm. Remy lives in Tremé, and so does Collette. We'll go there tomorrow." Patrick stroked her cheek and gazed into her face with such intensity she feared she'd collapse. "I'm afraid you're stuck with me, *cher*. C'mon. Let's try some dessert before we start your cha-cha lesson."

Chapter Twenty
The Plot Thickens

The next day, a harried, overweight police officer, his uniform spotted with grease and sweat, dragged a battered woman from the drunk tank into an interrogation room. Her bruised face gave silent testament to her epic battle in a queer bar. The cop led the woman into the grimy room, tan paint peeling from the walls, a bare light bulb the only illumination.

A grim-faced Eddie and Gino stood in wait. Three wooden chairs sat around a small, battered table. Eddie looked from the officer, a veteran cop with a beer gut and bad knees, into the woman's battered face. The officer pushed the woman down into one of the chairs, and Eddie nodded in appreciation. "Hey, man, thanks."

The uniform nodded back. "Anything for you, Eddie."

He walked away, leaving Eddie and Gino alone with Tinkerbelle. Eddie opened a paper bag, and the pungent fragrance of marijuana filled the room. He smiled at Gino, who spoke, chewing his gum all the while.

"Tinkerbelle, I'm told they found this bag of reefer on you. Captain Vitale, wouldn't you say this is enough to send her to the penitentiary for the next ten years?"

Eddie bobbed his head in agreement and moved closer. "Lieutenant DeLuca, I'd say even longer once the judge gets a look at her. I've made a study of women like her. They're always fishing in the wrong stream, always looking for ladies to pervert with their twisted ways. It won't go down easy for her when she gets to the pen. Those matrons use rubber hoses on gals like Tinkerbelle. I hear they can really mess a girl up. Then they'll put her with the other daggers, the ones that hate her. I doubt she'll make it out in one piece."

Tinkerbelle looked up at him, the fear obvious in her battered face. Perhaps her life in New Orleans had been hellish, yet a round in prison appeared to terrify her.

Eddie's expression betrayed nothing. "Tinkerbelle, I might could make all this go away. We'll put you in the infirmary for a few days, so you can get three square meals and let your bruises fade. After that, how about a one-way bus ticket out of New Orleans? Any place you want to go. Just imagine. You could take in the sun in Miami. All I need is one little favor, and I'll make this whole thing go away. Where's Louie Favre?"

Sweat rolled down Tinkerbelle's red face, her eyes wide with fear. "I don't know."

Eddie's lips drew back in a predatory smile. "Aw, Tinkerbelle. Don't bullshit me. You know where he is. Hell, do you really owe him anything? He lies, cheats, and pimps out every gal he meets. Shit. If you wasn't so ugly, he'd have tried to sell you, too."

She looked away. Eddie grabbed her chin and forced her to look at him. "Oh, come on, Tinkerbelle. You don't want to see me get nasty. Where's Favre?"

Tinkerbelle started trembling, her movements abrupt and violent. Gino pulled Eddie away from her.

"Eddie, she's having a seizure. We better get a

doctor."

A huge grin lit Eddie's handsome face. "Not until she tells us where Louie is."

****

A Cadillac enameled in glossy ebony paint came to a stop in Tremé, where shotgun-styled homes were drenched in the vibrant hues of the city—hot pinks, shades of turquoise and aqua, and every permutation of violet—and nestled next to each other on the street. The damp air was bathed in a hot mist, a Turkish bath of gumbo, fried okra, and collard greens.

Remy had garbed himself in a sports shirt and seersucker trousers. He jumped from the driver's seat, and swung the rear door open for Désirée and Patrick to alight. "I'm taking us to fellows who know everything that goes on in Tremé."

The trio walked past a home painted in vibrant purples and pinks. Three old men sat on the front porch playing a raucous game of dominoes, the Bakelite pieces shattering the silence as they clattered onto the wooden board.

"Throw down them bones, Junior!"

Two combatants battled each other while the other kibitzed from a third chair. "C'mon, y'all! Play again."

The soggy heat rendered the roof overhang useless in protecting the codgers from the sun, but they didn't seem to mind. By nine that morning, the trio of old-timers had already consumed half a tub of Falstaff beer. The brew anesthetized them to the weather. Plates holding the remnants of their breakfast, barbeque and red beans and rice, sat at their feet. They sat watching the world go by from their perch, passing gas, and gulping beer. The kibitzer, a Cajun, had even planned dinner. "My little gal is bringing us some fried catfish. Best y'all ever ate."

Remy addressed the old men. "Hey, y'all. My name is Remy. I stay on St. Philip. Folks say y'all know everything that's going on in Tremé. Have any of you seen a skinny white fellow in flashy clothes walking around here lately?"

The kibitzer's face brightened. "Yeah, I seen the guy, a real dude, smelling all fancy, dressed like a pimp. Ain't been around for a while, though. For real, I don't know where he's gone to."

Another fellow stopped the game long enough to make a suggestion. "You might could ask Buster Garnier. Buster has lots of white friends, and I seen him with that fellow. He stays down the street on St. Augustine."

Remy spoke to Patrick and Désirée in a low murmur. "I know Buster. He's a real hustler, knows everybody, white or colored."

The third man gave his head a violent shake. "No, Buster ain't been around for a while. I heard he's in Alexandria with his brother. Only other person who knows what's going on in the whole city is the blind woman, Madame Ruby. She might could help you."

Ten minutes later, Remy maneuvered the Caddie into the Quarter. Désirée sat back into the heavenly coolness courtesy of the Coupe de Ville's Frigidaire system.

Patrick thought a moment. "Could your uncle have already left the city?"

Désirée shrugged her shoulders. "No, I doubt it. Uncle Louie is too dumb to leave New Orleans. Besides, he would have called Mama if he left, but maybe if we find him before Vitale does, I can convince him to go away. He's not a good man, but he'd never murder someone."

They began their hunt into the Quarter, the car windows rolled down despite the ferocious heat. As Remy maneuvered the Caddie toward Chartres Street, a French refrain drifted from an alcove. Désirée's face broke out in a broad smile. "We've found her!" She tapped Remy on the shoulder. "Please pull up here."

When Désirée flung the door open, Patrick slid toward her as if to follow. She stopped him from alighting. "Let me handle this."

She took a deep breath before she strode up to the blind woman.

"Madame Ruby, it's Désirée. What you know good?"

The old woman hunched down in her chair and whispered, "I know a heap of stuff, baby, but ain't none of it good."

Désirée's stomach lurched. Madame Ruby might as well have punched her square in the stomach.

"One of Tinkerbelle's friends saw her in jail an hour ago. She told me that the bitch blabbed and told where they could find Louie. He's hanging around the Dew Drop Inn."

Madame Ruby had uttered the name of a magical bistro renowned throughout the South for its great race music. What was a white woman, especially a violent butch like Tinkerbelle, doing at the most famous black nightclub in the city? Madame Ruby must have sensed the question because she answered before Désirée could ask.

"Tinkerbelle was selling dope for Louie. He's got a

new lady friend, a shake dancer who works at the Dew Drop Inn. I heard they trying to get enough money to leave New Orleans. I bet you he'll be there tonight."

Désirée replied with an anemic "Thank you" before dropping a dollar in the accordion case. She stumbled toward the Caddie, praying all the while that her uncle's misplaced love for the city wouldn't keep him in New Orleans.

****

Late that afternoon, sunlight peeked through the slats in the Venetian blinds. The mottled light stripped Frankie's muscular body atop the rumpled spread. She rolled over on her side and stared at her beloved. Her luck in capturing the heart of the most beautiful and, surely, the most passionate woman in New Orleans still awed the girl. In her young life, Frankie had never met anyone with such an appetite for sex and such a talent for erotic improvisation.

They made love in the morning, honeyed love, dark and passionate. Opal whispered smoky endearments, and their amour stretched into the afternoon. By early evening, both were sated. Frankie's head reclined on her pillow, gazing into the face of the love of her life. Opal smiled back, her eyes dancing in the dim light.

"Daddy, I got something to talk over with you. I heard from Patrick Sr. He called all the way from Europe. He's going to leave his wife and wants me to marry him. I accepted."

Her words punched Frankie squarely in the gut. The girl broke into breathy sobs, with tears rolling down her cheeks. Try as she might, she couldn't stop them. "No, baby, please, don't do it."

Opal took her lover in her gardenia-white arms and whispered to her in a husky alto, "Don't cry, darlin'." She stretched her arms in a yawn, shook her mop of black hair, and then fell back onto her pillow.

Frankie broke into another round of tears. "How could you do this to me when you know how much I love you?"

The room went quiet, except for Frankie's bawling.

Opal glared at the girl, her patience strained. "Don't you understand? He's got all that money."

When Frankie finally spoke, emotion choked her voice, and she could barely speak. "Is that all you think about? Money? I'll give you every penny I have. Please, baby, don't do it. Money don't mean nothing."

The young butch watched as Opal slid from the bed, moved to her vanity, and angrily slathered her body with gardenia-scented lotion.

"'Money don't mean nothing?' Spoken like a poor person. When I was fifteen, a fellow once gave me two hundred dollars just to look up my kitty cat. That money kept me and my mama from starving." Opal stared at her reflection in the mirror. "My two-hundred-dollar days won't last forever, and I don't intend to end up some broken-down whore dancing in a rat-hole. I'm going to have a life, a place in the Garden District. When he divorces her, he'll marry me. People in New Orleans will have to be polite, even if they have to swallow their gorge. Don't you understand?"

Frankie sat up in the bed, her eyes dimmed by her waterworks. "But you're supposed to love me, baby, just me."

"I do, baby, I do." Opal slithered over to the girl, sat next to her, and kissed away her tears.

Chapter Twenty-One
Uncle Louie

A gravelly contralto booming from a loud speaker rolled down La Salle Street. The singer almost drowned out the noise from the raucous throng gathered outside the Dew Drop Inn.

A black man accompanied by a well-dressed young white couple darted across the street. Remy and Patrick slowed their pace for Désirée as she walked unsteadily in her stiletto pumps. The two men strolled toward the two-story building housing the Dew Drop Café Bar & Cocktail Lounge. They sauntered past a youthful crowd composed of people of color, but not entirely—New Orleans had always been the hub of after-dark miscegenation.

Patrons milled around the front of the place, smoking and laughing, unmindful of the moist heat. Some of the men wore iridescent sharkskin suits like the ones Louie favored. Others dressed in black linen against the heat. Young women with skin tones ranging from cream to sweet black swished past in gowns of fuchsia and peacock blue, their lips painted in vivid pinks and reds.

Patrick and Remy had garbed themselves in snappy sharkskin suits like cool cats. Désirée, clad in a spaghetti-strapped sundress, her hair pulled into an elegant upsweep, scanned the crowd of dark faces in a frantic search for Louie. Her eyes landed on a group of young white men, most likely Tulane frat boys, who jostled with each other. One glanced at a seductive beauty and chortled, "I'm hoping to taste a little brown sugar tonight."

Désirée glanced from one fellow to another, but none was her errant uncle. She perked up when she heard the gritty blues voice. After a second of listening to the vocals, she tapped Patrick's arm. "I don't see Uncle Louie, but that's Big Mama Thornton singing. She's his favorite. If anybody could get him out of hiding, it would be Big Mama."

Patrick took her arm and pulled her close. "Okay, we'll go in now, but remember what we agreed on."

She gave a nod. "I remember. Let Remy do the talking."

Remy exchanged cordial smiles with the other patrons, but then spoke through clenched teeth. "Don't worry. I know the owner. Once we find Miss Broussard's uncle, I'll drive him to the bus depot." He turned his face ever so slightly in Désirée's direction. "We've got to be careful, Miss Broussard. We're dealing with the police, understand?"

She nodded before averting her head. "I've got it."

The three made their way through raucous laughter, the damp air electric with kinetic energy, to a tuxedoed doorman who collected the dollar cover charge. Remy took charge, greeting the young man in polite tones. "Where y'at, man? We're looking for a white cat named Louie Favre. You know him?"

The young guy looked from Remy to Patrick before nodding. "Yeah, he's inside with Miss Angelique, the shake dancer."

Patrick held out a ten-dollar bill. "My friend, Louie is in a trouble with the police, and I know nobody wants to get his mess on them. If you let us in, maybe we can handle it for you. Please?"

The doorman dropped the ten in the cash box and waved them on. "Miss Angelique is dancing now. Y'all go on to the back of the house and get Louie. Excuse my French, but we don't need no shit from the police."

The trio made their way into a hazy maze of cigarette smoke and flashing teeth. Starched white cloths covered every table, and staff rushed up and down the narrow aisles. The band members wore electric-blue sharkskin, their hair conked, straightened with a lye solution, and then styled into shiny pompadours. Still, no one in the club noticed anything but the dancer as she undulated on the stage.

Miss Angelique looked as if a master sculpture had carved Venus out of a block of caramel. Her eyes glowed amber like a cat's, and she'd styled her ebony locks in the cropped curls of an Italian movie queen. A gold bikini barely covered her curves, her hips undulating in time with the drummer, her pelvis thrusting in time with each rim shot.

Désirée stared at the beauty, open-mouthed. "She's Uncle Louie's type, all right. I bet he stayed in New Orleans because of her. Now it's too late. I got to find him."

Remy kept his attention on the beautiful woman, a carnal smile dancing across his lips. "I'd stay for a lady like that, too."

Patrick gave an enthusiastic nod of his head. "I think a lot of fellows would," he said before suddenly remembering Désirée sat next to him. He answered her raised eyebrow with a sheepish grin. The trio abandoned the table for the backstage area.

Musicians in flamboyant garb and their female admirers packed the crammed area. Désirée's stomach almost bolted at the stench of fried chicken, perspiration, bourbon, and cigarettes. She looked around the place but couldn't see hide nor hair of her uncle until someone struck a match. Through the club's low light, Désirée caught sight of Louie, sharp as a tack in one of his signature iridescent suits. He was involved in an animated conversation with an older black man clad in a tuxedo. The tuxedoed gentleman pulled a cigarette and fished around his pockets for a light. Louie's Ronson flared in the dimness. "Now, Frank, I'm just saying Angelique is worth more money."

The tuxedoed man took a hit of his cigarette. "Louie, I been dealing with hooch dancers since before I opened this place, and I don't need a pimp to tell me how to run my business."

Before Louie could reply, the man called Frank spotted Remy and waved him over. The two exchanged a hearty handshake before Remy pointed to Louie and whispered in Frank's ear. Frank glanced at Louie and walked away with a derisive snort.

Désirée took Patrick's hand, and the two made their way toward him. "Uncle Louie."

When Louie turned and saw his niece with Patrick Renaud, his jaw almost dropped to the floor. "What are y'all doing here?"

Désirée pulled at her uncle's arm. "Bringing you a warning. You have to get out of the city right away, and I don't want an argument. The cops nabbed Tinkerbelle, and she's probably ratted on you already."

Louie gave a vehement shake of the head. "Tinkerbelle would never squeal on me. Besides, I can't leave without Angelique."

Désirée looked him square in the face. "Are you talking about that pretty lady, the dancer?"

Louie nodded. "I'm in love, *cher*. She's my woman. I can't leave her."

Tears rolled down Désirée's cheek. "No, not again!" She grabbed her uncle by the lapels. "She's your woman? Uncle Louie, I been hearing that same bullshit since I was six years old. How long you going to be with this one? How long before you drag her down like you did all the others? You can't marry her, at least, not in Louisiana. How you going to support her? By selling dope and pimping her out?"

She opened her pocketbook and handed him a roll of cash. "Take it. It's from Mama. Three hundred dollars, enough to get you out of the city and away to a new start."

Louie pushed her hand away.

Désirée seized his hand again. "If you really love Miss Angelique, leave her alone and get out of New Orleans."

From his expression, Désirée knew her words had struck their mark, but before Louie could reply, the house lights flashed on and off.

Louie hotfooted it out through the rear exit, then took off in a dead run. Before Désirée could follow him, Patrick stopped her. "Let him go, Désirée."

Remy rushed toward them, sweat rolling down his cheek. He pointed into the club. "The police are here, Miss Broussard, and we have to leave. We can't have Mr. Renaud involved in this."

Her stomach lurched when she saw Eddie walking through the club. Patrick grabbed her arm, and the trio exited the cramped backstage area.

Inside the bar, the crowd didn't greet the arrival of the police with quiet acceptance. "What the hell are the cops doing here? They need to keep their white asses away!"

Eddie stepped forward, looked around the room, and broke out in a smile. The mood suddenly lightened. Many in the crowd appeared to recognize the young police officer, who moved through the Dew Drop Inn shaking hands and backslapping with abandon. "Hey, Leroy, glad to see you. Norvel, how's your mama doing? Alphonse, when did you get back in town?"

It appeared as if Eddie knew everyone in the place. Then Frank, the tuxedoed owner, walked over, hand extended. "Eddie! Glad to see you, man. Big Mama finished her set, but she'll be back. Why don't you two fellows sit and enjoy the floorshow?" Frank snapped his fingers at a waiter. "Bring our guests some refreshments."

Eddie licked his lips at Angelique's undulations before turning to the owner. "Frank, as much as I'd love to stay, we got an itty-bitty problem. Someone told us that a bad actor named Louie Favre was here. Me and Gino need to talk to him."

Frank glanced at the beauty dancing on stage, then shook his head. "I knew that son-of-a-bitch was up to no good. He's in the back." He took the young detective's arm. "Eddie, you been coming here for a long time. I'm trusting that you won't make a ruckus."

Eddie met his concern with a raised eyebrow. "Frank, when have I ever caused you trouble? If anything goes down, we'll take it outside."

Miss Angelique ended her set with a frenzied set of hip lunges and dashed off behind a velvet curtain. Eddie and Gino followed.

Désirée, Patrick, and Remy had already sped out of the club before Eddie and Gino ambled toward the back of the house. They raced down La Salle to where Louie stood in wait, calmly smoking. "Uncle Louie, get in that Caddie over there. The police will be out here soon." She dug into her pocketbook and retrieved the wad of cash once again. "Like I said, here's three hundred dollars. This is for you to leave the city. Go, Uncle Louie, and don't come back!"

Remy spotted a black Ford with a white New Orleans Crescent affixed to the side. "Wait, y'all." He darted over to the police vehicle, pulled up the hood, and fiddled around before closing it. "A car won't get far without a distributor cap." He took Louie by the arm. "I'll drive you to the train station. Come on."

Louie pushed Désirée's hand away. "No." His eyes misted. He turned Désirée's head toward his and looked deep into her face. "No, boo, you done enough for me already. Now go on. I'll get away. Give that money to Angelique."

Stunned, Désirée took his arm in her hand. "Are you crazy? You can't get away on foot. Come on. Let Remy drive you to the bus station."

Louie suddenly took off running down La Salle. He called back to her over his shoulder. "Go home, *cher*, and forget about me! Tell Angelique I love her."

Switchblade in hand, Louie ran back to the Dew Drop Inn just as Eddie and Gino left the club. He yelled out into the night, "Hey, Vitale! I hear you've been looking for me!"

Eddie pulled out his revolver. He spoke, his manner calm, his voice gentle. "Louie, I've been waiting a long time."

The knife flew through the air and landed at Eddie's feet. Eddie pulled the trigger, and Louie fell to the ground. More shots rang out as Eddie emptied the chamber of his revolver into Louie's prone body.

Silence. Then the crowd encircled Louie's corpse, tentatively at first, then moving closer. Angelique, dressed in a silk wrapper, rushed from the rear of the club. The onlookers surrounding Louie parted for Miss Angelique. She wailed a loud, "Daddy!" before she collapsed in front of her lover's corpse.

It took all of Patrick's strength to keep Désirée from running back. "You can't help him. He's dead. It looked to me like he wanted to die. Come on, darling."

Désirée took a final look across the street. Eddie stood over Louie's body, his face devoid of all expression, no anger, no remorse, no joy. A shiver ran up Désirée's spine.

Chapter Twenty-Two
Truth

Louie's cadaver reclined on a steel table, his head resting on a wooden pillow. Light from a single bulb spilled over his thin body, which a sheet partially obscured. Patrick grasped Désirée's hand as they moved to the viewing chamber.

The idea of looking at her brother's corpse had unnerved Young Miss so much that Jim Dandy joined them, instead of her. When Claude pulled back the drapes blocking their view of Louie, Désirée gasped at the sight of her uncle's form. Jim Dandy bit his lip before he swiveled toward the viewing window. He stared down at Louie's body. "Désirée, you better thank God your mama ain't here. She couldn't deal with Louie looking so pale."

She gazed down at the corpse, its skin devoid of color. "I guess if you'd bled out on the *banquette*, you'd be pale, too, Jim Dandy. The papers printed all sorts of lies about him, but I expected them to. We were there and saw the whole thing."

When the police searched Louie's corpse, Mr. Yates's pinkie ring had somehow found its way into Louie's pants pocket, and Eddie Vitale became the hero of the day. The next morning, the *Picayune* had plastered the image of Eddie shaking hands with the mayor on its front page. His expression somber, Eddie looked resplendent in his police uniform. The caption read: "NOP Capt. Vitale Ends Misdeeds of Criminal Louie Favre."

Louie's death wrapped up the Yates murder with a bright red bow.

Désirée couldn't take her eyes off the corpse. "I read everything in the *Picayune*. No one wrote how Louie provoked Eddie into killing him."

Claude entered the viewing chamber and rapped on the window. "The undertaker is here to pick up the body."

Jim Dandy brushed his lips against Désirée's cheek. "I better be on my way, sweet pea. I need to check in with your mama after I talk to the mortician. She ain't doing so good since she heard the news."

He walked off, leaving Désirée to take a final look at her uncle.

"Gosh, Patrick, I wish I hadn't said all that stuff about Angelique, even if it was true."

Patrick looked down at the corpse. "You probably saved that girl a whole lot of grief."

She gave a tiny nod of agreement. "Well, Uncle Louie is finally at peace, or at least I hope so."

Patrick clasped her shoulder and led her away from the morgue. He took her arm when they mounted the steps and ascended toward the main floor. "I think your uncle died because he really loved that girl and didn't want to destroy her. He knew he couldn't change. I don't know if I could have done what he did."

She grasped his hand. "Maybe you could if you loved someone enough. I would have."

He gave a bitter laugh. "Maybe. I did love someone once when I was kid. I was nuts about a girl named Ina.

I met her in New York when I was in college."

Désirée's interest was suddenly piqued. "You had a lady love? Really? You've never mentioned your personal life. Do you want to talk about her?"

He looked at Désirée with mock severity. "Well, I might, but you have to swear my tale of woe won't end up in one of your stories."

She stopped walking, placed her pocketbook on a stair, and pantomimed crossing her heart. "Cross my heart and hope to die. I'll never tell another soul."

Bitter laughter rang through the stairwell. "Since you gave an oath, I guess I can spill the beans. Ina was brilliant and quite lovely. She wanted to change the world. She initially disapproved of my Southern roots, fearing I might be a bigot. She was a Jewish radical."

Désirée lifted an eyebrow. "A what?"

He pursed his lips. "You heard me. Ina was a Jewish radical, all fiery and passionate, especially for the rights of Negroes. Her being Jewish didn't matter a rat's ass to me, but Mama hit the roof when she found out. Ina's folks were pissed, too. You see, they weren't overjoyed at having a gentile for a son-in-law, especially one from the South. We broke up after I finished college. One day she wrote to tell me she'd found someone else. It devastated me at the time, but that's over. We still keep in touch, though, and Ina's traded in her political fire for working in the arts. I guess it was all for the best."

She took his arm. "Would you have died for her?"

He stared at Désirée for a long moment. "Such a melodramatic question, but I'll be honest. I wanted to die when Ina told me she'd moved on. Let's leave it at that. C'mon." They mounted the stairs in silence.

****

For all their disapproval, everyone was inconsolable at Louie's death, and guilt pervaded his wake. The pall set in as heavy as the humidity that blanketed the city. Young Miss paid for the casket and a decent burial. Louie's friends, black and white, packed the funeral mass. His body lay in state, surrounded by flowers, made up like a two-dollar whore, rosary beads tucked into his folded hands. Afterward, a group of jazz musicians marched before the coffin and played Louie's favorite tune at his interment. He'd been a skunk all his short life, but in death, Louie Favre went out in style.

After Louie's funeral, Patrick insisted Désirée take the remainder of the week off. Her mind had become such a jumble of confused thoughts and tortured emotions that she couldn't have typed the shortest memo. Still, she managed to put her thoughts on paper and compose a story about a con artist who got his final comeuppance. She vowed never to show it to anyone, and instead, had tucked it in the folder with the rest of her New Orleans short stories.

Three days after the funeral, thermometers rose around the city. The late July heat was its most oppressive when Désirée donned a simple sundress and trekked to Maison Renaud. Remy greeted her when she arrived. "Miss Broussard, I'm surprised to see you so soon after your loss. Mr. Renaud said you'd be off for the rest of the week."

"Yes, I know, he wanted me to take some time off, but I need to speak to him."

"Oh, well, he's at the Mason-Dixon Line. Perhaps you can talk to him there."

She made her way to Bourbon Street, unable to shake memories of the recent past: Yates's battered face, Louie lying dead in a pool of blood, Young Miss shaking with grief.

Désirée approached the doorman. "Excuse me, sir, but I was wondering if I could talk to Mr. Renaud, Junior."

The fellow looked her up and down, a greasy leer on his face. "You auditioning for a job, sugar? I'm sure Junior would love to see you."

Désirée ignored his suggestive manner. "Could you please tell Mr. Renaud that Désirée would like to speak to him?" She pulled out the card Patrick had given her the first night. "I won't take too much of his time. I just need to have a short word with him."

The man took the card, turned it over, and noted Patrick's signature. "He don't give these to just anyone. Follow me, sister."

Désirée glanced at the image of Lilly in an animal-skin print bikini before she followed the man into the cool darkness, down a corridor to a large door carved from a block of antique oak. The fellow knocked. "Mr. Renaud, a young lady needs a moment of your time. She says she's Louie Favre's niece."

A masculine voice that she knew so well answered, "Come in, Désirée."

Désirée entered an elegantly appointed chamber and perused the place. Patrick Renaud Sr. had had the walls painted soft amber and filled the place with a stunning collection of Greek and Roman antiquities. She looked beyond the shining glass bottles and crystal goblets to Patrick, who sat behind a massive desk, his face unreadable. He jumped up from the desk and rushed to her. "Sorry for the formality of the place. It's Daddy's taste, not mine. What are you doing here, darlin'? I thought I told you to take the rest of the week off after what you went through with your—"

"Uncle Louie. He's who I want to talk to you about."

Patrick rifled his pockets and tossed three hundred-dollar bills onto his grand mahogany desk before sitting. "I meant to give this to your mother. It should cover the funeral expenses."

She slid the bills back to him. "Patrick, I didn't come for money. When we first met, you said if I needed help, I could come to you. Well, I need help. That's why I'm here. How can I tell the world that my uncle never touched Mr. Yates? Nobody will believe me, especially with that ring the police found on him. I was right about Vitale. Uncle Louie may have been shit, but Vitale is worse. He planted that ring on him."

His gaze never left her face.

She swallowed hard. "Eddie was wearing Mr. Yates's ring. I saw it flashing from his finger when he came into the Starlight to mess with Mama. He planted it on Uncle Louie."

Patrick sat back in the chair, his hands folded into a pyramid. "What do you want me to do?"

She'd thought about the injustice from the moment Eddie Vitale had pumped her uncle full of lead. Her shoulders sagged when she realized the futility of trying to restore Louie's good name since he'd never had one. "I guess there's nothing you can do unless you know how to raise the dead. I just needed to talk to you. It's so unfair." She paused, as if searching for the right words. "There's someone else who knows what happened. The night we met, I went to the Starlight Lounge to see my mother. The Starlight is a friendly sort of a place, especially if you're, uh, different. Baby Ruth went there with Frankie. As you know, Frankie's an acquaintance of Opal Jordan, your father's, uh, friend."

Patrick's expression remained unreadable, but he leaned over his desk. "Go on."

They looked at each other for a long moment. Désirée hesitated. "I believe Baby Ruth might be dead. Maybe the police killed her."

Patrick remained silent. Désirée searched his face and saw nothing. Realizing the futility of her mission, she stood to leave. "Anyway, at least, you know. You're busy. I won't take up anymore of your time. I'll see you next week. Thank you, Patrick."

Désirée turned abruptly to make a hasty retreat, but Patrick bounded from his chair and placed himself between Désirée and the door. He took her face in his hands and stroked her cheek. They didn't speak for what seemed like an eternity. Then he pressed his lips to her ear.

"The moment I saw you, Désirée, I knew you were special. You can't begin to believe how much you mean to me. God rest his soul, Louie didn't deserve you. Don't worry about Baby Ruth. I found her, and she told me what happened. She's in a safe place. I'll look after her. I swear to you, I'm going to clean up this whole mess, but these things take time." He looked at her intently. "Darlin', sometimes a fellow like me has to deal with the scum of the earth like Yates and Eddie Vitale, and, sorry to say, Louie, too. I used him to round up some girls for one of my business associates. It wasn't right. That's just the way of the world."

Désirée gave him one sad look and walked away. "Goodbye again, Patrick. I'll come back to work on Monday." She closed the door and made her way down the dark corridor. She paused, savoring the air conditioning before she entered the steaminess outside.

Désirée heard a dark contralto whisper her name, "Désirée," and the potent fragrance of Jungle Gardenia engulfed her.

Opal Jordan walked out of the shadows garbed in a violet sheath dress, her black hair hanging in waves about her shoulders. She looked as glamorous as any starlet gracing the silver screen. "Hey, Désirée. What are you doing here?"

"Uh, well, uh, I needed to talk to Mr. Renaud, Junior."

When Opal took a step forward, Désirée caught her essence, a fragrance more potent than mere gardenia perfume. "What did you and Patrick talk about?"

Désirée swallowed, barely able to contain herself. She felt her eyes dampen, and she averted her face. "My Uncle Louie."

The raven-haired beauty appeared taken aback when Désirée spoke his name. "I'm sorry about your uncle, darling. I knew Louie, charming rascal that he was. It shouldn't have happened like that."

Désirée's eyes overflowed, and tears rolled down her cheeks, but she managed to utter a few words before pulling out her handkerchief. "Thank you very much. Uh, I guess I need to get going."

"I'm sorry to bring up unpleasant memories of someone you loved. You don't really have to go, do you? I'd hoped you'd stay. We could have some iced tea or even soda pop, if you want. Please, I want to talk about Frankie."

The mention of the young butch snapped Désirée back into reality. "I haven't seen her in a while. Mama tried to reason with her, but she refused to listen. She got into a fistfight, and Jim Dandy had to throw her out on her ear." She moved closer and whispered against Opal's ear, "Mama said she wasn't happy about you getting married to Mr. Renaud Senior. She's been drinking a lot."

Opal sighed, resigned to a reality she hated. "Drinking is one thing Frankie doesn't need to do."

Although the light in the foyer wasn't the best, Désirée saw regret in Opal's face. "Frankie never understood me and Pat. It's not like it is with Lilly and Eddie."

Désirée's shoulders sagged at the mention of her friend. "Lord, poor Lilly. I've known her all my life. For a cool kitty, she goes nuts over men, but Vitale is the worst of the worst. She loves his dirty drawers."

Opal paused, digesting Désirée's words. When she spoke, her voice sounded cool and smoky. "Lilly is young and passionate. Her love for that bastard is white hot. She can't stop herself." She moved a bit closer. "Désirée, your name means desire, doesn't it? Do you desire young Patrick?"

Désirée averted her head. Even Opal knew the truth. "I can't talk about him."

"Well, a little bird told me he has feelings for you, too."

Désirée's head whipped around so quickly she feared it would fall off her neck. "For true?"

Opal's face lit up for the first time. "For true, so

promise to take it slow with him. He's left more than one broken heart in New Orleans, but I think you'll be good for him."

"Me?"

"Yes, you." Opal's face darkened, and she took Désirée's hand. "I have a request. Your mother knows Frankie. Please ask her to talk to her one more time. Ask her to tell her that I love her. She doesn't need to be jealous about Patrick Senior, because he and I don't have relations, not really. Everybody thinks he's a big playboy, but his sugar's bad, so he can't get it up. One of the reasons he loves me is he knows I'd never mess around with another fellow. It would hurt his pride. He understands my need for special friends." Opal took a breath, then flashed a weak smile. "Frankie wouldn't listen when I tried to talk to her. Can you ask your mother to tell her that? Please?"

Désirée took her wrist for a moment. "Yes, sure I can."

She turned to leave, but Opal placed a hand on her arm. "When you visit the Mason-Dixon, can you stop by to say 'hey'? You see, I don't have any lady friends."

At that moment, Opal reminded Désirée of one of the curses of beauty, the insecurity of some women. "Well, then, I guess you have a new friend, Miss Jordan."

"I'm Opal, not Miss Jordan."

Désirée planted a kiss on her cheek. "Goodbye, Opal." With that, Désirée walked off into the heat of the day.

Chapter Twenty-Three
A Turn of the Card

The sultry July heat passed into an even hotter August and September. Thankfully, by the time the calendar read October, the temperature had dropped and fall arrived in New Orleans.

Songwriters have serenaded the world about the beauty of autumn in New York and April in Paris, yet Désirée had never read a celebration of the loveliness of fall in New Orleans. She'd always thought her magical hometown looked best clad in autumn colors, the ancient streets slick with rain. The beauty of the city pushed Désirée to write stories of jazz, the smells, the strange characters, and the passion. She filled the pages of her notebook with provocative tales that only a New Orleans native could spin.

The vibrant pace of life at Maison Renaud comforted her, and Désirée threw herself into her job in the weeks and months after Louie's death. Work was the only distraction from her grief and the mounting heat from her proximity to Patrick. He commandeered her thoughts both day and night. Thankfully, Patrick absented himself with frequent trips to Baton Rouge and left her in peace. Still, even when he was absent, she found a fresh rose sitting atop her desk each morning.

Samantha rarely entered her tiny office; however,

one afternoon when Patrick was away, she took a tentative step across the threshold. She wrung her hands and refused to look Désirée in the eye, but she managed to speak. "Frankie's back at Baby Ruth's flat on St. Peter."

Désirée placed a hand on her shoulder. "I've been there. It's a walk-up above an Italian deli, isn't it?"

For once, Samantha didn't pull away. "Things haven't been going her way. Even though the police are raiding all the bars, she's been out on the street, getting crazy drunk."

"Maybe I can talk to her."

The younger girl finally shrugged her off. "Don't waste your time. She won't talk to me, and I'm her friend. I doubt she'd listen to anything you'd have to say."

"Well, I made Opal a promise. I said I'd talk to her. I gave her my word. I have to try."

****

One Sunday afternoon, after mass, Désirée climbed the rickety stairs of the St. Peter Street flat. The door was ajar, but she rapped before entering.

The place consisted of a dingy room with vaulted ceilings, wallpaper peeling off moldy walls, the plank flooring scuffed. Someone, most likely Baby Ruth, had scattered boric acid and mothballs on the floor to detour the roaches from overrunning the place. An icebox, electric fan, and hot plate made the place livable. Beaded curtains gave the dim chamber the look of a cheap bawdy house. The flat smelled of empty beer bottles and the remains of half-eaten meals. The spicy scent of Italian salami wafted through the rafters from the ground-floor delicatessen.

Frankie reclined on a brass bed in the middle of the room.

Désirée took a step toward her. "Hello, Frankie. It's Désirée Broussard. Opal wanted me to talk to you."

Angry tears rolled down Frankie's face as she guzzled a bottle of Falstaff beer. The empties on the floor beside the bed told Désirée it wasn't her first one. "I don't know why she sent you. I barely know you. Besides, she's with that old man now and doesn't give a shit about me." The young butch's sobs filled the tiny room. "It's so bad, Désirée. I lost my woman. What am I going to do?"

In the last few days, Désirée's thoughts had remained on a pair of dark eyes and a sensual mouth that promised so much but seemed to deny everything. "I can't really tell you about love. I haven't been very lucky in that direction, but I know Opal cares about you. She told me about Mr. Renaud. She says they don't, well…they don't, you know, have intimate relations. Why don't you stop drinking, clean yourself up, and go to her?"

Frankie stared at the door through eyes watery with tears. "I don't care if they don't do nothing. She says she's going to marry him. How can I forget that?"

"I guess you can't, but why don't you stay away from bars for a while and forget about the booze? I check the *Picayune's* police ledger every day. The vice squad is working overtime, raiding every queer joint in the Quarter. They've hit them all—Mom's Society Page, The Golden Rod, Miss Dixie's, Hy's, and Lafitte's in Exile."

The girl turned her face from Désirée. "The cops haven't set foot in the Starlight, and they ain't going to.

Young Miss pays them to stay away." Her eyes filled with tears again. "Go away and let me sleep. I got to dream about my girl."

The young butch rolled onto her back and dozed off. Instead of abandoning her right away, Désirée picked up the trash littering the floor and washed the dirty glasses and chipped plates. She closed the door, descended the stairs, and dumped the trash into a can already overflowing with garbage.

She'd grown up around drunks. Frankie had chosen her path. The girl was lost. Opal or no Opal, Désirée made an oath to herself never to return.

****

Half an hour later, Désirée returned to her own flat. She jumped into the shower to wash away the sordid stench of her encounter with Frankie. Hot, soapy water slid down her body as she scrubbed. Her body ached at the thought of Patrick, his delicious voice buzzing in her ear and his Pour Un Homme de Caron-scented skin. Maybe touching oneself was a sin, but since she'd met Patrick, she committed the sin on a daily basis.

She fell back against the cold tiles and stroked herself, gently at first, but memories of Patrick swiveling his hips to a bongo beat made her touch more urgent. A vision of full lips spread into a dimpled grin intruded, and she gave in without guilt. Désirée convulsed into orgasm. The sensation, as powerful as it must be to barrel over Niagara Falls, carried her away. Satiated, she sobbed at the intensity of the release.

Désirée opened the bathroom door to the heavenly fragrance of smothered chicken over rice, fried okra, and cornbread. Her nose led her to her tiny kitchen. Lilly, dressed in a faded negligee, her platinum locks coiled around curlers, sat at Désirée's kitchenette table. She didn't look up from shuffling her deck of worn Tarot cards.

"I slaved over a stove for that bastard, and the son-of-a-bitch called to say he couldn't make it. You eat it."

Désirée's stomach growled, and her hunger overwhelmed her. She turned her attention to the delights sitting on her stove. Désirée grabbed the plate, plopped down on a chair, and devoured the food.

Lilly placed the queen of cups onto the table. "Désirée, this is your card." She arranged the cards on the kitchenette table, a profusion of swords, the devil, then death and the tower, the destruction of illusion.

"I don't like this, Désirée. These cards are bad, real bad."

Lilly's cooking held Désirée's mouth captive. She made short work of the okra and moved on to the chicken and rice, sopping up the gravy with the last of the buttery cornbread. After she'd devoured everything on the plate, she watched as Lilly shuffled the cards for the fifth time. A chill crawled up Désirée's backside when she looked down at the table. It didn't matter how many times her friend manipulated the deck. The same dark cards kept appearing.

"This is bad, Désirée. You better stay home for a couple of days and hide under a blanket."

Lilly shuffled the tarot deck. The cards continued their sinister message, transfixing both girls with their power. The telephone rang and broke the spell. Désirée gave a glance at her clock. "It's nine o'clock. The only person who'd call me this late on a week night is Mama or..." Her voice fell, and she couldn't utter Patrick's name.

Lilly turned over another card. "Something bad is coming, worse than when your uncle died."

Désirée took a deep breath before picking up the receiver. "Hello."

She made out the Johnny Ray song "Cry" over the screams of someone in the background. After a pause, she heard a familiar voice.

"Désirée, it's Mama. Come to the bar. Frankie's here, drunk as all get out, causing every kind of shit known to man."

"Why should I care about Frankie? Let Jim Dandy toss her out on her ear."

The voice on the other end seemed agitated. "It's not Frankie I'm worried about; it's that Renaud girl. She won't leave her friend, regardless of the danger. I'm asking you—I'm begging you—to get her out of here."

She remembered her promise to Patrick. "Mama, I'll be there in a few minutes."

She turned to Lilly. "I have to go out. Patrick's sister is in trouble. I swear I won't be long."

Désirée rushed into her bedroom and grabbed a pair of Capri pants and a sweater.

Lilly stormed after her, the tarot deck in hand. "These cards are terrible. They're worse than when Louie got killed."

Before her friend could say another word, Désirée had slipped on a pair of flats and was racing toward her door. She turned back to Lilly, giving her friend a long look. "I'll be home soon."

The moment she opened the door, she heard the tension in Lilly's voice. "Don't say I didn't warn you."

Chapter Twenty-Four
Dead Reckoning

Throngs of people crowded the streets of the Vieux Carré that night, yahoos spitting out rude comments, drunks pissing in alleys, and lowlifes hustling cigarettes and loose change.

Désirée trekked through the Quarter, ignoring leering johns and glares from jealous girls. Her focus remained on rescuing Samantha, but something kept nagging at her, something deep in the pit of her stomach kept saying, "Bad things are about to happen. Go back."

She refused to listen to her gut. It was just a feeling, after all, and folks would think she was nuts if she mentioned it. She continued to walk through the dank humidity as she made her way to the Starlight.

Boisterous young fellows and a few girls in varied degrees of masculine dress packed the club. Frankie, one eye blackened, sat on a bar stool under the watchful eye of Samantha. The battered butch sang along with Johnny Ray, aping his exaggerated, over-enunciated style. She wailed long and loud, and in her drunken state knocked over her beer mug. "My baby left me for an old man. What am I going to do?"

A furious Young Miss mopped up the foamy mess before it spread over the counter. "If your baby had to listen to your shit day in and day out, it's no wonder she left your sorry ass. I would've left you, too."

She spied Désirée making her way through the crowd and whooped. "Well, thank you, Jehovah. She keeps playing 'Cry' over and over again. I hate that frigging song. Get Samantha out of here before Frankie goes crazy."

Désirée whispered into the girl's ear. "Samantha, c'mon, we have to leave. If your brother finds out about this, you'll be in hot water."

The girl shook her head. "I can't desert her. She's my only friend."

Frankie placed a wobbly arm over Samantha's shoulder. "Where y'at, Daddy-O? What you know good?"

Samantha waved off Jim Dandy when he approached and attempted to pull Frankie up from her bar stool. "You're bothering these good people. We have to leave."

The drunken girl plopped down hard and pushed Samantha away. "Don't wanna go home. Wanna stay here with my friends." She gestured to the crowd, most of whom ignored her.

Jim Dandy called to her from behind the bar. "Listen, you dumb bitch, you won't have any friends if you keep this mess up."

Désirée didn't relish dragging a drunken girl all the way to St. Peter Street, but a walk in the heavy night air would sober her up. "Jim Dandy is fixing to throw you out on your ear. Samantha and I will help get you home. Come on."

Frankie folded her arms in defiance and sat hard on the stool. "I'm not going nowhere."

A muscular butch called out to Frankie, "I don't

give a shit about your baby. Just stop playing that song."

The drunken girl swiveled around and yelled out to the young woman, "Kiss my ass and tell me the flavor!"

The angry butch marched over to Frankie, blood in her eyes. "What did you say, bitch?"

Jim Dandy rushed from behind the bar and pushed the girl away from Frankie. "We don't need no more crap in here tonight."

A femme rubbed her breasts against the red-faced butch. "Come on, baby. Let's go home."

Jim Dandy yanked Frankie from her stool with one furious jerk. Désirée placed her arm under the drunken butch's while Samantha took the other, and the two girls steered her toward the door. "We got to get you home before you start more mess."

The girl broke down once again. "Don't you understand? My woman went and left me. It's killing me."

Désirée pushed her forward. "Yeah, I know. It's killing me and Samantha, too."

Frankie suddenly came to a dead stop and refused to budge. "It ain't right that she's getting married to that old man. My baby is supposed to be with me. She belongs to me. I can't live without her."

At that very moment, the house lights flashed on and off.

A voice yelled, "Shit! It's the police. They got a paddy wagon outside."

A high-pitched scream punctuated the chaos. Uniformed officers appeared at the club's rear and front entrances. A masculine young fellow grabbed a plump femme and kissed her. Five cops in uniform walked through the club, shining their flashlights into the crowd.

Désirée stood in place, unable to move. Young Miss stepped out from behind the bar, eyes blazing, with Jim Dandy following. "Ain't this a bitch? I've been paying y'all to stay away for five years. You crooked bastards are worse than thugs. At least they stay paid off."

At that moment, Eddie walked into the bar with Gino right behind him.

Eddie faced off with Young Miss, grinning all the while. "I'd keep my mouth closed if I was you. I could've shut this place up tighter than Dick's hatband a long time ago, but you stayed open because of me." He looked around the club and then turned back to her with a smile. "Don't worry your pretty little head about it. We're just running in the cross-dressers."

She hissed at the young detective. "Go to hell."

Eddie's broad grin angered her even more.

Young Miss grumbled to Jim Dandy as she took her place behind the bar. "Just like the police. Why do they have to do us like this, Jim Dandy?"

Eddie moved into the center of the bar. "Into everybody's life a little rain must fall, dear lady." He called out to the crowd, "All right, most of you have been through this before. You've violated Municipal Code 14240, 'the wearing of clothes other than the type worn by the proper sex' and Municipal Code 17983 'consorting for the purpose of a lewd assignation, lewd dancing, dressing in the attire of the opposite sex.'"

Désirée pushed Samantha and Frankie into a corner near the counter and stood in front of them in an attempt to conceal the two girls. She watched as the police dragged away boys in female drag and young women in masculine clothes.

Two effete young men wore men's clothing, but were made up to the hilt with Pancake, lipstick, and nail polish.

Eddie pointed to the fellows. "Pick up those fruits."

A uniform pushed them to the door.

He gave the crowd a quick once-over and released those dressed appropriately with a wave of his hand. Eddie stopped in front of another boy in full drag. The kid rolled his eyes and received a slap on the head for his defiance. "Don't roll your eyes at me, motherfucker. I'm not the one in a dress."

Another boy wore toreador pants, his shirt unbuttoned to the waist. Eddie stared at the kid, his expression revealing nothing. He motioned to a uniformed cop. "Check his underwear."

The cop pulled down the toreador pants, revealing a pair of women's panties. Eddie gave a nod, and the police officer dragged the boy off.

Two terrified young women, both feminine in dress and manner, held each other. Eddie glowered at them. "Here for some cheap thrills? Get out and don't come back."

The girls sobbed with relief as they ran out into the night.

Eddie scanned the bar one more time, but stopped the moment his gaze fell upon Désirée, who'd remained frozen in place. His teeth glinted in the dim light, as if he'd caught the brass ring, the mother lode. He looked up to the heavens, his blue eyes sparkling. "Jesus just smiled down on me."

When Eddie placed a restraining hand on Désirée's

shoulder, Young Miss summoned every ounce of the maternal instinct she'd ignored since her daughter's birth. She marched up to him, took her daughter into her arms, and enveloped Désirée in a motherly embrace. "You stay away from my little girl. Even a blind man could see she's not queer."

Eddie spoke through clenched teeth. "Young Miss, go back behind the bar. I've got police business to take care off. Me and her need to have a chat about a mutual friend."

Désirée's brows knotted together, and she sighed in frustration. "Mama, go on. I'll be fine."

Young Miss shrugged her shoulders and took her place behind the bar. "He better not touch a hair on your head, baby."

At that moment, Eddie noticed Samantha huddling with Frankie in the dark corner behind Désirée. He strode to Samantha, grabbed the girl, and pushed her toward the exit. "Fancy meeting you again, Miss Renaud. Under normal circumstances, I'd run your little dyke ass to jail, but I guess tonight ain't normal. Your brother is an acquaintance of mine, so I'll let you go. Get the hell out of here."

Samantha extended her arms to Frankie. "Please, let me take her with me."

Eddie pulled her away from her friend and pushed her toward the exit. "No, she's going with us. Now you go on home."

The girl meandered to the threshold, lingered for a bit, but then walked away. "Don't hurt her."

Eddie answered her with a laugh. He fixed his eyes on the drunken girl and noted the bulge on one side of her pants. "Hey, fellows, this one's packing." Eddie whispered in the drunken girl's ear, "I guess Opal likes her loving on the strange side."

Young Miss barged from behind the counter, shaking with rage, her face mottled crimson. "Take Frankie away, but leave my daughter here. She just came down to help me out."

Eddie and Désirée couldn't take their eyes off one another. He turned his back to Young Miss. "I just need to talk to her."

A confused Frankie suddenly emerged from her drunken stupor and turned to Désirée. "Hey, what's going on? You said we was going home." The intoxicated girl focused her eyes on Eddie. "Hey, I know you. You took that old fellow's ring, and I seen you wearing it." She gave a drunken snort, giggled, and then shouted to the crowd of police. "Hey, y'all, I seen…"

Before the girl could say another word, Eddie hit her with such force that she flew across the room and crashed head first into the bar.

The room went silent.

Then Frankie groaned. "Who hit me?"

A cop helped her to her feet. She managed a couple of unsteady steps before she collapsed and fell back to the floor. Désirée pushed her way toward Frankie, but Eddie barred her with a powerful forearm. He spoke through clenched teeth. "The bitch made me do it."

Gino pulled Eddie off to the side. "Let her go, man. She ain't worth the trouble."

Eddie turned to his partner, his smile gone. "No, she knows something."

Gino shook his head. "So what? We're in the clear for sure." He passed the black wallet to Eddie. "This fell out of the bulldagger's pocket. She must have rolled Yates that night and was too dumb to get rid of it."

The tension between the two men evaporated the moment Eddie saw Yates's initials on the billfold. He exhaled, then crossed himself. "Mary, Mother of God, thank you!"

Gino chomped down on a piece of gum. "The girl's so drunk she can't say shit. Anyway, who's going to listen to a dyke?"

Eddie nodded, then pushed Désirée into the grip of a sweating police officer. "Take her to the tank."

Young Miss's screams filled the air. "You're not taking my baby."

Désirée called out to her, "Mama, don't worry. Just bail me out."

Gino watched Désirée's retreating form, then took a long look at his partner. "I wish to hell you hadn't done that, Eddie. Young Miss is going to be pissed, and we got the problem of that drunk dyke. You don't know your own strength, do you? You pushed her headfirst into the bar, but with all the confusion, nobody saw you do it. Anyway, she'd already got into a fight, had a black eye, so she ain't nothing we need to worry about."

Eddie relaxed his shoulders. Gino gazed into his face as if searching for something, perhaps a modicum of regret. He didn't see any. "Eddie, it's finished. We're home free. The fellows from the *Picayune* are out there with cameras. Come on."

Eddie straightened his tie and walked out from the club. A photographer flashed a camera at him. "Over here, Eddie!" The young detective responded with a glorious smile.

Chapter Twenty-Five
Night Court

Masses of queer humanity packed the Broad Street lockup. Most were male, young men in every kind of feminine garb, including full drag. Others wore men's clothing but used heavy applications of Max Factor makeup to signal to johns.

Désirée sat in the women's holding cell along with the other prisoners of the evening assault: street prostitutes of every hue, public drunks, B-girls, with a few butches from sundry raids sprinkled in. The police had even arrested a couple of regular girls who'd made the mistake of wearing dungarees to bars that evening.

The cell stank of perfume and puke. Some of the more defiant women smoked and laughed as if it was a lark. Claude sat stone-faced and alone, muttering to herself. "Young Miss needs to tell the police they arrested somebody's mother."

Désirée looked around the cell and noticed the absence of a familiar face. Samantha's surname had rescued her, and she'd managed her escape, but where was Frankie? Probably sobering up in the drunk-tank and annoying everyone unlucky enough to be around her. Désirée wished to hell she had listened to Lilly's warning. *"These cards are terrible. They're worse than when Louie got killed."*

Yes, they sure were.

Someone cleared her throat with a hacking noise. Désirée turned to a muscular butch with a pack of cigarettes rolled in her shirtsleeve, lust burning from her eyes. Butch women had approached Désirée before, and she'd never had a problem, but this woman had a dangerous glint in her eyes. If she had designs on her, Désirée soon destroyed them.

"I hope to hell you're not thinking about messing with me. My pimp would kill you if you tried."

The butch looked away.

Suddenly, the scent of lavender cologne sliced through the funk. The hair on Désirée's arms stood up, and the temperature in the packed cell dropped precipitously.

A darkly handsome fellow with blue eyes strolled up to the holding tank. He scanned the captives, spied Désirée, and strode up to her. "Miss Broussard, we need to talk," Eddie whispered to her through the bars. "All you have to do is tell me what I need to know, and I'll make everything disappear."

Désirée hissed at Eddie, "I saw what you did to Frankie. She was drunk. Why didn't you leave her alone?"

Eddie moved in closer. "You didn't see shit. Besides, she's not who I'm asking about. Come closer."

She hesitated before taking a step toward him. In the blink of an eye, Eddie shoved his hand through the bars and grabbed her. "Did your bulldagger friend talk about a ring?"

Désirée tried to pull away, but he had her forearm in a vise. "She was too plastered to do anything but sing the blues over her girlfriend."

Eddie released her. "For your sake, I sure hope

you're telling the truth." His lips puckered into a smirk. "Hey, baby, you still wet over that Renaud fellow?"

She felt a flame heating her face and averted her head before she cursed him out.

Eddie grabbed her chin through the bars and turned her face back to his. "I bet he's just as messed up as his daddy." He chuckled at her expression. "I know all about the senior Mr. Renaud's proclivities. Like father, like son. I'd be surprised if young Mr. Renaud doesn't want to do some strange stuff to you. I sure would." He gazed into her face as if searching for her soul, then startled her with his bitter laughter. "Shit, you know all about it, don't you, girl? It's a shame you're stuck on that fellow. A pretty gal like you, we could've had a lot of fun together."

The matron walked to the cell, jingling a string of keys, a couple of uniformed officers at her heels. A drunken woman puked in a corner. She grimaced at the smell, then announced, "Okay, girlies, time for night court."

Eddie strolled off, whistling all the while.

****

Peeling paint and mold formed intricate lacework on the courthouse walls. The court stank of drunks, urine, and bodies covered in the funk of nervous sweat. Young Miss and Jim Dandy sat in wait on a wooden bench as those caught in the raids walked in.

With his hair slicked to one side over his freckled face, the young judge looked like an Eagle Scout, and despite smoking like a chimney, he had a well-scrubbed, all-American air about him. A wedding band flashed from his left finger, and his lips pursed each time he sentenced one of the "criminals."

"That will be twenty dollars." The judge turned his ire on a youthful drag queen. "Sir, have you read the Good Book? 'Men, leaving their natural use of women burned in their lust toward one another.' Young fellow, you are living a scandalous life of depravity and vice."

Désirée stood in wait for the bailiff, her hands shaking more from worrying about Young Miss than going before a judge. Her mother had been so cocksure about paying off the police, yet look what happened. She wondered what kind of reception she would receive from Lilly after her friend had warned her the cards were bad. Désirée had promised she'd be right back, but fate changed everything. It was two in the morning, and the bailiff had yet to call her name. The thought of Patrick's reception scared her the most. In spite of his declarations of caring for her, how would he handle seeing her name in the *Picayune*?

She wasn't particularly religious, yet she couldn't stop a silent prayer. *Dear Virgin Mary, when this whole mess is over, I'm going to live the life of a nun.*

When Désirée finally took her place before the bench, the judge quoted a biblical verse as if by rote. "Romans, chapter one, verse twenty-seven. 'The woman shall not wear that which pertaineth unto a man, neither shall a man put on a woman's garment, for all that do so are an abomination unto the Lord.' You got something to say for yourself, young lady?"

Before Désirée could answer him, the judge said, "If I was your daddy, I would've beat the sin out of you. I pity your poor parents."

She heard her mother's angry yelp from the back of court, followed by a low bellow that she knew came from Jim Dandy. The pair jumped from the bench and marched up to the judge, followed by a short, chubby gent with pomaded hair. Désirée recognized him as the family lawyer.

The diminutive fellow piped up, "Your Honor, I am the attorney of Mr. and Mrs. Pierre, the young lady's relations. Mrs. Pierre had requested that Miss Broussard assist her with the removal of a misguided patron. We were just informed that she died during the raid."

Désirée gasped loud enough for the judge to drop his cigarette. She turned to Young Miss, who gave her a curt nod.

The attorney noted the interplay. "It's true, Your Honor. The girl is deceased."

The room swirled around Désirée, but she managed to stay erect.

Before the diminutive lawyer stepped up to the bench, Young Miss, her face a mask of rage, whispered to him. The attorney buttoned his suit jacket and strode up to the judge. "Your Honor, please note that Miss Broussard is attired in ladies' side-zippered pants and a woman's blouse. She is a model of femininity, sir, the victim of circumstances and over-zealous policing. Mr. and Mrs. Pierre have requested you release her, and in view of the circumstances, drop all charges. Her name must not appear on the City Ledger, either."

Perhaps the tears streaming down Désirée's face softened the judge's heart, or maybe her youthful beauty swayed him. Perhaps the cash the tiny lawyer had slipped him before court, along with the threat of a lawsuit, made him more inclined to be merciful. For whatever reason, the judge pursed his lips and said, "Yes, perhaps we should give this lovely young lady the benefit of the doubt." His expression suddenly turned benevolent. "Miss Broussard, I hope I never see you in here again."

Désirée walked into the hallway with her mother at her heels. Young Miss pulled a handkerchief from her pocketbook and handed it to Désirée. "I'm so sorry about Frankie, but no one saw what happened."

The girl's tears continued, unabated. "I saw it, but with all the excitement, I guess nobody else did. She said something Vitale didn't like, and he hit her so hard her head slammed into the bar. Of course, it won't matter what I say, since she was so very drunk, but I'm sorry for that poor girl."

Young Miss closed her eyes. "I should have known. As soon as my attorney gets Claude out, I'll call the mayor. I helped him get elected, so he owes me. You get some sleep and forget about what happened."

Désirée stared at her, dumbfounded. "Mama, how am I going to forget what happened? I just found out that poor drunken girl is dead, and no one's going to do a thing about it." She wiped her nose with the handkerchief and folded it. "Your handkerchief's got a pound of snot in it. I'll wash it for you, Mama."

Young Miss embraced her daughter. "Keep it, darling. I have a feeling you'll need it. Jim Dandy can drive you home."

Désirée shook her head. "No, you need him with you. Besides, the walk to the Quarter will clear my head."

Young Miss gazed into her daughter's face. "If you think so. I'll call you as soon as I can. Now I've got to take care of Frankie's body. Believe me, darling, this isn't over yet."

Désirée moved past the few unhappy souls loitering in the hallway and walked down the courthouse steps. She looked into the early morning sky and admired the magic of New Orleans in those hours before the sun devoured the dark. Though the dawn had yet to make an appearance, somewhere a bird warbled a cheerful tune, perhaps in celebration of being free. Although she wasn't much of a singer, she felt like joining him. She'd never felt so thankful to be alive.

Chapter Twenty-Six
The Stroll

Désirée crossed Broad Street and marched down Tulane Avenue at a clipped pace, past the large turn-of-the-century brick relics lining the street. If she hoofed the three miles to the Quarter, she'd make it to her flat in time for a shower and an early breakfast. Of course, she'd call Patrick first and ask him to break the news of Frankie's death to Samantha.

She walked in the pre-dawn light and thanked the Virgin that the sun hadn't yet made an appearance. The fragrance of frying bacon hit the air. Her stomach growled, propelling her thoughts of the pot of grits soaking on her stove. She planned to devour a whole plate of grits, smothered in butter, with eggs and bacon on the side, and wash it down with a glass of milk. Afterward, she'd sleep for the rest of the day.

Living suddenly meant more to Désirée than anything in the world. She passed an all-night diner and smelled brewing coffee with chicory, then gave a quick prayer to the Virgin. *Thank you, Our Lady, for keeping me alive and living in New Orleans.*

Désirée felt a momentary pang of sadness over Frankie's death, but it quickly disappeared at her exhilaration for possessing a beating heart.

South Rampart turned into North Rampart. The chirping ended. Except for the sputter of an auto engine, there was a strange quiet in the air. Désirée shivered despite the early morning heat. Something evil hid in the morning darkness. Lavender, the fragrance she'd grown to hate, wafted through the coffee-scented air. A masculine voice whispered her name, shaking her into reality.

"Hey, Désirée, come over here."

When she didn't look back, the voice became more insistent. "Hey, girl, I'm not playing. Come here. I need to talk to you."

Perhaps Eddie only wanted to talk, but she couldn't chance it. Even without seeing him, the heat of his rage burned hot enough to consume her like a marsh fire.

She picked up her pace, dashed past two drunken men. One upchucked in the gutter while puke covered the other. Neither would be able to stop Eddie from beating her to death.

The sun finally cracked through the dimness. She felt her strength ebbing, but gathered her courage and turned around.

Except for the drunks, the street was empty. Eddie had disappeared like a vampire with the dawning of the morning light. Désirée gasped in relief and continued her trek. He'd given up and she was free—but was she? Maybe he'd returned to Broad Street for a patrol car. Yes, he must be driving. She might be fast, but she couldn't outrun an automobile.

In the distance, Désirée heard the roar of an engine moving toward her, so she darted into a narrow alley. A baritone voice murmured behind her when she passed an alcove. "Hey, sugar."

Her heart stopped. She turned. A fellow had dropped his trousers and pointed his erection in her direction. "You ever seen anything like this before?"

Désirée rushed away, running until she could run no more. Winded, she stopped and looked up at a street sign proclaiming Canal Street. Her breathing returned to normal, and for a moment, she relaxed. Then, she heard a tire squeal and looked back at a black police car making its way down the street. A group of domestic workers moved toward her. She joined them in an attempt to make herself invisible.

The car slowed to a crawl. The driver cracked the glass and yelled to the crowd.

"Hey! Have any of y'all seen a pretty white girl in pedal pushers?"

A stout fellow dressed in the checkered pants and white tunic of a cook pushed her behind him. He yelled out to Eddie, "No, chief, ain't seen nobody this early in the morning."

The police car raced away. A relieved Désirée nodded to the cook and said a hasty, "Thanks, y'all," before she made her way toward the Quarter.

The nightwalkers, gamblers, drunks, and prostitutes stumbled toward their homes while others began their day under the rays of the morning light. Désirée had eluded Eddie, at least for now, but where could she go? He knew where she lived, or he might even wait for her at Young Miss's house. Her tears threatened to return, but she kept walking.

A few more blocks and the sounds of the Quarter welcomed her. She watched as a group of sewer workers descended into the bowels of the city. A drunk staggered down pavers and crawled into one of the city's all-night taverns. Désirée continued her trek all the way to Governor Nicholls.

Maison Renaud emerged in the early morning stillness, haloed by the rising sun. Désirée followed a woman dressed in a snowy-white housekeeper's uniform as she ambled toward the rear entrance.

The domestic turned to her, an expression of shocked recognition on her face. "What are you doing up so early, Miss Broussard? Ain't you working later today?"

Désirée grasped the woman's hand. "Please let me inside. I have to speak to Mr. Renaud."

The domestic nodded, pulled a key from her pocketbook, and motioned toward a heavy oak door with leaded-glass inserts. "C'mon, baby, follow me. You look like you been through it. Let's get you some coffee."

The woman unlocked the door and led Désirée through a darkened entry lined with shelving for purses, racks for coats, stands for umbrellas, and tiled flooring for wet galoshes.

They made their way to the dimly lit kitchen, where a tall figure in a T-shirt and chinos fiddled with a coffeepot. When Patrick turned, his shocked expression revealed all. "Désirée, I looked all over for you. When Samantha told me what happened, I went to the Starlight and then to the courthouse, but I couldn't find you. Where were you, baby?"

Désirée gave him a feeble smile. "Vitale followed me. I think he wants to kill me. Well, I…oh, dear God, Frankie's dead."

She collapsed into his arms.

Chapter Twenty-Seven
The Morning After

When Eddie and Gino entered the superintendent's office in the afternoon, he'd blanketed his desk with newspapers. Heroic images of Eddie and Gino leading raids throughout the Quarter shouted from every front page. "Look at this, boys. Y'all are as big as movie stars now."

Eddie appeared tired, out of sorts, and in desperate need of a shave, not his usual picture of sartorial magnificence.

If the superintendent noticed anything untoward with either detective, he didn't mention it. "Fellows, guess who just called? Earl Long, soon-to-be-governor-again Earl Long. That jackass hasn't been sober in thirty years, but he was raving about the great work you did cleaning up the Quarter. I didn't mention old Earl to the mayor, since he's also running for governor, but he was pleased as punch, too." The chief paused to dip his fingers into his tobacco pouch. "The fly in the ointment, however, was a nasty call from the owner of the Starlight. Young Miss nearly chewed my ass off because you fellows arrested her daughter. Vitale, she said she told you the girl wasn't queer. On top of everything, she was mighty pissed about that dyke who died, too."

Eddie gave Gino a sideways glance, pursed his

lips, then spoke, his voice husky and dark. "Sir, Miss Broussard was wearing dungarees."

"Her mama said they had a side zipper. Men's dungarees don't have 'em."

Eddie snorted angrily. "Oh, so I guess I better learn the finer points of ladies' apparel. Regarding that dagger, folks should be celebrating in the streets. One of Louie Favre's gang, a homicidal lesbian at that, is dead. Like I told the *Picayune,* New Orleans is safe again."

The older man packed his pipe with fragrant tobacco. "Well, the girl being a criminal didn't matter to Young Miss. My ears are stilling ringing because of Désirée Broussard. Shit, I hope to hell never to hear her name again. I swear Young Miss threatened me with everything but the electric chair."

Gino looked at his partner. Eddie ignored him. "Sir, did Young Miss happen to mention that she and Désirée Broussard were relations of Louie Favre? The judge let her go, but I have a bad feeling about that gal."

The superintendent puffed the perfumed smoke into the air. "Leave her alone." He placed his pipe down in an ashtray, then folded his hands into a triangle. "Vitale, I know you got plans beyond the force, and I applaud them, but you were supposed to be raiding the queer bars for show. Folks don't like it when a kid ends up dead and a regular girl gets picked up for doing nothing."

Eddie jumped from his chair. "Sir, I'm telling you—"

"Sit down, Vitale."

The two men eyeballed each other for a moment.

Eddie sat as commanded.

The older man spoke in a calm, assured voice. "I said, leave the Broussard girl alone. That's an order. Her mother is a holy terror. That was bad enough, but then I got a call from Patrick Renaud, Junior. Boy, did that young fellow give me what for. He said the Broussard girl works for him, you followed her, and now she fears for her life."

Eddie jumped up from his chair. "Sir, that's bullshit!"

The older man ensnared him with a cold glance. "Sit down, Vitale. I'm not going to tell you again." The superintendent calmly lit his pipe. "Renaud called the mayor, but I think I can make it right." The chief puffed away. "Look, you killed Louie, shipped Tinkerbelle to parts unknown, and the girl who stole Yates's wallet is dead. It's over. Is that understood?"

Eddie and Gino exchanged a glance. Then Eddie nodded. "Yes, sir."

The superintendent put his pipe down, then broke out in a grin. "Good. Reporters from the *Picayune* and the *States-Item* are on their way with photographers, and, I might add, some fellows from Channel 6 will be here soon. Y'all are going to be on the television, so get into uniform. Enjoy your celebrity as long as you can."

Gino jumped up and gave the superintendent's hand an enthusiastic shake. "We really want to thank you, sir." He pushed Eddie to the door. "Let's go and get ourselves spruced up."

They left the office only to find themselves surrounded by fellow officers. The young detectives accepted the hearty handshakes and pats on the back with aw-shucks modesty. No one seemed to notice

Eddie was uncharacteristically quiet. Something was eating at him, but if Gino knew what, he didn't let on.

Chapter Twenty-Eight
At Last

Désirée awoke to muted whispers drifting from an adjoining corridor. Except for a streak of illumination from a ribbon of sunshine invading through the heavy drapes, darkness enveloped most of the room.

Her head shot up from the pillow, her eyes focused on the vast catchall of a chamber. Ornate furniture from previous decades filled the space. Oriental carpets covered the oak floor. A master furniture maker had upholstered plush parlor chairs in crimson damask. A Tiffany lamp bathed a corner in a peach-colored glow. The fragrance of hothouse magnolias filled the warm air.

When Désirée pushed the covers back, an alarm rang in her ears when she realized she was only clad in her panties and bra covered by a gossamer-light nighty. She relaxed when she remembered a smiling servant undressing her before coaxing her into the massive bed, but she pulled the sheet around her at a quiet knock on the door.

The heavenly aroma of fresh coffee and toasted bread suddenly overwhelmed the cloying magnolia scent. Remy carried a silver platter with a pot of the dark brown nectar, along with creamer and a sugar bowl. A serving woman followed with a tray of club sandwiches and fried potatoes. The servants positioned both atop an oversized nightstand next to the bed.

"The cook made these special for you, Miss Broussard. She said you better eat everything on that plate and get your strength back."

Remy nodded to the serving woman as she exited the room, then said, "I know you had quite a night, but now you've had some rest. Mr. Renaud will look in on you after you finish lunch."

"Lunch?" She glanced at an antique clock tick-tocking away in a corner. Shocked, she pushed at the covers and put her feet toward the floor. "Lord, it's twelve-thirty already. Mama must be hysterical. I have to call her."

Remy took a step toward her. "Don't worry about your mother. Mr. Renaud has already been in touch with her." He pointed to a simple navy frock draped across a padded chair. "She stopped by while you were sleeping and brought you a change of clothing. Eat your lunch, miss. I'll send a gal to run your bath in a few minutes."

They exchanged a long look before Remy opened the carved door and exited. The moment he left the room, Désirée fell on the sandwiches like a starving lioness. She inhaled every morsel and drank hot coffee to her fill. Relief rolled over her like a blanket, bringing with it a sense of protection.

Désirée pulled off the band that held her locks in place, and her hair cascaded past her shoulders like a chocolate waterfall. She heard a gentle rap and a familiar voice. "Désirée, it's me."

Her heart lurched the moment his voice drifted into the room. The door opened and Patrick stood at the threshold, holding her in place with his gaze. They faced each other in silence, words unnecessary. Then he smiled, his dimples lighting his cheeks. Although she wanted to turn away, his grin made it impossible.

"I've never seen you with your hair down before. You're so beautiful."

She felt her face blazing.

Patrick took a tentative step into the room. "Your mother told me what happened during the raid. I'm so sorry."

Désirée finally averted her head and fiddled around with the coverlet. "Why are you sorry? You didn't do anything. Vitale did."

He moved toward the bed, his steps slow and measured. "You went to the Starlight because I asked you to look after my sister. That monster could have killed you."

"But he didn't kill me." Désirée choked at the thought and couldn't speak. She remembered his sister and almost jumped up from the bed. "Is Samantha all right?"

Patrick smiled again, his teeth glinting white in the dim light. "She's fine and staying in a place Vitale will never search."

The two gazed at each other, the air thick with tension. Désirée realized her vulnerability, the thin nighty the only protection in her state of undress, and raised the coverlet to her chin. "Things have gotten worse. Vitale asked about that ring Mr. Yates was wearing because he thinks I can ruin him. I'm sure he'll figure out Samantha knows something. Of course, he can't cross you, but I guess I'm expendable."

He gave his head a shake. "Uh-uh, darling, not to me. I'm afraid you'll have to endure my hospitality until I work out this mess. Your mother brought a change of clothes, but you'll need more. Feel free to wear some of Samantha's until I can arrange to pick up your things. My sister has closets filled with fashionable dresses my mother bought her, but she despises them. I'm sure you'll find something that suits you."

He licked his lips before striding about the room. "This is the guest suite. We've rarely used it since my grandparents passed, so please forgive the furnishings. You'll have to stay here until we sort things out. Now, let me run your bath."

Patrick paused at the foot of the bed, his eyes never leaving her. Her hands shook, her pulse rose, and the overwhelming desire to hide under the covers nearly overcame her. Patrick didn't say a word, just opened a door leading to God-only-knew-where and walked in. Désirée heard the rush of water and thought, *Goodness, there's even an adjoining bathroom.*

He returned a couple of minutes later. "Let me see if I can stir up a robe for you. I'll be back."

The moment he left the bedroom, she darted to the adjoining room to relieve her aching bladder. The claw-foot tub, filled with hot water, sat on a throne of white tile. Her body rallied at the thought of soaking in it. She twisted her hair into an upsweep, then secured it with hairpins she found on the counter. Off went the nighty and her bra and panties.

Désirée tested the water with her big toe. Patrick had managed to find the perfect temperature. She slid into the mammoth affair and lay against the gleaming porcelain, her eyes closed in silent prayer. *Dear God, please let this moment last forever.*

A knock at the door interrupted Désirée's reverie. She remembered Remy's promise to send a maid and called out to her, "Come on in."

The door opened, and she heard a gentle tread on the tiled floor as the servant approached. Gentle fingers gripped her shoulder. She looked up into Patrick's grinning face, his dimples caressing his cheeks. He stood next to the bathtub, chenille robe in hand. "I told you I'd bring a robe."

If he had been another man, Désirée would have screamed at the top of her lungs, but she didn't say a word when he knelt next to the tub and picked up a washcloth and a bar of cold-cream-scented soap. Patrick worked it into frothy suds before circling her back with the cloth.

His robe dropped to the floor. He'd forgone his shirt, and her eyes remained fixed on his muscular chest. Perhaps Michelangelo had risen from the dead and sculpted his body from flesh and blood instead of marble. She cast an eye downward and snapped her head back almost immediately. Although he wore pajama bottoms, the rise at the opening signaled his arousal. She felt her warmth between her legs and couldn't stop shaking.

"You're trembling, Désirée. Don't be scared. Everything's going to be all right."

She turned her face to him. "No, it won't."

He knelt next to her. "Then kiss me. It'll make you feel better. C'mon, baby. Just a little one, please?"

Désirée had dreamed about kissing him, sampling his lips, since the moment they met, but her insecurity took over. "Huh? But—we shouldn't, should we? After all, I work for you." Yet she knew he felt the same attraction she did. Would he be satisfied with a chaste smooch? "Oh, well, I guess it's okay if we do it this once." She gave Patrick a sweet, closed-mouth buss on the lips.

Patrick shifted his body, and Désirée felt the warmth of his breath. "No, baby, not like that, a real kiss."

He slid his mouth over Désirée's, their kiss as sweet as a summer melon, just the way Désirée always imagined. She rolled back, savoring Patrick's lips on hers.

Patrick murmured in her ear. "That's not the way you kiss somebody, Désirée. You know you're supposed to use your tongue. That's what makes it feel good. Like this."

Patrick's tongue tasted of honey, peppermint, and everything delicious. When she met it with her own, the kiss's sweetness increased tenfold. He traced the contours of Désirée's face with his lips before he kissed her again with even more passion. Désirée felt a hand caress her bare breasts.

Half-heartedly, she spoke words she didn't believe. "We shouldn't, Patrick. Really, we shouldn't."

He placed his lips on her neck. "If we don't, I think we'll both die from the strain of holding back. You don't know how hard it's been working next to you for almost three months, wanting you but not being able to say so. I thought I had self-control, but I guess I don't. Maybe it's wrong, but I have to be with you, darling."

Désirée found herself lifted from the tub.

Patrick stood her on the white tiles, his eyes on her nude body. "Oh, my God, you're so beautiful."

He dried every inch of her with a fluffy terrycloth

towel, whispering tawdry endearments the entire time. He swept her up into his arms and nibbled her neck, his lips as soft as satin feathers. Patrick moved his mouth upward and used his tongue to make gentle love to the inside of her ear.

She put her cheek on his chest. He smelled of citrus cologne, and the warmth of his body ignited a hunger she hadn't felt in two years. Since their first meeting, her desire had deepened. Désirée had been a virgin when she met Johnny, but now she was a woman, with a woman's needs. She lay in stillness, caressed by the warm, perfumed air. Patrick tilted her head upward toward his face. Although they were alone, he spoke in a whisper, his beautiful voice, dark and husky. "Désirée, I have to have your lips."

He moved his lips over hers and separated them with his tongue. The kiss deepened, their tongues entwined. Without warning, Désirée's body came alive, and she became the aggressor. She threw her arms around his shoulders and ravaged his beautiful mouth with her tongue as if she were a rampaging warrior exploring an unknown universe. Time abandoned them, and they kissed for an eternity, until he exclaimed, "Damn, baby, I'm not sure I can control myself."

"Then don't."

He wrapped his arms around her and carried her into the bedroom. Their time had come.

Chapter Twenty-Nine
The Garden District

Members of New Orleans's Sicilian community had lauded the name Willie Corolla for years. Old-timers pointed him out as an example of pulling oneself up by the bootstraps. They spoke of his rise from paperboy to running his family's furniture business by age seventeen. He'd made his fortune, courted a beauty from a genteel but cash-strapped family of impeccable lineage. Willie married the poverty-stricken beauty after making her father solvent.

Willie renovated his bride's rundown familial home in the Garden District and transformed it into an opulent villa with marble steps and columns. He bowed to every wish of his lovely wife. They'd packed the home with the finest European furnishings and created one of the greatest showplaces in the South. Still, despite his elegant suits and genteel manner, there were those in New Orleans who considered Willie a thug. Of course, no one with a brain would say so to his face or even in polite conversation.

That morning, Lilly garbed herself in a simple floral sheath. She'd made herself up like a Hollywood glamour girl and scented herself with Shalimar perfume. Lilly climbed the marble steps leading to Corolla Manor. She took a deep breath before she rang the doorbell.

A regal black woman in a black uniform opened the hand-carved front door.

Lilly greeted the housekeeper, a nasty smirk on her lovely face. "Hey. I'm looking for Miss Bianca Corolla."

The woman's expression betrayed nothing. "Miss Corolla is with her mama and Mrs. Lula Vitale. They're in the dining room addressing wedding invitations."

Lilly's lips twisted into a pout. "Oh, they are? Would you please tell Miss Corolla that Lilly Thibodaux needs to talk to her about something very important?"

The housekeeper opened the door wider. She gestured toward a brocade settee in a huge foyer. "Please come in and have a seat."

The entryway's huge size dwarfed Lilly's entire apartment. Lilly plopped down on the sofa, awestruck by the elegant European-crafted furnishings and crystal chandelier blazing in the coffered ceiling. She'd never seen such a show of wealth and, for an instant, lost her resolve. How could she compete with all this?

The maid returned, her cool demeanor unchanged. "Miss Corolla will see you now, Miss Thibodaux. Please come with me."

Lilly followed the woman past a sumptuous living room with recessed walls painted a buttery yellow and filled with elegant furnishings, portraiture, and statuary. The serving woman opened two massive French doors that led to the huge dining room decorated with a tasteful eye and accented with artful arrangements of roses and gardenias. The floral fragrance overpowered Lilly's perfume.

The grandeur encircling Lilly overwhelmed her.

She thought about abandoning her mission and high-tailing it out the door, but she didn't. Lilly had promised herself she'd fix Eddie Vitale's little red wagon, and this was the day to do it.

Three women sat at the table, and Lilly recognized them all—Mrs. Corolla and her daughter from their photographs in the newspaper, and Lula Vitale from the pictures Eddie carried in his wallet.

Mrs. Corolla reminded Lilly of Grace Kelly, regal and exquisite, her profile as patrician as a princess. Lilly scrutinized every inch of her daughter and found her wanting. Unfortunately, the daughter, Bianca, possessed less-than-average beauty. Although pleasant enough to look at, the girl took too much after her father to be pretty. Yes, nothing about her was earthshaking in the looks department, although she did have a trim figure. What Eddie saw in Bianca had been a mystery to Lilly until she saw the opulence surrounding her. Eddie wanted to be a part of this, and Lilly planned to make sure he never would be.

The moment she entered, Lula Vitale glared at her with blue eyes matching those her handsome son possessed. Lula's lip curled involuntary, and Lilly despised her on sight.

Lilly refused to let a bunch of women intimidate her. She thrust up her celebrated bosom and flashed a smile. "Hello, ladies. My name is Lilly Thibodaux."

The room went silent. Her reputation obviously preceded her. Lilly took a deep breath. "I didn't come here to beat around the bush."

Mrs. Corolla tittered sweetly and pointed to a chair. "It's a hot day, Miss Thibodaux. Would you like to take a seat, perhaps some refreshments, iced tea?

Lemonade?"

Lilly shook her head. "No, ma'am, nothing for me. I'm here about Eddie Vitale. You see, Eddie and me are in love."

Bianca gave a loud gasp, but Lilly ignored her. "He adores me, and I'm crazy about him. Everything was hunky-dory until he told me he's going to marry your daughter, even though he doesn't love her. Isn't it just like a man to promise a girl the moon, bring her cash and a few trinkets, and then treat her like shit when she falls for him?"

The room went silent for a long moment as the three women digested the news. A tearful Bianca blurted out, "Would you please leave my house?"

At that moment, Lilly saw the pain in the girl's face and realized the poison of her words, but she couldn't take them back. Instead, her shoulders stiffened, and she stuck her chin out in defiance. "Well, excuse me. I was just telling you something you needed to know, woman to woman. Do you think I like doing this?"

Bianca rushed from the room. Mrs. Corolla rose, her voice calm. "I'm afraid I'll have to ask you to go."

Lilly didn't move. "Do you really want your daughter to marry a man like Eddie Vitale? He's screwed half the girls in New Orleans, even the colored ones."

Lula glanced at Mrs. Corolla and then turned to Lilly, daggers in her blue eyes. "I knew about you and thought Eddie would have the sense to break it off, but I was wrong. What did you hope to gain from this? Did you enjoy tormenting an innocent girl who has done nothing more than love my son?" She appraised Lilly, a nasty smirk on her face. "You're a cheap whore, aren't you? Well, Eddie will be here at any moment, and if you know what's good for you, I suggest you listen to Mrs. Corolla. You need to leave. Now."

Lilly darted out of the room and rushed down the corridor to the front door, where the housekeeper stood holding it open. She dashed down the steps just as a grinning Eddie came sauntering toward the house. His smile disappeared the moment he saw his paramour. "What the hell are you doing here? What the hell?"

She pushed past him. "What the hell do you think I'm doing here, daddy? Better go inside. Your fiancée is waiting."

Lilly ran off, her laughter hollow and empty.

****

Two hours later, Lula and Eddie sat across from each other in the Commander's Palace, a famed Garden District eatery. Although Lula's lips spread in a grin for the benefit of anyone watching, her face remained flushed with unspoken fury, and Eddie knew her anger wasn't close to abating. "Boy, you don't know the hell I went through after that mess. Bianca is devastated, and her mama wasn't too happy either."

Eddie dipped a piece of crusty French bread into a steaming bowl of turtle soup. "Wait until I get my hands on that slut. Nobody'll pay a cent to see her take her clothes off."

Lula pounded a fleshy hand onto the table. "Stay away from her. That's an order. Don't touch a bleached hair on that floozy's head. You're just like your daddy. He had an eye for trashy whores, too."

Eddie lit a cigarette and inhaled. "Damn it, Mama. I'm not like him, or Sal either. Both of them weren't worth the powder it would take to blow them up. I've got dreams, Mama, and nobody is going to mess them up."

His mother took his hand. "We're going to have to sort this thing out with Bianca. That gal stirred up a hornet's nest, but I managed to ease it over. I told them she had it in for you because you arrested her for drugs. I think Bianca believed me." She gripped his wrist. "Marrying Bianca is a golden opportunity, your chance to be somebody in this city. You can't mess this up."

When he looked into her face, Lula's blue eyes had turned to steel. "There are no lucky breaks, Eddie, especially in New Orleans. Just like I've always told you, you've got to grab for what you want; otherwise, the world will destroy you, and you'll end up half a man, just like your daddy. You can't afford regrets, just keep your eye on the brass ring, darling, and above all, don't mess up anymore. I'll ease things with Willie and Bianca, but you forget about that stripper."

"Yes, Mama." Eddie took another drag on his cigarette. "I have another problem, Mama, and it doesn't concern Lilly. I've gotten myself into a bit of a tiff with Patrick Renaud. It's about his daddy's girlfriend and the dead dyke. I didn't touch a hair on that bitch's head, but he doesn't believe me."

Lula stirred another teaspoon of sugar into the rich brew of coffee, chicory, and cream. "Patrick is upset with you about a drunken lesbian? For true? Well, we can't have that. I'll call Patrick Senior when he comes back from Europe. Me and him are tight from the old days. I'll chat with Willie, too, and patch things over, so you fellows will be as right as rain before you know it, but, baby, no more screwing up. You hurt Bianca real bad, and you know she's Willie's heart."

Eddie relaxed into his chair, his anger forgotten. "Aw, Mama, Bianca loves me. When she cools down, I'll go to her on bended knee and tell her what a lying whore Lilly is." He grinned at his mother. "I'm getting that brass ring and putting it right in your lap. One day, you'll be the queen of New Orleans."

Lula patted her son's beautiful hand. "One day? Baby, I'm already the queen. I gave birth to a prince, didn't I?"

Chapter Thirty
Goodbye

The limousine came to a languid stop in front of a pillared mansion on Canal Street, a grandiose mortuary reminiscent of the Tara Plantation in *Gone with the Wind*. The liveried driver opened the rear door, allowing his four passengers to alight. Désirée's feet touched the sidewalk. Patrick took Désirée's hand and whispered into her ear, "Thank your mother for handling the funeral details. Opal is in no shape to bury that poor girl."

Désirée shrugged her shoulders. "Mama figured it was the least she could do." She watched as Patrick helped Opal from the luxury of the back seat.

Opal stood on shaky legs. She took a tentative step toward the mortuary, but swiveled around instead and threw herself into Patrick's arms. "I'm sorry, but I don't think I can go in."

He released her with a gentle pat on the back. "Samantha felt the same way and didn't want to come either. We'll give Young Miss your regards. I'll have Emile drive you home."

The two women locked eyes for a long moment before Opal took a step toward the black limo. Désirée gave her arm a squeeze. "Frankie's friends are inside, waiting to say goodbye to her. I think you need to be with them."

Neither woman turning away. Finally Opal glanced at the massive mortuary and gave a heavy sigh. "Yes, of course, I can't disappoint them, can I?"

When they walked up the marble steps, uniformed ushers with gloved hands swept open the massive doors of cherry wood and leaded glass. Désirée stifled a gasp when she entered the oak-paneled foyer. Scarlett O'Hara could have swooped down the grand staircase without raising an eyebrow, but today Miss Scarlett would have been lost in a sea of grief.

Organ music wafted through the hush, floated through the corridors, and ascended toward the ceiling. The mourners straggled into the viewing room, all dressed in their best, some in sequins, others in threadbare tuxedos. Most of the bereaved were kids from the Starlight, still in shock that one of their own had met such an untimely end. A few still sported bruises and black eyes from the raid. Young Miss stood on one side of the door of the viewing room while Jim Dandy took his place on the other.

When Désirée entered, Young Miss took a step toward her and cradled Désirée's face in her hands. "The only thing I can rejoice about is that monster didn't hurt my baby." She looked back at Jim Dandy who nodded in her direction. "I guess it's time for us to go in."

The viewing room smelled like a perfumery, a battleground of bouquets, perfumes, and aftershaves. A wooden coffin shrouded in sprays of flowers rested on a dais.

Opal balked once more at entering. "I just can't look at Frankie in that coffin."

Désirée covered Opal's hand with her own.

"C'mon. Let's go over to her."

They looked into the coffin where the girl lay in state, garbed in a simple navy dress, her hair brushed forward into bangs and cheek-curls to conceal the bruises. The embalmer had masked her black eye with Pan-Cake makeup and had applied lipstick, eye shadow, and rouge. Opal gave a loud gasp at her lover's appearance. "She looks like a wax work." No one would ever connect this ladylike corpse to the vibrant butch everyone mourned.

Opal mopped up her tears and blew her nose before taking a seat between Désirée and Patrick. She spoke in a whisper, talking more to herself than her companions. "Why didn't the cops throw her in the drunk tank? She would've slept it off, and we could've talked."

Désirée pressed her lips to Opal's ear. "Don't worry. Patrick will take care of the son-of-a-bitch who did this. I swear he will."

The woman bestowed a weak smile on Désirée, but then withdrew into her thoughts. Désirée's own musings so consumed her that she didn't notice at first when two young ladies entered the room, one a lovely blonde in a navy-blue frock, the other a petite brunette in black, her hair carefully arranged beneath a cream-colored beret. The dark girl looked striking in her stylish dress and heavy makeup. She sauntered over to the coffin in heels, her hips swaying all the while.

Désirée's jaw dropped, and she gave Patrick's hand a squeeze. "My goodness, Samantha brought Baby Ruth."

He shook his head. "No, darlin', it's more likely Baby Ruth convinced her to come. Baby Ruth and Frankie were close."

She looked at him, confused. "Where has Baby Ruth been?"

Patrick whispered. "He, uh, she, has a friend, a cigarette girl who worked at the Mason-Dixon Line. I thought staying at her flat was a bit dangerous, so I found a place for her where the police would never look."

Recognition of the newest mourners sent a wave through the chapel. The room suddenly erupted in whispers. Désirée heard a current of murmurs and ignored them.

"That gal must have just come to town. I ain't seen her before."

"I bet she's going to work for the Renauds at the Mason-Dixon."

A boy sitting in the front murmured to a friend, "Hey, is that Baby Ruth? Ain't seen her in weeks. Who's the gal with her?"

Patrick squeezed Désirée's hand. "Samantha refused to join us. Now I know why."

Except for the organ music, silence again cloaked the room. Without warning, a gasp went up from the front row, and heads turned toward the door. The funeral director entered, followed by two young men from the New Orleans Police Department, Captain Edward Vitale and Lieutenant Gino DeLuca. Both men wore black armbands and carried their hats in hand. Gino, the beefy fellow in a rumpled suit, seemed ill at ease, but his handsome, blue-eyed partner appeared quite confident.

Désirée's blood turned to ice.

Young Miss gave a low howl. "What the hell are you two doing here?"

Eddie looked around the room and whispered, "Paying our respects."

Her face flamed. "You got your nerve, you cold-hearted bastards."

Muffled grumblings broke out among the mourners when Eddie and Gino strolled past Young Miss. Eddie scanned the room, curled his lips at the assembled queers, and then smirked at Gino. His leer evaporated the moment he spied Désirée. He stared at her, his eyes like two blue caldrons of burning hatred.

The intensity of his glare so frightened Désirée that she grabbed Patrick's hand. She felt him stiffen. "He won't do anything to you, darlin'."

Eddie's face reddened. He took a deep breath before turning his attention to the two girls who stood near the coffin. He greeted both with a smile. "Good evening, ladies."

He barely glanced at the petite blonde, but kept his gaze on the dark girl.

When he didn't appear to recognize her, she relaxed. "Good evening, sir."

When Eddie looked down at Frankie's body, a hint of a smile danced across his lips and twisted into a ribald smirk. Perhaps it amused him that someone so consumed with masculinity would spend eternity in a dress.

Patrick abandoned his seat and walked to the two young men.

"Lieutenant DeLuca, Captain Vitale, I'm afraid you've distressed Désirée. I'm going to have to ask you boys to leave."

Eddie paused for a moment, a retort on his lips, but he decided against it. He nodded, and the detectives left without a word.

Young Miss waited until Eddie and Gino were out the door. She glanced at the funeral director before she addressed the crowd. "I've been asked to say a few words. Frankie was a good kid, tossed out on his, uh, her ear by her mama and daddy at fourteen. You all know she would've given anybody the shirt off her back and wouldn't have wanted us to mourn her. We'll bury her and have the repast at the Starlight."

****

An hour later, the morticians laid Frankie to rest in one of New Orleans' famed above-the-ground graves. Her body would molder for a few years until some poor graveyard worker would sweep her bones into a bag and lay them in the back of the chamber.

Patrick and Désirée motored off immediately after the funeral. Despite the sadness enveloping the limousine, she had to bite her lip to keep from giggling. Samantha had showed a bold side Désirée never suspected she possessed. The girl had slithered into the viewing room in her outfit and fooled Eddie Vitale. Désirée could barely stifle a laugh.

Chapter Thirty-One
After the Repast

Samantha and Baby Ruth clomped down St. Claude Avenue, an unsteady Samantha maneuvering in heels, undulating her hips, and managing a reasonable approximation of a slither. Her makeup looked straight out of Hollywood, her ensemble seductive yet chic. Still, despite her flawless disguise, Samantha glanced over her shoulder every third or fourth step. It appeared the events of the day had unnerved her. "Vitale's going to kill me like he did Frankie. I know it."

Baby Ruth took Samantha's gloved hand in her own. "Now, you stop it. There's no way the bastard knew who you were. I saw the way he stared at your ass. The son-of-a-bitch didn't even look at your face. What can he do to you anyway? You're the one with a rich brother and an even richer daddy. I don't have nothing, nothing at all, but he doesn't know what I saw. Besides, I think he's trying to get to that Désirée girl. You can tell she's on his shit list by the way he looked at her. Mr. Renaud said she found my earring. The one that fell off when I ran away."

Samantha shoulders slumped. "For true?"

Baby Ruth sighed. "For true. She's in big trouble with that Vitale fellow."

Samantha kept walking. "Well, my brother is crazy about her, so he'll take care of her." She slowed down her pace. "It wasn't just Vitale, Baby Ruth. I hated seeing her in that casket."

Baby Ruth tightened her hold on Samantha's hand. "Yes, terrible, wasn't it? You'd think, if the embalmer was going to doll her up, he'd have picked a more flattering shade of lipstick."

Samantha appeared shocked by Baby Ruth's words. Then she looked into her friend's face and saw the mirth there. Both girls broke into peals of laughter. "You're the devil, Baby Ruth, but I guess you're right. I'm just a big ol' scaredy cat."

Baby Ruth squeezed her arm. "Oh, come on, Samantha. You're the bravest girl I know, and now we're best friends forever, aren't we?"

Samantha gave her new friend's cheek a warm kiss, then wiped away the lipstick with her handkerchief. The girls walked up the steps of a huge camelback shotgun house painted in bright permutations of pink and purple. A loving hand had arranged wicker furniture on the polished boards of the pillared veranda, a nod to Southern hospitality. Samantha gave the leaded glass door a rap, then pushed it open. "Aunt Collette, we're back."

They pulled off their heels and trod carefully on the varnished parquet floors that led to the living room. "Aunt Collette, I—"

Samantha stopped dead in her tracks. Patrick and Désirée sat, hand in hand, on an overstuffed chaise in the drawing room with its mishmash of hues as garish as the exterior—a pink ceiling, bright turquoise walls, and sunshine yellow molding. Crocheted doilies bedecked the overstuffed chairs and davenport, and hand-tinted photographs of generations of Collette's ancestors looked out from every space. A few modern flourishes had been added, such as glass vases from a wealthy client, along with a framed image of the Virgin Mary.

Collette jumped up from a plush parlor chair upon seeing the girls and rushed toward them. She wrapped Samantha in a motherly embrace, released her, and dragged her toward Patrick and Désirée.

"Look who's here, baby. Your brother and his lady friend stopped to see the two of you. Why don't y'all visit while I check on dinner? Samantha baby, we're having your favorites—catfish, green beans, candied yams in praline sauce, buttermilk cornbread, and peach cobbler for dessert."

Collette caressed Samantha's cheek and gave Baby Ruth a nod, smiling brightly all the while. "I got my little girl back, and I praise the Virgin for it. I'll see y'all in a minute." She left the room.

The four young people sat in silence, unable to voice their thoughts. Finally, Désirée spoke. "It was good to see you at Frankie's wake, Samantha. I thought you were brave not to run from Vitale, even if the prick didn't recognize you."

The stress of the week bubbled up. Samantha's lower lip trembled, and she broke into tears. Baby Ruth's arm encircled her waist. "Don't worry about Vitale, darling. Mr. Renaud rescued me from a fate worse than death and brought me here. He'll take care of everything, I know it."

A confused Désirée looked from Baby Ruth to Patrick. "You brought Baby Ruth here?"

Patrick's face colored. "It was the least I could do. No one would ever look for her at Collette's."

Collette's voice drifted from the hall. "Come and get it, y'all. Dinner is served in the kitchen."

Baby Ruth placed her head on Samantha's shoulder.

Désirée took Patrick's hand in hers before rising from the sofa. "You heard the lady. It's time to eat."

****

Collette possessed the largest, cheeriest kitchen in Tremé. She'd painted the high ceiling bright yellow. The walls were scarlet, with red-and-white-checked linoleum flooring. The place smelled of coffee, banana pudding, ripe loquats, summer peaches, and strawberries. Copper pots hung from a rack above Collette's pride and joy, a bright red Gaffers and Sattler stove.

Désirée, Patrick, Baby Ruth, and Samantha sat around the kitchen table, fully sated, their stomachs bursting from Collette's sumptuous food. The only sound was satisfied groans.

Patrick smiled up at Collette, his dimples lighting up the room. "Collette, that was fabulous."

His hostess's grin matched his in wattage. "Anything for you, darlin'."

Collette turned to Désirée. "Patrick saves folks all the time."

Désirée placed her head on his shoulder. "Yes, Miss Collette, I know."

Collette chortled at the lovebirds. "But you haven't heard it all, sugar. Baby Ruth, tell them your story and be honest like you was with me. A lot of us have seen it all, but others need to know the truth, no matter how or what."

Baby Ruth sputtered a reply. "Well, I, uh…"

Samantha nodded her head in encouragement.

"My real name isn't Baby Ruth. It's Babe Ruth, like the baseball player. Daddy didn't want no girls, and when he saw that thing between my legs, he figured he had a son. Only thing is, he had a daughter, but they didn't know it until I could walk and started playing with dolls. Daddy used to beat me something horrible, and Mama was afraid he'd kill me. When I was twelve, she gave me to this man, thinking he'd take care of me. He told her he'd be good to me, only he wasn't."

The room went silent. Baby Ruth dropped her eyes. Collette rose from her chair, walked over to Baby Ruth, and took her chin in her hand. She lifted the girl's face up to hers. "Tell them what happened, darling."

Baby Ruth responded with a wry smile. "When I turned fifteen, I ran away from him and got me a job at the Lucky 13 before Mr. Renaud bought it. That's where I met Frankie, at the Lucky 13. She had a specialty act with another girl where they'd do it on a mattress in front of men." She stopped talking and turned to Collette.

Collette giggled. "Go on."

"It was a big joke to Frankie, easy money. We became friends, and I started B-drinking. After Mr. Yates got killed at the Starlight, Mr. Renaud tracked me down." She spoke in a giggly whisper. "That fellow who brought me to New Orleans had pictures of me and him together, nasty ones. I took them with me when I ran away. I showed them to Mr. Renaud, and he said, 'How interesting, Baby Ruth. I'm acquainted with this fellow and his wife.' Next thing I knew, I had all this money, and Mr. Renaud is sending me to cosmetology school. He's my knight in shining armor."

Désirée clasped Patrick's hand.

Baby Ruth's mood darkened, and Désirée knew the sobs would start. "But now Frankie's dead."

Collette took Baby Ruth in her arms. "Everything's all right, darling. It's all right to cry over a friend. It's God's honest truth. The world is hard for colored people and queers."

"Ain't that the truth, Miss Collette."

She gave Baby Ruth a gentle kiss on the head. "This has been a day for tears. Maybe tomorrow will be better."

****

The next afternoon, Patrick maneuvered his Caddie down narrow Quarter streets and turned onto St. Marc. Once he'd parked, he walked toward the faded awning of the Starlight Lounge. When he crossed the threshold, it took a moment for his eyes to adjust to the smoky darkness.

Then he crossed the cement floor, picking his way through tossed cigarette butts and gum wrappers. He strode over to the bar and took a stool. Young Miss had recognized him the moment he walked in. "What's your poison, Mr. Renaud?"

He murmured his reply, mindful of those around him. "Whatever you have on draft is fine, darlin'."

Young Miss gave him a sly smile before pumping Falstaff beer into a chilled mug. "It's on the house, Mr. Renaud, or should I call you Patrick? I went to Désirée's place again and picked more clothes for her." She pursed her lips, and then moved closer. "My baby asked me to give you something else, too, all her writing. You're lucky. She never shares it with anybody. She must trust you." She placed a portfolio stuffed with papers on the counter. "Please, take care of this. It means the world to her."

Patrick colored slightly. "Uh, well, I'm honored."

Young Miss noted his blush and smirked. "When I was at Désirée's flat, I checked in on her neighbor. Lilly, the gal who lives next door, is missing. Looks like somebody tossed her place real good."

Patrick's mouth twisted into a grimace. "I'm afraid Lilly made a foolish mistake and had to leave. Her life's in danger."

Young Miss wiped down the bar. "From Vitale?"

Patrick gave her a nod before taking a sip of beer. "Yes, ma'am."

She crossed herself. "Lord have mercy, that girl has the world's worst taste in men."

He licked the suds off his lips. "Don't worry about Lilly. She'll be safe."

She grabbed a beer bottle and took a gulp. "I know my little girl is a smart kid, but it means a lot to me that you're looking after her. I wish somebody had looked after Frankie."

Patrick looked around the club. Young Miss watched as his eyes locked on a young butch sharing a rum-and-Coke with a nubile femme.

"That's the trouble with kids like her. They don't have family to take care of them. Her folks threw her away when she was fourteen, and she was on her own." She plopped the beer bottle on the counter. "Lord knows I can't criticize her parents. My mamma did the same thing to her own flesh and blood."

Young Miss handed Patrick the photograph of the young Marine enshrined on the bar. "That's my brother Virgil, smartest kid you'd ever meet, a real gentleman, only Mama thought being cultured meant being weak. She liked her other son, Louie, better. One day she caught Virgil kissing another boy, said a bunch of hateful things, and threw her baby out. When she finally came to her senses, we couldn't find him. It happened during the war. Joined the Marines to show her he was a man. He had to lie about his age in order to get in." She polished the glass over the portrait, then placed it back on its usual perch. "Those medals don't mean nothing when the one you love comes back to you in a casket." Young Miss poured him another mug. "Remember that the next time you get pissed at your little sister."

Patrick didn't say a word.

Chapter Thirty-Two
Pride Goeth before a Fall

Patrick reclined in the butter-soft leather of a club chair. For once he agreed with his daddy, who detested modern décor and liked the comfort of traditional furnishings.

He held up to the light a cut-crystal glass filled with amber liquid and admired the perfection of the beautiful goblet. The prisms reflecting from the facets bounced off the walls, painting them in vivid hues. Patrick took a deep sip, savoring the taste before knocking back the rest of the liquor. A rap at the door roused him from his reverie. "Come in."

Eddie entered, dressed to the nines as usual, a grin on his face. Today, however, Patrick noted something different about him. The young detective looked as if the events of the past days had knocked him down a peg. His cockiness had abandoned him, and for once, he seemed a bit nervous.

Patrick pointed to a chair. "Thanks for coming, Eddie. Take a seat and have a drink with me."

Eddie stood in place, his hands folded in front of him. "No, sir, I'm on duty."

His host gave a dark laugh. "Aw, come on, Eddie. A drink would do you good. Besides, when has a member of New Orleans' finest ever turned down free liquor?"

Eddie grabbed a bottle of Jack Daniels, poured two fingers into a glass, along with a splash of water, and gulped it down. "Where's your partner, Willie?"

Patrick chuckled. "He's on a clean-up mission, mopping up your messes."

Silence invaded the space. Patrick poured himself another drink, brought the glass to his face, and inhaled the fragrance. He took a sip, savored it with a sigh of pleasure, and then placed the glass atop a marble coaster.

"Best bourbon on earth. They distill it in small batches with a special yeast. It takes seven years to perfect. It's a favorite of my daddy's. Of course, I didn't invite you here to discuss bourbon."

Eddie played with the brim of his hat. "Well, I wanted to apologize for that little misunderstanding at the viewing parlor. I wouldn't upset you for the world, sir, but that dyke ran with a rough crowd and put your sister in danger."

Patrick took another sip as he assessed Eddie. "That girl couldn't say boo to a goose, just a kid pretending to be tough, and now she's dead."

Eddie's mouth tightened. "Well, sir, I believe she was part of Louie Favre's gang, and you know what he did to Mr. Yates."

Patrick gave another chuckle, a dark cynical one. "I know what the police and the newspapers say Louie did to Mr. Yates. A coward like Louie would never have done anything to a big fellow like Boyd Yates. He was just a low-level pimp."

Eddie stiffened. Patrick appeared to enjoy his discomfort as much as he did the taste of his bourbon. "You see, Eddie, I had other information, a story from someone who was in that alley that night, someone you didn't see when you and Gino beat him up."

Eddie's blue eyes grew to twice their size, and Patrick chuckled. "Don't be scared. Boyd Yates was a mean, drunk son-of-a-bitch. I heard he provoked you. I'm not sorry he's dead, or Louie either. Somebody would have killed him sooner or later, so you might as well get the glory."

"Patrick, sir…"

Patrick's voice remained calm, but his anger began to escalate. "Shut up, Eddie. The sloppy way you killed Yates is what bothers me."

Eddie stared at him, uncomprehending. "But I didn't kill—"

Patrick bounded up from his chair. "Don't tell me that shit. Somebody was watching and saw the whole thing. Willie knows everything too. Funny, I smelled the thug on you when we first met. I let it go because, if you do business in New Orleans, you have to deal with thugs, but I didn't like it."

Eddie's anger finally bubbled to the surface. "Somebody who's had everything handed to him wouldn't understand! That cracker insulted me!"

Patrick shifted his body closer to Eddie. "You killed that drunk over bullshit. Man, you had it all…charm, good looks, ambition, everything. Women love you. They'd vote for you in droves. Hell, they'd even name their kids after you. Colored folks like you, too…remarkable for a member of the police force. You'd get the Sicilian vote and wouldn't have to raise a finger. With Daddy and Willie Corolla in your corner, the sky was the limit, but guess what? You fucked it up. Couldn't hold on to your temper, could you? Couldn't keep your pants zipped, either. Now the damage is done, and sorry, but I can't have it."

It took Eddie a moment to absorb his dashed dreams. "Well, at least I don't have sexual deviants in my family. I'm not talking about that little dagger you call a sister either. Yeah, I know about your daddy and all his twisted shit…Junior."

Patrick's face was expressionless until his smile returned, but it was anything but warm. "There's that temper again. Boy, you're going to regret saying that about my family. Oh, yes, you will. I know you think of me as Junior, the jolly son who does his daddy's bidding, but I'll let you in on a secret." Patrick leaned over and whispered, "I've never been jolly."

Tension crackled in the room as the two men took each other's measure. After half a minute, Eddie spoke. "Where's Lilly?"

"Ah, Lilly, a very impetuous young lady. You should have had enough sense to break up with her a long time ago. Now she's blabbed everything. I'll do one thing for you…get her out of New Orleans and give her money to keep her mouth shut."

Eddie plopped in the chair. "Where is she?"

Patrick shook his head. "Where you can't get your hands on her. Let everything calm down. Hopefully, you'll stop this craziness, and maybe we can come to a deal, but you can forget about being mayor." He took another sip of bourbon and kept his gaze on the young detective. "I know you tried to sweet-talk yourself back into Bianca's arms, but Willie won't have it and neither will I. I have to protect her from the likes of you. Care for that drink now?"

"No."

He ignored Eddie's words and refilled the glass. "No? You probably need one."

Eddie's mouth twisted into a determined sneer. "No, sir, I don't need a drink. Bianca loves me. She'll come around. Her mama's angry for now, but she'll come around too. Like you said, sir, I had everything, and I'll get it all back, with or without you. Mr. Renaud, I have my eye on you, your dyke sister, and that little whore you're screwing, Miss Désirée Broussard. Maybe she's pretty, but she's Louie's relation, so she must be a bad apple. As for you, you may have money, but I have the police."

Without warning, Patrick's hand smacked hard on the desk. "Are you threatening me?"

Eddie smirked. "Maybe."

Patrick's shoulders relaxed. "You know something? I think it's time to say *adieu*. Goodbye, Eddie."

Eddie stormed out of the office and slammed the door with such force he didn't hear Patrick dialing his rotary telephone.

A female voice answered from the other side. "New Orleans Courthouse."

Patrick whispered into the receiver. "Operator, please connect me to the police, Lieutenant Gino DeLuca. Thank you."

Chapter Thirty-Three
Collette's Home for Wayward Young Ladies

Désirée hissed under her breath. "You ungrateful heifer! Patrick has saved your neck! He's done his best to keep Vitale from finding you. He put you up at a hotel, even arranged a flight to Havana to get you out of New Orleans, all so that crazy bastard won't kill you." She stopped in her tracks and glared at her beautiful friend. "Girl, what went through your head, pulling a stunt like that?"

Lilly gave a defiant toss of her head. "You'll never understand. I love Eddie, even if he's a lowdown skunk. What do you think he told Bianca Corolla?"

Désirée grabbed her arm with such fury it caused Lilly to wince. "Girl, you are a piece of work. What does it matter what he told her? Forget him and concentrate on getting out of town before he kills you. While you're here, mind your Ps and Qs. This isn't a hotel, and Collette isn't your maid."

Lilly pulled her arm away with an angry grunt. "I know how to act."

"Bullshit."

Désirée rolled her eyes at her friend, then moved to Collette's drawing room. Lilly followed Désirée, her hips swaying lazily as she slunk across the carpeted floor. Patrick and Collette sat huddled together in a corner. They broke apart the minute Désirée entered.

No one said a word when Lilly sauntered into the room. The swish of her crinoline petticoat cut through the silence.

Samantha sat on the chaise, looking bored as a block of wood, but brightened up considerably at Lilly's entrance.

The blonde beauty slid onto a parlor chair upholstered in costly French brocade, thrust her shoulders back, her abundant bust line on full display. She simpered as she crossed her shapely legs. "Thank you for letting me be your guest, Miss Collette. I swear I won't give you a moment's worry."

Collette's jaw had dropped the moment she set eyes on Lilly. "My goodness, girl, you should go to Hollywood, California. I bet you'd give Miss Marilyn Monroe a run for her money. I saw that movie, *The Seven Year Itch*, and loved it." She rushed over to her guest and took Lilly's face in her hands. "But you're prettier than she is. Welcome to my home."

Collette stepped away from Lilly. "If I didn't have to go to the restaurant tonight, we'd stay and talk about your dancing at the Mason-Dixon Line. I hear it's a real swanky place. Maybe, one day, they'll let me in there. You never know."

The room went silent once again, and Patrick looked away. Collette continued, "Anyway, I have two plates in the oven, and the spare room is all set up." She pinched Samantha's cheek. "My little girl is spending the night, so you won't get lonely."

Patrick eyed his sister before turning his attention to Lilly. He shifted in his chair. "Collette, perhaps we should—"

Without a second thought, Désirée jumped into the

conversation. "What a wonderful idea, Collette. The girls can keep each other company. Patrick, why don't you and I leave, so the young ladies can become better acquainted?"

Patrick appeared stunned by Désirée's words. "Uh, yes, of course. Samantha, call if you need anything. Remy can bring it."

He stood, gave Collette a gentle kiss on the cheek, and then took Désirée's arm.

"Have a pleasant evening, girls."

****

Désirée and Patrick made their way to his Cadillac. She'd bundled herself against the chilly weather, and Patrick's icy demeanor made the nip in the air even worse. He didn't bother to conceal the edge in his voice. "Are you encouraging my sister's infatuation with that woman?"

Désirée pulled her arms away from Patrick, her walk defiant. "No, but I think she'll keep Lilly distracted enough that neither one will get in more trouble."

He thought for a moment. "I don't know. You might be right. And of course, Lilly's preference seems to be men."

Désirée relaxed; her anger dissipated. "So far, at least. As long as we can keep her away from Vitale, she'll be safe until you can get her out of town. Why in God's name did she pull that crazy stunt? I'm afraid of what he'll do if he catches her."

He grasped her hand so firmly she winced. "I understand your fear, darlin'. The bastard made a threat against my family. I suggest you call your mother and warn her."

Désirée took in his words with a gasp. "Are you saying that Vitale plans to harm Mama?"

His silence told her everything she needed to know. "I'd hoped we'd be free of him after he killed Uncle Louie, but I guess I was wrong."

Patrick pulled her to him. "Don't you worry about a thing. Willie and I won't allow that bastard to hurt you or anyone you hold dear. We have someone watching him day and night. I'll take care of you, baby."

She threw herself into his arms, but a niggling fear remained.

****

An hour later, Lilly slithered around Collette's kitchen in satin mules and a matching robe, a carnal smirk on her face. Her naked breasts almost popped out of the delicate fabric. "I couldn't stand wearing that dress another moment. Crinoline is so scratchy."

It took all the self-control Samantha possessed not to gape at her. She'd never seen a woman so free, so devoid of even an ounce of false modesty.

Samantha nibbled on a plate filled with fried shrimp, Creole rice, candied yams, and creamed spinach. She pointed to the huge stove occupying one corner of the spotless kitchen. "Collette left plates in the oven. Why don't you get you something to eat? There's strawberry lemonade, too."

Lilly demolished everything on her plate. After she'd plowed through her own food, she cut a swath through Samantha's yams and washed everything down with a glass of lemonade. Samantha sat spellbound as Lilly waxed poetic over the food.

"Oh, my goodness, Samantha. This is the best

shrimp this gal has ever eaten. What do you think Collette put on them to make it so good? Mama used to sprinkle a pinch of garlic on hers, and they were almost this tasty."

Without warning, Lilly belched with such ferocity that she startled Samantha. Her face turned bright red, and she answered Samantha's startled look with a giggle of embarrassment. "Oops, sorry. Hope you don't think I'm a pig." The beautiful dancer lowered her lids, and Samantha's heart almost leapt from her chest. "I bet Eddie would think I was."

At the mention of Eddie's name, Samantha rolled her eyes. "Don't talk about him."

Unfortunately, Lilly didn't choose to hear her. "Sometimes I hate the son-of-a-bitch. He probably told Bianca Corolla that I was crazy or something."

She suddenly stopped talking, her lips quivering as if she'd break into tears. Samantha gazed into her beautiful face. "Golly, I don't know what to say. You look tired. Maybe you need a nap. Don't worry, I'll clean up the kitchen. Collette likes everything to be spick-and-span."

Lilly slithered toward the spare bedroom. "Yes, sleep would be good."

****

When Désirée and Patrick returned to the Maison Renaud that afternoon, she bussed him on the cheek, giggled nervously, and said, "Patrick, I need to use the little girl's room. I'll be back in a minute."

Instead of moving to the powder room, she used the telephone in Patrick's office. "The Starlight Bistro, the best cocktail lounge in New Orleans, Young Miss speaking."

The moment Désirée heard her mother's voice, she bit her lip to avoid breaking into sobs. "Mama, it's me. I just wanted to let you know I'm okay. Patrick is taking good care of me. I got the suitcase. Thank you so much, darlin'. Maybe I can come to see you later, only…"

Young Miss sighed into the phone. "Only what?"

Désirée began trembling. "Oh, Mama, please, watch your step. I worry about you and the police."

Her mother cackled into the phone, but couldn't conceal the tension in her voice. "Don't fret about me as long as I have Jim Dandy. Vitale came by asking about you, but I didn't tell him shit. The bastard made your stepfather mad enough to spit, and I thought the two would come to blows. I swear if Vitale hadn't been packing a gun, Jim Dandy would have kicked his ass all the way to Broad Street."

"Did he threaten you, Mama?"

Young Miss met her question with silence and took a pause before answering. "We'll talk about it later."

Désirée screamed into the receiver. "Mama, you tell me right now what he said."

After what seemed like an eternity, Young Miss finally spoke, her voice calm. "Like I said, don't worry about me, baby. I can take care of myself. I've got Jim Dandy and my pistol. That's all I need."

Perhaps Young Miss thought her words would comfort her daughter. They didn't. Désirée sobbed into the phone. "No, please, Mama, you can't do that. I'm staying low for a while, not leaving Maison Renaud. Let Patrick handle Vitale." She paused for a moment. "Please, Mama, don't do anything rash. Kiss Jim Dandy for me. Tell him I love him. Goodbye, Mama."

When Patrick entered the office, Désirée had broken down, tears still rolling down her cheeks. He swept her up and wrapped his arms around her. "What's wrong, baby?"

"Vitale. He dropped in on Mama. She wouldn't tell me what he said, but I could tell he scared her." She wiped her face with a tissue, then blew her nose. "Tears and mascara don't mix. I must be a mess."

He turned her face up to his. "The most beautiful mess I've ever seen."

****

Samantha sat alone in the guest bedroom, a spacious chamber Collette had decorated for her when she was a child. She'd painted the high walls in soothing tones of pale yellow and placed Samantha's favorite toys, a kaleidoscope, jump rope, and erector set atop the old bookshelf holding the girl's best-loved volumes.

The homey New Orleans feel of Collette's house hadn't consoled her. Her only friend, Baby Ruth, had hidden herself away. To make matters worse, the woman she adored mooned over a no-good lover. Long, leisurely baths relaxed her, so Samantha sat in the tub to soothe her nerves. The soak worked its magic. She dried off, changed into her pajamas and was in the middle of brushing her teeth when she heard a rap at her door.

"Wait a minute, please." Samantha spat out the toothpaste and rinsed her mouth before opening the portal. A Shalimar-scented vision in a sheer pink negligee greeted her.

"Sorry to bother you, sugar, but I'm lonely. Can I come in?"

Lilly didn't wait for an answer. Instead, she strolled inside carrying two glasses of a frosty yellow brew that she placed on a nightstand before throwing herself on the bed. "I'm bored, too. I need somebody to keep me company. Try some of that lemonade."

The girl took a sip and promptly coughed. "This is the strongest lemonade I've ever tasted."

Lilly giggled wickedly, her laughter husky, filled with dark sensuality. "Don't think I'm being bad, but I slipped a little vodka into it. Have another sip. It'll loosen you up."

The glow of a Tiffany lamp illuminated the room, tinting the yellow room in shades of peach. Samantha marveled at how young Lilly looked without the heavy makeup, with the downy skin of a child. Lilly rolled onto her side and ran a finger down Samantha's arm.

"I hate not being able to work, hate it. I'm bored." She turned toward Samantha, a wicked leer spread across her lips. "And horny. C'mon, kiss me. I know you want to."

Samantha moved her mouth from Lilly's cheek to her lips. She feared pushing too hard, but she needn't have worried.

"No, you can do better than that. Come on, Samantha. Kiss me good."

Lilly's lips smelled of minty toothpaste and tasted like a summer day. Within a few minutes, Samantha's pajamas and Lilly's negligee lay on the floor.

The two girls moved together, ensnared by their mutual need. Their passion escalated until both of them could no longer hold it. Then, out of the blue, Lilly moaned the one name Samantha never wanted to hear.

"Eddie!"

Chapter Thirty-Four
Falling in Place

The bedroom shutters allowed faint slivers of light to penetrate the early morning darkness. Désirée rolled over and stared at a slumbering Patrick. In sleep, he looked like a child, a tousle-haired innocent. They'd made love the night before, rhythmical, horizontal ecstasy. He took his time. The sex was slow and easy, so both of them could savor every moment. Patrick whispered things she'd never heard before, dark endearments that thrilled her. Then, when she was in orgasmic throes, he murmured, "I love you, Désirée. Marry me, darling."

She hadn't answered. Her passion made it impossible to utter a word. Instead, she closed her eyes and threw herself into an odyssey of delight. In the illumination of daybreak, she realized, once and for all, she'd die if she lost him. If she had to sacrifice herself for Patrick and her mother, so be it.

Désirée climbed out of bed while Patrick slept. She bathed, applied makeup, and donned one of the creations Young Miss had sent, a hunter green sheath with a low décolletage. A quick visit to her little office yielded two pieces of elegant linen stationery embossed with the Renaud watermark.

Dearest Mama,

When you read this letter, I'll be dead. I pray

everything will go as I have planned. I cannot live any more knowing that you and Jim Dandy are suffering because of me. You know I love you and Jim Dandy too much to let that disgusting man mess with you anymore. Please do not worry about me. Maybe God will understand that this is for the best.

Don't be angry. I went after Eddie Vitale to protect you. Yes, the Commandments say "Thou Shall Not Kill." I never wanted to kill anyone until now. They will find me at the Lucky 13. I gave my stories to Patrick, but please, if you have a moment, read them. I think you will get a kick out of some of them.

Regarding my burial, I saved up $675.00, and it is in a cigar box in my locker. Put me in the crypt near Uncle Louie. I guess I am more like him than I thought. Please kiss Patrick for me and tell him I loved him. I have to protect you all.

Goodbye, Mama,
Your Désirée

She pulled out the other sheet of stationery and wrote away, her eyes filling with tears.

My darling Patrick,

Goodbye, my love. Please don't hate me for what I have done. I had to protect you and Samantha from that monster. Hopefully, I will kill him because, if I don't, he will destroy my family and might even kill you one day. I won't have you or Samantha hurt because of him. I am meeting him tonight and will look him straight in the eye before I shoot him dead. If he kills me first, then forgive me because I failed.

Goodbye forever, my love. I love you more than you can imagine. By the way, my answer would have been yes. I would have loved to marry you, but it was not to be. Think of me sometimes.

Désirée

Désirée folded the letters in two, slid them into scented envelopes, and slipped them into her pocketbook.

She tiptoed into the still-dark bedroom carrying a pot of coffee and a plate of buttered toast she'd purloined from the kitchen. Désirée positioned herself next to the side of the bed and gazed at Patrick in silence, watching as a sliver of sunlight fell on his face. Finally, Patrick opened his eyes. He moved toward her side of the bed, rested his head on his arm, and appraised her, his hunger evident. "You're up early, aren't you? Why didn't you wake me?"

She settled herself on the side of the bed. "After our shenanigans last night, I thought you might need some extra shuteye."

He closed his eyes as if remembering their erotic play. "We were naughty, weren't we?" Patrick sat up, smiling. "You're all dolled up. You look good enough to eat. I was hoping maybe we could play some more."

Désirée yearned for the comfort of his arms, but she refused to let him weaken her resolve. "As much as I'd like to, I have to check on Lilly and Samantha. I brought you coffee from downstairs."

He grabbed at her breast. She pushed his hand away with a snicker. "Let me be on my way, so I can come back to you."

Patrick bounced from the bed, his nude body so muscular and beautiful Désirée couldn't tear her eyes away. He moved toward her like a giant cat, his arousal obvious. She jumped up and circled him like a panther, her warm breath against his cheek. "Somebody looks awful social this morning." Suddenly she remembered the task looming before her and sobered. "I'll be back later, I promise. Enjoy your coffee, darlin', and think about how much I love you."

****

Instead of having Remy drive her, Désirée took a taxi to Collette's house. The cabbie's eyebrow arched upward when she said Tremé, but his expression turned into a smile when she flashed a wad of bills under his nose. "I'll need you to come back here in an hour."

She braced herself before knocking on the front door. A clear-eyed and sober Lilly, dressed in a pale pink silk wrapper, opened the portal.

Lilly gave her friend a sniff of disapproval. "Are you checking up on me or something?"

Désirée nodded. "Sure am. Lilly, please tell me you behaved."

The beautiful stripper didn't speak, but bit her lip before looking away. Her silence confirmed the worst of Désirée's suspicions, and she could barely stop herself from exploding in rage at her friend's actions. "So this is the way you repay Patrick for saving your life? Why her, when you can have every hard-on in New Orleans? She's just a kid."

Her friend waved Désirée past the threshold. "C'mon in. I have some coffee on the stove. Miss Collette left this morning, and Samantha won't leave her room. We can talk in the kitchen."

Désirée followed Lilly into the kitchen. "I blame myself. I know how randy you can get, but I thought big cocks were your thing." She took the percolator from the stove and poured herself a cup of joe.

Lilly sat in silence, smoking a cigarette. Finally,

she spoke. "It was just for a lark. Lots of gals have, you know, messed with gals. Nothing to it."

Désirée allowed herself a chortle. "Bullshit, Lilly. Tell that crap to somebody who doesn't know you like I do. You loved it, didn't you?"

Lilly answered with a reluctant nod. "I had a good time, but it doesn't mean I'm queer, just open-minded."

Désirée noticed a slight tremor in Lilly's hand. "But what about Samantha? She's not experienced, and she's crazy about you. The poor girl must be devastated."

Lilly took another puff of her cigarette before she snuffed it out in an ashtray. "She'll get over it. Anyway, I have other things to worry about, more important than a rich dyke. Mr. Renaud ordered me to go to Havana until this mess blows over. His daddy owns a casino there, and he's booked me into a club. I've never been to Cuba, but I hear it's a fun place. Opal bought me some clothes, and I'm flying to Havana this afternoon. I better get ready."

She rose from the table and sauntered off, leaving Désirée to question the wisdom of telling Patrick what happened between Lilly and his sister. The thought of his icy expression convinced her to keep mum. Confessing would only make things worse between the siblings.

Désirée staggered away from the kitchen, barely able to place one foot in front of the other, her eyes blinded by tears. She found a telephone sitting in an alcove. She took a deep breath, picked up the telephone receiver, and dialed "O" for operator before making the most difficult call of her short life.

"Excuse me, but can you please connect me with

the police headquarters?"

A pause. Then the operator spoke, "Yes, ma'am."

A male voice answered, "New Orleans Police. Officer Mouton speaking."

"May I please speak to Captain Eddie Vitale?"

"Okay, he's around. Hold on. I'll get him."

Silence, then after half a minute, she heard a click followed by the voice she'd learned to despise. "Captain Vitale speaking."

She took a gulp of air. "Sir, it's important that you listen and don't say anything. This is Désirée Broussard. I told you I'd keep quiet about what I know, but you wouldn't listen. I'm tired of you messing with my family. I want you to stop. I'll meet you at the Lucky 13 at ten tonight. I'll be alone, and we'll talk this out."

Dark laughter poured from the receiver. "The Lucky 13? I'll be waiting for you, darling."

Eddie had tried to make his voice congenial, but his innate coldness seeped through the telephone. Désirée knew she'd be dead by the end of the meeting, but so would Eddie.

She had no way of knowing that, the moment their conversation ended, Eddie ran to Gino's desk to share the good news. "You won't believe it. Désirée Broussard called. She wants to meet me at the Lucky 13 at ten." He looked down at his manicured nails. "The minute she's gone, my worries are over."

Eddie strolled away, whistling, and didn't hear Gino making a call.

"Mason-Dixon Line? I'd like to speak to Mr. Renaud please. Tell him Gino DeLuca is on the line."

****

Désirée mopped away her tears and reapplied her makeup. She found Samantha sitting alone when she returned to the kitchen. She joined the girl at the table. "Lilly told me what happened. I think it shocked the poor girl that she liked it so much."

Samantha's face turned red. "I suppose she hates me for what happened, or says it didn't mean anything? She called out for him."

Désirée turned her gaze on Samantha. "You want me to tell you what to do, don't you? I can't. Lilly's a regular gal, not like you. She's gone on Eddie Vitale, and nobody can do a thing about it."

She covered a piece of toast with strawberry preserves. "Crazy in love, that what's she is. My mother spoke to her landlady. She said someone broke into her place and ripped up her pretty frocks. When I told Lilly, she cried for a bit but said she knew Eddie did it because he loved her. She told me she didn't mind because she loved him, too. You can't fight something that powerful." Désirée inched closer. "I know visions of Lilly are dancing in your head like sugarplums. You dream of romance, but it won't happen with her. I've seen it before with Lilly and her men. They hate each other one minute, then love each other the next. Someone might end up dead, but it won't be him."

Désirée's words hit Samantha squarely in the gut. The girl averted her face and began to sob.

"Maybe I should have kept my opinion to myself. I'd love to stay with you, but I promised your brother this would be a brief visit. Samantha, I need a favor." She pulled two sealed envelopes from her pocketbook. "One is for your brother. One is for my mama. Promise you'll give them both to Patrick, but not until

276

tomorrow. Please, swear you will."

Samantha took the envelopes. "Why don't you give them to him yourself?"

Désirée never had mastered the art of lying, but decided to try. "It's a surprise for both of them. You see, well, your brother proposed, and I decided to say yes."

Samantha gasped at the news, thought about it for a second, and broke out into a huge smile. "My parents will probably have a conniption fit. Guess it doesn't matter, does it?"

"No, it doesn't matter what they think." The honking of a car horn intruded. "There's my cab. I'll have to be on my way."

Samantha stared into her face. "All right, I understand, but I feel like you're holding something back from me. You don't have to, you know."

Désirée returned the girl's gaze for a brief moment, then looked away. She knew she couldn't tell anyone about her plans. "No, I'm not holding anything back, but if you'll excuse me, my cab is waiting."

****

When Désirée returned to Maison Renaud, she found a shaven and rested Patrick waiting in his office. His eyes gleamed, and his lips spread into a wide grin, revealing the dimples she so adored. He plopped on a chair and pulled her onto his lap.

"I've been waiting all morning for you, darling. I heard from my parents. They're coming back in two days. I called Collette's place and told Samantha. She wasn't pleased, but she'll get over it. Now, about that question I asked. Will you marry me, baby?"

Désirée gazed into the face of the man she loved.

He looked at her with an expression of such sweet earnestness that words almost deserted her. "Patrick, I'd hoped to tell Mama first."

He broke out in laughter. "Does that mean you will marry me?"

She turned her face away from his. "I'm not planning on marrying anybody else, sugar."

He buried his face in her neck and couldn't see the frown that crossed her brow.

"I need to see Mama. After all the mess she's had to deal with, maybe I could visit her this evening, spend some time with her before she goes into the club. I know she'll be thrilled by the news."

He hesitated. "I don't like the idea of you going out without protection. I'll have Remy take you and wait."

She giggled, praying it didn't sound forced. "I'll have Jim Dandy to watch over me. You don't have to worry about me with him around."

Patrick massaged her leg, then allowed his hand to trail up to her thigh. Despite the turmoil of the day, Désirée relaxed her head against his chest. "What are you doing?"

He placed his lips against her ear. "I'm just returning a favor from this morning."

His fingers, like those of a jewelry thief, slid her panties to the floor.

The lovers stared at each other for what seemed an eternity. Then Désirée, overwhelmed by lust and need, placed his hand between her thighs. "Come on, baby. Do me."

Patrick fingered Désirée's silken vulva until it was slick. He stroked the lips, keeping his fingers on the place where the sensation was the strongest.

She closed her eyes and purred like a kitten. "You're so good to me, so good." Her hips moved in rhythm with his fingers. He pulled his hand away and, pushed by a throbbing between his own legs, carried her to the sofa. "Darling, please don't deny me. I'll die if you do."

She puffed a sigh. "Well, we can't have that."

****

A few hours later, Désirée emerged from her own bathtub, cleansed from her afternoon of carnal delights. With the blinds down, no one would know she'd returned to her flat. Stillness wrapped her cottage, and she didn't run the radio or phonograph. She'd hated lying to Patrick, but she knew what lay before her.

Désirée pulled out a gift from Lilly, a black skirt with a deep slit up the side and paired it with an off-the-shoulder red blouse courtesy of her mother. Instead of pulling her hair into a ponytail, she let it fall in waves past her shoulders, then applied her makeup heavier than usual. She clipped on a pair of ruby-red hoop earrings that finished the look with the perfect amount of sluttish panache. When she'd finally achieved the wanton tone she wanted, she called for a cab.

Désirée walked away mouthing a silent prayer. *Dear Virgin Mary, please help me get Mama's gun, even if I have to steal it.*

Chapter Thirty-Five
Not-So-Grand Finale

Revelers packed St. Marc that night. Désirée ignored the catcalls from the sailors and frat boys looking for action and strolled into the Starlight. Conversations turned to whispers the moment she crossed the threshold.

"Damn, she looks like a movie star."

"Nah, she's a stripper."

"Bet she's one of those dancers at the Mason-Dixon."

The butches whispered among themselves. The young fellows admired her feminine beauty as they would a movie star. She looked flawless and untouchable.

"Nah, that girl ain't no stripper. She's Young Miss's daughter, not her sister. I knew something was up with that gal. Regular girls don't hang out in queer bars."

"Young Miss must have been a baby when she had her."

Young Miss slammed a Pink Lady onto the counter and seemed more harried than usual. She turned to a bubbly femme who flirted with two butches. She didn't notice Désirée's approach.

Désirée leaned over the counter, oblivious to the femme.

The femme rolled her eyes and looked away.

Young Miss placed the drink on the bar, turned her head, and caught sight of Désirée. The older woman's face flamed, and she stormed over to her daughter. "Girl, I should beat your behind real good. Why are you here? Have you lost your mind?"

Désirée spoke in a whisper. "No, Ma, uh, Young Miss, I haven't lost anything. I need your help. Can I borrow the gun you keep under the bar?"

Young Miss's eyes blazed. "What the hell do you need the gun for? You're sleeping with the most powerful fellow in the city."

Désirée felt heat coming to her face and averted her head.

Her mother kept up her rant. "Don't deny that you're sleeping with him. I've seen that dreamy look on your face before."

Désirée kept her head down. She couldn't meet her mother's scowl. "Patrick's not always around. I have to protect myself, don't I? Please, Ma, uh, Young Miss, just for tonight. I feel nervous."

"Jesus Christ, do you even know how to shoot a gun?"

"I can shoot, at least with a rifle. Remember, I used to hunt quail and chucker with Jim Dandy before Johnny and I started seeing each other."

Young Miss folded her arms. "A pistol isn't for hunting quail. I'm not helping you get yourself killed, and that's the end of it!"

"But, Mama, I mean, Young Miss—"

A second later, someone screamed, "You bitch!"

A bar fight had erupted between two drag queens, and they struck blows like seasoned prizefighters.

Young Miss ran into the fray. The timing was perfect. Désirée darted behind the bar, grabbed the pistol, and dropped it in her pocketbook.

Only Claude witnessed the theft. The old woman hadn't reached her usual catatonic state yet, but she didn't seem to care about anything except her drink.

****

A few minutes later, Désirée sauntered into the Lucky 13. She took a deep breath before venturing into the stinking void, also known as the kitchen. The ancient cooks ignored her as she slipped past them into the darkness.

The Lucky 13 was different from her previous visit. The place was a tomb, no unmet desires, no whimpers of frustration, or final satiation, or rage. When she advanced beyond open doors and empty rooms, she heard no moans of pain or pleasure. Finally, she stopped, her feet hurting from the high heels. As she stood in wait, she wondered, once again, if she could kill someone in cold blood. Before she could ponder it further, the scent of Agua Lavenda Puig cut through the funk.

Eddie strolled past her. Désirée stepped back, watching him from the darkness. She wondered if she had the courage to confront a fellow like him.

Eddie glanced at his wristwatch before stepping through the gloom. He took care with his movements, as if mindful of the semen-stained floor. A door opened. Mistress Adele stood in place. "Are you here to see me, my handsome fellow? I have some time for you."

He strolled through the dim light, unaware that someone was watching him.

Désirée took a deep breath, then moved toward him through the darkness. She walked with a seductive thrust of her hips, her red peasant blouse accenting her breasts, her dark hair streaming past her white shoulders.

Eddie stared at her as if he were looking at an apparition. "What are you doing here, baby? Don't tell me somebody like you needs money. You need to get out of this place and never come back."

The girl sighed, then replied in a timid murmur, "You're looking for me. It's Désirée, Désirée Broussard."

He squinted in the weak light, and his eyes widened. The lovely creature before him was the prey he'd stalked for so long. "For true, that's you, Désirée? I wasn't sure you'd show up. Shit, I thought you were pretty, but I didn't know you were beautiful. It's a shame to kill you."

Désirée yelled out into the darkness, "I don't know what I did to make you hate me so much, but here I am. I can't have you messing with people I love."

He pulled a revolver from his shoulder holster. "And I can't have you blabbing to everybody about that ring. Shit, I didn't even mean to kill that peckerwood."

Désirée opened the pocketbook and felt for the gun. Her hands shook so violently she realized she couldn't go through with it. At that moment, she knew she was staring into the face of her killer. "If you're going to shoot me, then do it, only stop messing with my family and leave the Renauds alone. You're not powerful enough to destroy them, no matter what you think."

Eddie answered her with a nasty chuckle. "Still

mooning over Patrick Renaud, are you? He's not worth it, but I guess you'll never really know."

He hesitated for a moment before aiming his gun at her. Désirée closed her eyes, preparing for death. A shot rang out…

A groan, a thud, silence.

Désirée stood in the darkness, wondering if this was death—no angelic voices or demonic screams, just silence.

She opened her eyes and looked down at the floor where Eddie's crumpled body lay, blood oozing from a small wound in his chest.

She heard a masculine voice say, "Okay, fellows, let's take him away."

Désirée stared, unable to speak or move. Mistress Adele stood in the threshold, a small caliber pistol in her hand. She nodded in Désirée's direction and smiled like a butter-wouldn't-melt-in-my-mouth schoolmarm before closing the door. Mistress Adele had once told Désirée that the Lucky 13 was dangerous for a pretty girl. She hadn't lied.

Four toughs, following the direction of a beefy fellow wearing two-tone shoes, chewing on a wad of gum, lifted Eddie's body onto a sheet and carried it off. "Be careful, y'all. You don't want to spill anymore blood or get it on your clothes."

Désirée recognized the fellow. One of the toughs grumbled, "Okay, Gino, we got him now."

Gino? What was Vitale's partner doing in the sordid halls of the Lucky 13?

She stood, unable to move. A familiar voice whispered her name. "Désirée, come with me."

Patrick walked out of the darkness, calm, collected,

dressed in dungarees and a black T-shirt.

"You silly, silly girl. Thank God Samantha read your letter, or that mad dog might have killed you."

Désirée shook uncontrollably. "I, I, oh, God, I—" She took a step into the void, swayed, and collapsed into his arms.

****

When Désirée finally revived, she found herself reclining on a leather chaise. She had a vague memory of Patrick carrying her to his office. She looked up. He'd taken his place behind his desk.

"Patrick, please let me explain."

"No." His lips tightened. When he continued speaking, his voice sounded as if he'd packed it in ice. "You did something very foolish tonight, Désirée, and I could wring your neck."

He stood up and pushed the chair away. He paced the room, his movements those of a caged panther.

"Willie and I had already planned to take care of the bastard. Does that shock you? Well, they put down mad dogs, don't they? His partner tipped me off about your call to Vitale. If he hadn't, you might be dead."

Désirée attempted to speak, but words failed her.

Patrick glared at her with such intensity that she looked away. He took her chin in his hand and turned her face back toward his. "Look at me, girl! You could have been killed, and what would I have been left with?"

"I'm sorry."

"And what about your mother?"

She sputtered out a weak, "I said I'm sorry," before breaking into sobs.

He shrugged his shoulders as if in resignation.

"Okay. I'm still trying to figure out how you got in the place."

"Through that nasty kitchen."

Patrick poured a shot from a bottle of Courvoisier and brought the small snifter glass to her lips. "Sip it."

Désirée managed to take in a mouthful of cognac before coughing it up. "I still think this stuff tastes terrible."

Patrick remained as cold as a Frigidaire. "One more sip. Then I'm taking you home."

"Yes, sir." She took a swallow, then fell back on the chaise. "I gave Samantha two letters, one for you and one for my mother. I have to get them back."

He moved closer. "Yes, I know. I read both of them. Your mother will never see hers. I burned it. You were willing to die for me?"

"Yes."

She smelled the familiar fragrance of his cologne and his sweet breath against her cheek.

"Baby, I couldn't have handled you dying. It would have killed me deader than a bullet."

Désirée whispered to him, "Madame Adele told me there's death in the Lucky 13."

He nodded. "She didn't lie." Patrick stroked her hand. "Now, let's go home, and we'll talk about it in the morning." He whispered against her cheek, the permafrost gone from his voice. "You're sleeping in the guest room. You need some rest."

Tears poured down her face. "I don't want to sleep alone. How can I rest after seeing that?"

He pulled a handkerchief from his pocket and mopped away her tears. "My poor baby. Eddie Vitale isn't our concern anymore. He was too dumb to realize that his partner wouldn't be part of his craziness anymore. He didn't stand a chance." He shook his head. "I hate this business, but the fool messed with the wrong cat, a deadly mistake. Eddie could've had a bright future. I guess all this was bound to happen, but it's a mess." He slid onto the chaise. "Désirée, after they, uh, settle this, I'm afraid we'll have to attend his funeral. I'm not looking forward to it." He looked her in the face. "Swear that you'll never tell another soul about this—ever."

Désirée looked him straight in the eyes. "Of course, I swear. I won't tell anyone."

"Not even your mama?"

A throaty giggle escaped her lips. "Especially not her."

"You won't write about what happened?"

The tension evaporated with his words, and she laughed. "Never. No one would believe me anyway." She looked around and found her pocketbook on the floor next to her. She handed him Young Miss's pistol. "Could you give this back to Mama? I kind of borrowed it without her knowing."

Patrick took the gun and flipped open the empty bullet chamber. Désirée gasped and fell back onto the chaise.

He gave her a stern look. "In the future, darlin', leave the gunplay to others. Lord knows I'd wanted to spare you this." His fingers danced across her forehead. "I know you did everything for me, Désirée, but you'll never forget what it's like to see someone die. I pray, in time, it will be a distant memory." His eyes misted. "Now let's go home."

They exchanged a lingering look before Désirée

offered her lips to him. It was a proposal he couldn't refuse.

Chapter Thirty-Six
The Morning After

The *States-Item* carried the story of the death of a valiant young police detective the next day:

An anonymous tip led authorities to Canal Street where they discovered the body of Captain Edward Vitale. Captain Vitale, a vice officer with the New Orleans Police Department, was involved in a lengthy investigation of illicit narcotics trafficking. Vitale was the son of the late Pasqual Vitale and Mrs. Lula Vitale. He was a leader in the Sicilian community and the fiancé of socialite Bianca Corolla. Archbishop Joseph Francis will officiate at the funeral mass at St. Louis Cathedral on Saturday.

****

On the afternoon of Eddie Vitale's funeral mass, the spires of St. Louis Cathedral loomed high and black against the gray skies. A fleet of limousines snaked through Jackson Square, displacing the artisans who normally sold their goods there. Throngs of mourners moved toward the Cathedral as the crème de la crème of New Orleans society rubbed shoulders with the working class.

It seemed that everyone in the city knew Eddie Vitale and liked him. The mayor and his lovely wife entered the church, followed by the superintendent of police. The superintendent looked especially spiffy in his uniform, his badge worn upside down, as was customary.

Samantha and Baby Ruth watched the proceedings from across the Square. Both girls had dressed in heavy angora sweaters and woolen skirts against the chill in the air. They sipped hot chocolate from steaming mugs while they viewed the mourners walking into the Cathedral. Their interest picked up when Patrick Renaud, Sr., arrived accompanied by his beautiful wife.

Both girls moved closer, craning their heads to get a better look. The limo stopped, and a liveried driver exited and opened the passenger door. A darkly handsome fellow in his late forties alighted from the rear, followed by a demure brunette in a black fur coat.

Samantha snickered as her parents mounted the church steps. "The hypocrites. They wouldn't have rubbed shoulders with a mere policeman. Daddy said they had to be there because of Lula Vitale, but I know he's full of shit. Mama wants to show off the new coat she bought in Paris. Daddy wants everybody to know he's alive and kicking. They're both full of shit. Last night he told Mama he wanted a divorce, and she nearly had a cow, but she's acting all calm and collected now, putting on her public face. I wish they'd stayed in Europe and never come back."

Indeed, Mrs. Renaud looked stunning in an ebony sheath, several strands of pearls encircling her neck, her dark hair tucked beneath a black beret.

Baby Ruth nudged Samantha. "I bet your mama spent a hundred dollars on that dress, probably got it at the Maison Blanche."

Samantha took a generous gulp of hot cocoa. "A hundred dollars is nothing for Mama, and she's too big a snob to buy her dresses in New Orleans. She has her clothes specially made for her in New York City."

Baby Ruth tilted her head to the side. "New York, huh?" She turned back to her companion, a pout on her beautiful lips. "New York doesn't mean nothing to me. I've never been there."

Samantha gave her head a disinterested shake. "New York is a fabulous city, especially for femmes like you. They're sophisticated there, and everyone dresses up in the finest fashions. I'll take you there for Easter vacation."

Baby Ruth's eyes widened; her lips arched into a smile. "For true?"

"Yes, for true. I've never lied to you, have I? Daddy promised me a lot of money to shut me up. Maybe I can talk him into sending us to Havana, too."

Baby Ruth's face suddenly darkened. "Isn't Lilly dancing in Havana?"

Samantha turned to her with a smirk. "Why are you bringing her up? You jealous or something?"

Baby Ruth's face flamed a bright shade of crimson.

Samantha giggled. "Lilly's old news. Patrick sent her to Havana. She's probably hooked up with a fellow there. Anyway, I'm over her." She turned to Baby Ruth, a sly grin on her face. "I can't wait to show you New York. I'll take you to the Village, so we can meet some beatniks."

The petite girl gave Samantha a nudge. "For true?"

Samantha answered with a nod. "Of course."

Baby Ruth gave her friend a hug. "Golly, I'm going to New York. Guess I need to rustle up some new frocks." She gazed long and hard into Samantha's face. "Be honest with me. Are you sorry about staying here in New Orleans, instead of going to college in New York?"

Samantha shook her head. "Of course not. I like Newcomb despite some of the more stuck-up girls." She winked at her friend. "Besides, I wouldn't leave you, you big donkey."

Baby Ruth's face flamed. Then she lowered her lashes in a display of virginal demureness. Before she could respond, Samantha pointed to a Cadillac limo snaking its way toward the Square. "Look, there's Patrick and Désirée."

Another limousine pulled up, but the chauffeur remained behind the front seat. The rear door opened, and a grim Patrick stepped out. He held out his hand for Désirée. She emerged from the car, chic in a black tailored suit and veiled hat, her face emotionless.

The two girls didn't speak at the sight of Samantha's brother and his lady love. Perhaps they remembered the ugliness of the past few days. The two girls shared a secret neither would ever tell another soul.

Finally, Baby Ruth turned her gaze back to the funeral procession. "They could say a million rosaries for his soul, but I bet Vitale is burning up in hellfire right now, with Mr. Yates and a whole bunch of other folks."

Samantha placed her arm around her friend's shoulder. "I don't know, Baby Ruth. Maybe there's no such thing as hell. Maybe living in New Orleans in the summer is hell enough."

Baby Ruth took a sip of her cocoa. "Maybe."

Chapter Thirty-Seven
Joyeux Noël

The rainy autumn gave way to a chilly winter and New Orleans Yuletide. The windows in Godchaux's, Gus Mayer's, D.H. Holmes, and Maison Blanche glittered with mechanical elves and winking Santa Clauses. Evergreen wreaths hung from every door and masked the smells of the city. Drunks found themselves welcome in local taverns that normally barred them. Christmas carols rang out from every corner, and though it hardly seemed possible, more music than usual flooded the New Orleans streets.

A bout of arthritis forced Madame Ruby to play her rousing two-steps in the warmth of local bars. Even the Duck Girl got into the spirit of the season. A tinsel wreath circled her head, and she donned a festive cape that flapped behind her when she skated through the Quarter alone. She left her ducklings at home.

In the weeks after Eddie's death, the Lucky 13 changed hands, along with the Mason-Dixon Line, both bought by one of the wealthier men in the city. Mistress Adele departed New Orleans for places unknown. Some whispered that a benefactor had bought her a little house in Las Vegas, but, of course, everything about her was gossip. Who really knew?

Two days before Christmas, the lobbies of the great hotels of New Orleans all blazed with pine trees,

Christmas lights, turtledoves, plump cherubs, and wreaths festooned with glossy waxed fruits and berries.

The hotels and restaurants of the city feted New Orleans' finest, and the champagne flowed.

Evergreen garlands adorned the massive walls that kept the world away from Maison Renaud. The staff festooned the mansion with Christmas decorations, and the place was ablaze with lights. A giant pine covered with the finest Italian ornaments graced the Maison's gargantuan entryway.

A gaudy aluminum tree, with tinsel and bubbling Christmas lights, twirled in a corner of the Starlight, far from the tasteful Yuletide opulence of the Renaud residence. The youthful patrons wore their best duds for the occasion, with some of the girls and boys sporting wintry corsages. Rock 'n' roll blared from the juke box, and the kids hooted, hollered, and finger popped to the infectious beat. Claude sat alone, ignoring everyone.

Young Miss served heavily spiked eggnog from a crystal bowl, along with roast turkey with all the fixings and a huge frosted cake, courtesy of Miss Collette, who watched over the proceedings, beaming the entire time. Perhaps the offerings were modest to some, but for the guests, this was the closest they'd get to Christmas dinner with their families.

Désirée had garbed herself in a red satin sheath, an exact match of her mother's dress. The only difference, besides age and hair color, was the oversized diamond ring that flashed from Désirée's right hand. Female hearts had broken throughout Louisiana when the local papers buzzed with the news of the upcoming spring nuptials of Mr. Patrick Renaud and the young widow, Mrs. Désirée Broussard. Still, if anyone had invited the press to the Starlight that evening, a curious reporter might have noted the absence of the soon-to-be groom's parents. Both had graciously declined to attend the party since they were planning a huge Christmas shindig for the upper echelon of New Orleans society. All who knew them marveled at the strength of their marriage.

Upon their return to New Orleans, Patrick's parents were shocked with the miraculous change in their normally taciturn son and rebellious daughter. For once, Patrick seemed happy, and Samantha had transformed into a model child in poodle skirts and angora sweaters. The elder Renauds made a decision to keep to themselves any issue they might have with their son's intended and her family.

That evening, Samantha eschewed feminine dress and wore her customary dungarees and crimson bomber jacket. Her companion, a delicate blonde, had gowned herself in emerald green. She wore a pair of gaudy rhinestone earrings that almost overwhelmed her delicate features.

Someone put on LaVern Baker singing "Tweedlee Dee," and the dancing began. Glasses filled with bourbon-spiked eggnog clinked in noisy toasts, and the youthful patrons stuffed themselves with the tasty grub. The festivities had so heated up that no one noticed when Samantha handed Patrick a hefty envelope and he escorted his fiancée out of the club.

Désirée stared into his face, now completely unreadable. "What is it, Patrick?"

Without warning, a boyish smile appeared on his beautiful mouth. "I have a Christmas Eve present for you."

She couldn't stop herself from chortling. "Another present? Goodness, I only gave you some jazz albums and books, but you've bought me everything—a car, a fur coat, a ring. You've spent a fortune on me."

His eyes twinkled, giving him the look of a mischievous child. "This gift didn't cost a penny, just a few stamps and a call to a friend." He handed her an envelope. "Open it."

Désirée gazed into his face before opening the plump packet. Inside she found something that looked like a contract, with a handwritten note.

Dear Désirée,

I hope I'm not being too forward by addressing you by your first name. I realize that Southerners often are formal in their business dealings, but I have a hunch you aren't. Pat shared your fabulous work with me, and I must say I haven't been so intrigued by a novice writer in quite some time. My other Random House editors share my enthusiasm. I've enclosed a contract. Please have your lawyer peruse it. We at Random House want to start working with you right after the holidays. Feel free to call me at your convenience. Pat has the number.

Sincerely,
Ina Silverstein Ruben

The contents of the letter rendered Désirée speechless. Her heart beat with a wild rhythm. Her eyes shimmered with unshed tears, but not a word escaped her lips.

Patrick moved closer, his lips almost touching hers. "I take it you liked what was in the letter. Ina called me a couple of weeks ago and sent me the contract. I'm so proud of you, darling. I have just one request. When you write the next one, can it be as Désirée Renaud?"

Désirée answered him with a slow, sweet kiss.

What could be better than that?

A word about the author…

Lee René is the *nom de plume* of a jazz-loving author of historical romances, Young Adult and New Adult novels. She had the good fortune of being born in one of the most diverse cities in the world, sun-kissed Los Angeles. The City of the Angels is more than just palm trees, toned bodies, and beaches—it's a fusion of people, languages, and cultures.

In her past literary life, Lee worked as a lifestyle writer for magazines in Los Angeles, San Francisco, New York, and Vancouver, as well as an entertainment journalist and movie reviewer in print, on-line, and on radio in the Los Angeles area. She's a student of American history and her works are usually set in the past. When she is not writing away, Lee spends her time watching movies from the golden era on TCM, delving into history, or enjoying classical music, jazz, and gothic literature.

It's her sincere wish that lovers of dark romances will join her on her journey.

Thank you for purchasing
this publication of The Wild Rose Press, Inc.

For questions or more information
contact us at
info@thewildrosepress.com.

The Wild Rose Press, Inc.
www.thewildrosepress.com

To visit with authors of
The Wild Rose Press, Inc.
join our yahoo loop at
http://groups.yahoo.com/group/thewildrosepress/